FAIRHAVEN'S FORSAKEN

Susan Fernandez

Goose Rocks
Publishing

For my father,
whom I always wanted to make proud

FAIRHAVEN'S
FORSAKEN

Chapter One

I walked out of the woods at the edge of town, shooed away the crows that followed me.

"Sorry, guys," I murmured. "Not today."

Continuing alone sucked – I already felt like I was going to throw up. But the last thing I needed was to look like more of a freak if the crows attacked anyone who upset me.

Other figures headed down Capestone Road in the mist. I pulled my hood lower over my face, though I wouldn't be able to hide much longer.

And there it was. The two-story brick building squatted before me, rows of windows staring down.

I gritted my teeth, slipped through the front door, found myself surrounded by a dark sea. Most of the kids wore black or gray, a sort of unofficial dress code apparently. I wore my usual kind of outfit, the only one deemed appropriate by Sister Claire: a simple gray dress with buttons down the front, black stockings, and a pair of worn shoes.

I ducked into the office on the right and pulled my hood down, feeling exposed. The woman at the desk smiled.

"We never get new kids here, so I'm pleased to welcome you to Fairhaven High," she said. "Of course this year we have two, so you'll have company, though it looks like Mr. McGrath won't be joining us until tomorrow." A bell rang. "Don't worry, you're allowed to be late on your first day. I'm Mrs. Tinsley. If you have questions you can stop in any time."

She chattered on. I grew more anxious. I'd hoped to get into class early enough to hide in the back, like the coward I was.

"I'll walk you to your first class." She handed me my schedule. "Then they'll find you a student to show you around for the rest of the day."

I followed her down the empty hallway, fighting the temptation to run back out the front doors. We slowed in front of a classroom door. She opened it. I had no choice but to walk through.

Every face in the room turned. Mrs. Tinsley went to whisper to the absent looking, older man in front. I stood alone, fidgeting.

"Holy shit, it's that weird girl from the abbey," someone whispered.

I felt my cheeks burn. I tried to find something to look at besides the kids who stared at me, but there was nothing on the walls. The room felt like a cell.

Mrs. Tinsley patted me on the shoulder as she left, said, "Good luck, dear."

I was going to need a lot of luck.

The teacher cleared his throat.

"Well, as you all see, we have a new student starting her senior year with us. What is your name?"

"Eva Blackwell."

"I'm sure Ms. Blackwell would find it helpful to have someone guide her around for the day, show her where to find everything. Who would like to volunteer?"

Complete silence. Some of the students looked down, avoiding my eyes. Some watched me with obvious distrust.

"Surely one of you would like to help?" the teacher said. He tugged on his tie.

Someone snickered in the back.

"I can find my way," I muttered, desperate to sit down.

"Nonsense. Molly, how about you?"

A girl with straight blond hair in the front row looked up, frowned at me.

My stomach twisted. Molly wore a prim, button-down sweater with a matching skirt, her hair hung neatly on either side of her face. She cleared her expression and smiled at the teacher. "Of course I'll help."

"Excellent," he said. "That's all settled. Oh, I'm Mr. Edwards. Why don't you sit over there next to Oliver."

Relieved, I shrugged off my coat, sank down low in the seat. Out of the corner of my eye, though, I saw kids sneaking looks at me.

Mr. Edwards paced in front of the chalkboard the whole class. He went over the syllabus, wrote out math equations…was generally more excited about the subject than his students. I looked over at Molly. She appeared much the same as she had eleven years ago, the first time I'd seen her, when she'd stared at me from across the wall in the woods.

The bell rang, jarring me out of the memory. Everyone began to file out. Time to face Molly. I pulled my things together and went out to the hallway. Kids walked by, looked at me curiously, but Molly was nowhere to be found. I sighed. So this was how it was going to be. Great.

Then I realized I had no idea where I was supposed go.

It wasn't complicated: two floors made a u-shape around a courtyard in the back. But by the time I got to the other end of the building on the second floor, the bell had already rung.

For the second time, I walked into class late.

"I realize this is your first day, but I don't tolerate tardiness in my class." The teacher barely glanced at me. "This is your only warning. Next will be detention."

I stammered out an apology as I noticed Molly in the front row. My insides burned. All I wanted was to smack that smug look off her face. Instead, I took an empty seat near the window.

I just needed to reach the end of the day.

I managed to get through the next couple of classes without incident, started to feel sure I'd make it, when I hit the break in my schedule. Lunchtime. Sister Agnes had explained how everything worked, so I knew generally what to expect.

The cafeteria was already busy with groups of friends, eating and talking noisily about their first day back. Most of the tables were full. At the ones with empty seats, the kids shut me down with baleful looks.

"Oh my god, there she is."

Conversations shifted as more kids noticed me. No one cared if I heard.

"I thought she was homeschooled. Why's she here?"

"She obviously should have stayed in whatever dungeon she came from. I mean, look at her."

I walked stiffly to an empty table in the back, pulled out my lunch.

People stared.

"My dad said when she got dumped on the abbey doorstep the nuns had to keep her 'cuz no one else wanted her."

I hunched my shoulders, tried to focus on my food. Senior year stretched interminably before me.

*

When school finally let out, low, heavy clouds had drifted in, a steady drizzle falling. The dreariness was a comfort as I pulled my hood up and started home.

It wasn't a good day, but I made it through. I knew how to navigate solitude — this would be just another form. At least, it would be once the other kids got over the novelty of my presence. Which I was sure would happen soon. I hoped.

I'd thought I was alone on the street, but when I felt an itch along the back of my neck I turned to find someone behind me. Damp hair clung to his forehead. Green eyes stared at me, sent a strange fizzle across my skin.

I snapped my head back around. I didn't recognize him from school — but then I had made an effort to avoid eye contact with anyone. What was he doing? I'd passed most of the houses. Was he following me?

My heart skipped to double time. I sped up, glanced behind me again.

No one was there.

I stopped. The street was empty.

Awesome, just what I needed. Kids had probably dared each other to get close to me. At least I'd scared him off.

The moment I stepped away from the road, into the woods, I breathed easier. After a while, I neared the edge of the lawn where the branches bent over the path opened up. Ragnarok Abbey loomed before me. The mist off the ocean drifted past the building, everything darkened to a subdued gray by the rain. The abbey looked forbidding. But it was the only home I'd ever known.

I headed up the front steps, across the porch. Inside, I passed Sister Claire.

"Good afternoon, Sister," I said softly.

Claire inclined her head toward me without actually making eye contact and continued past, crossing herself as she did so. That was the best I could hope for out of her.

So I went on, certain I'd find a warmer welcome from the others, who'd be anxious to hear how the day had gone. When I got near the reading room, I heard my name and paused.

"I know, but I'm really not sure Eva belongs there," Mary said.

"She'll be fine, don't worry. It'll be good for her to get out of the abbey." Agnes, no surprise – the two were inseparable.

"But what about—"

"It's long past time, Em, honestly."

"Don't you remember how it was, though, even from that first night? We all know that kind of thing could happen again." I crept closer. I'd never heard much about that first night beyond: a man no one got a good look at left me on the porch. "Lord, I still can't believe we heard her crying over the noise of that storm."

"When Sebastian picked Eva up—"

"Everything just stopped. The storm went eerily quiet right then, I swear." Mary's voice was hushed.

"That was a coincidence."

"Nothing coincidental about the vase, Aggie."

Agnes was silent.

"Things don't just go flying through the air on their own."

"Sisters." Helen's stern voice cut in, made me jump. "That's quite enough of that."

Her footsteps sounded from deeper in the room. I eased back down the hall and pretended to come in again, trying to shake borrowed memories. I found the three of them perched on the couches wearing pleasant expressions as though nothing had happened.

"You're home!" Mary's face lit up with a smile.

"Oh sweetie, how did everything go?" Agnes asked. "It wasn't so bad, was it?"

Helen watched me intently, trying to read the answers on my face. To see them so worried made my throat tighten.

I turned to put my bag down against the wall, took a deep breath, turned back with a smile.

"Everything went just fine."

"I knew it would," said Mary. She pulled me in for a quick squeeze.

"Of course it did," Sebastian said as he walked in, wrapped his arm around my shoulders. "There was no reason to be so nervous." He smiled down at me, his warm brown eyes framed with wrinkles.

It's always been unclear to me how Sebastian ended up in the unorthodox position of running Ragnarok, as opposed to one of the nuns. He'd always been vague when I asked, but I've long suspected he was brought in to replace Sister Claire – which would account for some of her animosity.

"How were the other kids?" Agnes asked. "Did you make any friends?"

"Everybody seemed pretty nice," I replied. "There was one girl who even volunteered to help show me around."

"Well that's wonderful dear." Mary patted my arm.

Helen still watched me, her brows drawn together in a frown. She'd always understood me better than anybody.

"You must be awfully tired, Evie," she said. "We're just happy you're back and you survived your first day." She left it at that, thankfully. "We were discussing what we should make for dinner in honor of your new beginning."

Right.

"Ooh, yes," said Mary, practically bouncing, "how does corn chowder sound? It's perfect for a rainy day like this."

"That would be great, thanks."

"Do I have time to get some reading in before dinner, Helen?" asked Sebastian, who'd been spending more and more time these last few years cooped up in his study.

"Of course," she answered, then smoothed a piece of my hair back. "You, my dear, should go rest." I was about to argue, but she added, "You've had a long day. The three of us are more than capable of getting dinner ready."

We usually had about ten nuns in residence, though only six now – visiting nuns rarely stayed through the dark season. When things were quieter, the five of us ate dinner together, the few other nuns preferring to eat alone.

They went to start cooking, while Sebastian, satisfied all was well with his little family, went off to his study. I trudged upstairs and flopped down on my bed, exhausted.

I'd had about all I could handle – I was ready for the world to leave me alone for a while.

*

After dinner, when everyone had dispersed to their rooms, I finished my homework with the silence of the abbey gathering around me until I heard a soft knock.

"Evie, can I come in?"

"Sure."

Helen stepped into the glow of lamplight.

"I left a lunch for you in the fridge for tomorrow." She pulled down the sleeves of her black dress, the kind everyone wore for day-to-day work around the abbey.

"Thanks. You didn't need to do that."

"You know," Helen began, while I stared as hard as I could at the floor, wishing she wouldn't ask about school. She cleared her throat. "Well, I know you weren't keen on trying school in town, but hopefully you'll start to see how much more you can learn from the teachers there than from us. Did you, ah," she dropped her eyes, her long fingers fiddling with her cuffs, "I mean, nothing strange happened, right?"

"No, Helen. It was fine."

"Good. Of course it was. Anyway, I just wanted to say I appreciate you giving it a chance. Goodnight, sweetheart."

"Night."

She disappeared into the hallway. I sighed. I'd rarely seen Helen flustered. Apparently I wasn't the only one feeling weird about this whole thing. I tried to cheer up. After all, it could always be worse.

I turned off the light, soon felt the tug of sleep pulling at me.

Then I tugged back and everything shifted.

I stood in my room, looked down at my body still on the bed. This felt nothing like a dream. It felt real, but...different.

A flicker of light at the window caught my eye, a flash of lightning out at sea.

I wandered down the stairs, out a side door to go watch the storm. On the path to the beach I marveled at the brilliance of what I saw. All the details were crisp, the world lit with a silvery light that seemed to shine out from the inside of things.

The clear, shimmery light shifted across the ocean with its own currents, thousands of tiny sparks shooting into the air from the spray of crashing waves. Slender blades of glowing sea grass swayed with the wind in swirling patterns.

I took a deep breath, tasted the salt in the damp air. This was more vivid than any dream...or nightmare...I'd ever had.

I looked out over the water at the storm gathering in the distance. Dread crept in as jagged lines of lightning struck at the sea. A low rumble of thunder reached me. With all my attention focused on the storm, I felt a jolt of surprise when a voice spoke at my side.

"Danger is coming, child, as sure as that storm is."

A figure stood beside me, oddly shadowed so I couldn't get a good look at it. There was something steely in the voice.

"And it's headed straight for you. Beware the wings of darkness lest they devour you."

A cold thread of fear slipped down my spine. "What is it? What's coming?"

Silence.

"What should I do?"

"You must prepare. You must be strong." The voice relented, warming as it whispered around me. "When the shadow threatens to consume, remember the strength you hold inside yourself, child."

The whisper died, and I realized I stood alone, empty sand stretched away on either side. With the storm almost upon me, I fled to the abbey, fear driving me quickly back to warmth and safety. I hurried up to my room, looked down at my body.

A loud crash of thunder sounded, and I shot up in bed, my heart booming in my chest. I tried to steady my breath, slowly lowered myself back down. I felt the storm break over the shore, thunder cracking above the building.

I knew with absolute certainty: something was coming for me.

Chapter Two

The beauty of the clear morning was lost on me. I trudged along the damp path, staring at my feet, my insides all twisted up. When the big brick building came into sight, my breath quickened. The words of warning from the beach faded with more pressing fears.

I tried not to look at anyone as I walked toward the bend in the hallway where my locker was. But I didn't seem to blend in well. Conversations died when people noticed me. They all turned to stare.

With so many eyes on me, my legs felt like they no longer worked quite right.

"What a freak," someone whispered.

I heard a giggle in the now quiet hallway.

"Gran taught me how to ward off the evil eye when she heard the Blackwell girl was here."

"Yeah, my mom said there's something unnatural about her."

"Maybe that's why her parents got rid of her." Molly's voice rang out.

The air was sucked out of me – that struck an old nerve. What if my parents had somehow known I was different and that's why...

I clamped my jaw, kept my gaze straight ahead, managed to make it to my locker. I stood there, trying to get myself under control as humiliation flooded through me. My fingernails dug into my palms. My hands shook.

I closed my eyes, felt a storm rise inside me. It was as though all I had to do was let go of it, and it would tear through everything around me. My hair blew against my face; papers rustled, a gust of wind rushing through the hallway.

Suddenly I stumbled as someone knocked into me.

"Ow, hey." I rubbed my shoulder.

"Yeah, whatever," he muttered. I caught a glimpse of dark green eyes in a face I recognized before he disappeared around the corner.

A wave of embarrassed anger swamped me. He hadn't even bothered saying sorry.

But the rude encounter with my stalker wasn't enough to distract me from what I'd almost done. I'd called that wind up. I wasn't entirely certain how I'd done it, but I had to be more careful. If anything strange happened, everyone would suspect me. I was lucky nobody noticed.

The first bell rang. I walked to my seat in class and realized the morning outside was no longer clear. Dark clouds roiled in the sky, the wind blustering against the building.

I knew, without a doubt, I made that happen.

My hands trembled as I sat down. I hadn't done anything strange, even accidentally, in years. Certainly nothing so drastic. My breath started to come faster. I was afraid I'd hyperventilate. Affecting the weather? How was I supposed to deal with this? I was a freak.

I put my forehead on the cool desk, closed my eyes, concentrated on slow inhales. Right now I was at school – that was enough of a problem to deal with.

When I raised my head, I found the office secretary had interrupted. She spoke in a hushed voice to Mr. Edwards. Standing near them was the kid who'd knocked into me in the hallway. The kid I'd seen yesterday.

He stared at the back wall as though none of us existed. His untidy hair was dark brown, his eyes a deep green – the color of fir trees in the shade. A summer tan lingered, and he was well muscled, though lean. I might've found him interesting looking...except he was clearly an ass.

He dropped his gaze suddenly to meet my eyes. I looked down, blushing. Why did he have to look at *me*? And with such a strange expression? I was irritated with him all over again for making me feel like an idiot.

"We're very happy to have Mr. ah..." Mr. Edwards trailed off with a blank look.

"McGrath," supplied Mrs. Tinsley. "Tristan McGrath."

"Right. Of course. We're very happy to have Mr. McGrath join us as another new student. I'm sure the kids will help you catch up on what you missed yesterday."

The secretary left. I had a moment of grim amusement. The kids here didn't like newcomers. He'd be marked as another outsider, that easy self-assurance knocked out of him.

"Who might be willing to show Mr. McGrath around for the day?"

Every girl in the room immediately shot her hand up.

Okay, so much for justice. It wasn't outsiders they didn't like, it was just me.

I supposed I could see why the girls were eager to have a chance to talk to him. He was striking...in a scruffy, mysterious sort of way. If you liked that sort of thing. And I absolutely didn't.

Deep down, I knew some of my irritation came from the hope that had briefly bloomed in my heart that I'd have company. Another outsider, one who didn't know any of the rumors about me.

I pushed the thought away. He'd already proven he was just like the rest of them.

Mr. Edwards picked a girl in the front row, Sarah, with pretty brown hair she wore in a ponytail. Tristan sat down in the empty seat two rows over from me.

Molly twisted to peek at him with a smile, but he took no notice of her. When she turned back around, she caught me watching her. She flushed, her eyes filling with spite. Once again I was back to that day in the woods, eleven years ago.

I'd been lonely – the nuns never let me play with kids from town. I'd wandered along the stone wall until I came to one of the iron gates, the path on the other side a short-cut to town. Helen had clear rules about not leaving the property.

A noise from the tree above caught my attention. Perched on a branch, looking down at me, was a large crow.

"Hello."

He spread his wings and cawed.

I sat on a rock near the wall, tucked my legs underneath me, held out my hand. He flew down to land on my arm. His feathers were soft and shiny.

He cocked his head, fixed one glassy black eye on me. I smiled, told him my name, happy to have a playmate. He climbed up my arm to settle on my shoulder and called out again.

More crows floated down from nearby trees. Soon the black birds surrounded me. I laughed at their stories of the wind and the trees, stroked the feathers of the ones I could reach.

All around, yellow daisies shot up and unfurled, their bold, sunshiny color bright next to the dark birds.

A pebble clattered against the rock, unsettling the crows.

Two girls stood on the other side of the gate.

"I told you we could find her. And she does look weird," sneered the taller one with braids.

The crows went eerily still, watching the girls with the same intensity I did.

"Do you think she's crazy, Molly? Everyone says she is."

Molly just picked up another rock, threw it over the wall at me. The crows flew up in a pack, cawing angrily, flapping around the girls.

They fled, shrieking, while the crows scattered into the trees. I started to cry, my arm stinging where I'd been hit. It began to rain as I climbed off the rock and ran home.

With a fair amount of effort, I dragged myself out of

the memory to concentrate on the chalk lines scrawled across the board. The problems were clean. The answers simple. If you followed the formula everything worked out. Why couldn't my life work like that?

My next class was abuzz when I arrived: Tristan was there. With only two or three classes for each grade at any given time, there'd be no avoiding him.

The bell rang. He continued to stand in front, unconcerned.

"I take it you're our new student," said Ms. Chadwick. She shook his hand. "It's not often we get new faces in town."

I tried not to roll my eyes.

She grabbed a book. "You'll have to read an additional chapter tonight to catch up, ok?"

"That won't be a problem." He smiled at her. His voice was warm, faintly accented.

She gestured toward me. "There's a seat open behind our other new student."

He walked down the aisle and slid into the seat without looking at me. My neck prickled. I didn't know if he was staring at the back of my head. Awesome.

The discussion began about what we'd read. I raised my hand, answered the first two questions, but then I noticed the dirty looks the other kids shot at me. After that I kept my head down, even though the questions were easy and no one else volunteered answers.

The hours ticked by. Soon enough I followed everyone to the cafeteria, which doubled as the gym, off the back end of the main building.

I pulled out my lunch, opened a book, and concentrated on ignoring the table closest to mine. Molly, Sarah, and two others whose names I didn't know, sat down. There was also a girl with long brown hair pulled back in a braid named Lisbeth – the other girl from the rock-throwing incident.

And, of course, Tristan.

I hoped their choice of location wasn't deliberate, that I was being paranoid.

"Tell us, Tristan," Molly said, her voice sugary sweet, "where do you live?"

"I'm with my grandmother a little outside of town, just past that nunnery on the beach."

"Oh, that's Ragnarok Abbey," Molly supplied, disdain heavy in her voice. She began to say something else. I held my breath – but the other girl interrupted.

"Where did you live before coming here?"

"Yeah, where is your accent from?" asked Lisbeth.

"I was born in a town further inland, but when I was four my parents started spending a lot of time in Scotland where my aunt and uncle live. I ended up there for school, summers here."

"Why did you come back now for school?" she pressed.

"About a year ago my parents died. I returned for the funeral and stayed so I could live with my grandmother. With my parents gone, she doesn't have anyone else to look after her. I took a year off from school to travel with her. Then this summer she decided to move here to be closer to the sea. So here I am."

The whole table was rapt. I'd forgotten I was pretending to read. I quickly dropped my eyes back to the book before anyone caught me eavesdropping.

"You poor thing," Lisbeth said.

He shrugged.

"Yeah, that must've been really hard," Molly added.

"Well, anyway," said the other guy, "you'll like Fairhaven. It's kinda boring, but we'll introduce you around. Everyone here is nice." Oliver — that was his name. I wasn't sure his assessment of the school was entirely accurate.

"If you don't mind my asking," said Lisbeth, "why did you miss our first day of school?"

"My grandmother wasn't feeling well. Missing school is one of the perks of taking care of her." He smiled.

"That's so sweet of you," said Molly, clearly anxious to stay in the conversation.

A kid with a halo of curly hair joined them. Nathaniel — the boyfriend of one of the girls, I guessed. I so didn't want to learn their names and relationships. But it was hard not to be aware of everyone in such a small community.

"Hi, Katie." Nathaniel kissed her on the cheek. "Hey guys. What did I miss?"

"Tristan was just telling us about himself," Katie answered.

"Yeah? Where are you living? I didn't even hear of anybody moving into town this summer."

"We moved into a cottage up on Bellewood Drive."

"Really? Up past the abbey? Wow, that's kinda spooky out there."

"Yeah — have you heard about Fairhaven's Forsaken?" asked Molly.

"No, I guess not."

"We've heard it's haunted, but nobody's ever been inside," Sarah said, lowering her voice.

"The abbey? I thought people lived there," Tristan said.

Molly gave a scornful wave. "Well, the nuns do. Though not very many are left there anymore."

I was frozen in my seat, the bite I'd just taken of my sandwich suddenly too hard to swallow in my dry mouth. I knew what would come next, and I wished I were anywhere else but there.

"I guess the place was always creepy and everyone from town avoided it, at least that's what my mom said. Then, like, seventeen years ago...on some dark and stormy night," Molly added with flair, clearly enjoying the attention, "a stranger came to town, left a baby on the doorstep. Ever since, we've heard stories about weird things happening there. That's why we call it the Forsaken."

"Nuns don't strike me as the types to believe in ghosts and hauntings," Tristan said, cocking an eyebrow.

"Who knows what the nuns think about it," Sarah dismissed. "Besides, we don't think it's ghosts or anything like that making it cursed...it's the girl who was left there."

"That's right," Molly said. "Nobody knows where she came from, or if she's even human."

"Molly," Lisbeth said, "don't be ridiculous. Of course she's human."

Did they think I couldn't hear them? I stared at a point on the table, tried to remember to breathe. I felt light-headed, my skin prickly.

"Say what you like, Lissie, but you and I both know she's a freak," Molly snapped back. She turned to Tristan. "Eva doesn't belong here." Out of the corner of my eye, I saw her gesture at me. "See, nobody wants to be near her. Some say the nuns keep her in the basement because even they're afraid of her. It's only right to warn you, since you have to sit near her in English. You should be careful and stay away from her."

I felt their stares. Tears blurred my vision. The one person here who might have given me a chance...

No. I blinked quickly to clear my eyes.

I couldn't pretend they weren't all looking at me. I raised my eyes, tried to keep my face expressionless.

I knew Molly watched with a cruel smile, but my gaze had caught on Tristan's. I couldn't look away. There was none of the revulsion I'd expected, just a small frown. He looked almost...impressed? No, that couldn't be right.

Oh no. No, it was worse: it was pity. His green eyes burned into mine. I tried to stare back in challenge, though I'm sure I failed miserably. The moment stretched on. The people around him began to shift uncomfortably, but Tristan didn't look away.

I kept my gaze locked with his as I stood up slowly, not breaking contact until I grabbed my things. But I still felt their eyes on me. I began to move away, and it was like I walked underwater, a pressure on my chest making it hard to breathe.

Relieved laughter broke out at the table behind me. I kept my eyes on the door, while all around me the colors bled out. The world went cold.

Finally I pushed through the heavy door, into the quiet hallway. I closed my eyes, leaned against the wall, wondered if I should fake being sick and go home. But I didn't want to be bullied; I didn't want Molly to win.

Instead, I spent the rest of lunch hiding in the bathroom.

That'd show her.

When the last bell eventually rang, I hesitated. The quickest way to Tristan's cottage would be to cut through the abbey property. I wasn't sure he'd know that...or if he'd want to risk the Forsaken, I thought sourly...but I absolutely didn't want to run into him if he did. So I lingered, though every inch of me ached to leave.

Once the school cleared, I walked out, drew my coat tighter. The wind still howled, the sun lost behind the clouds. It felt more like the end of October than the beginning of September.

I passed the last house at the edge of town and a strange sensation tickled the back of my neck. Like I was being watched.

I stopped, looked around.

The wind ripped through the trees, loose leaves blowing about. I didn't see anything in the woods or on the street. My hair whipped across my face, the air cold against my legs, so I dismissed the feeling and hurried on.

I turned onto the path. The trees pressed in around me, unnaturally close, empty of the familiar feel of the animals that should've been around. There was something menacing in the turmoil of the forest. It caught at my breath, my legs slowing even as an itch to run tightened my chest.

There's nothing out there, I told myself. Why didn't that make me feel better?

The sound of flapping wings had me spinning around, searching for what might be up there. But I didn't see anything. Only trees.

Okay. So don't be silly. Just keep walking. Just ignore what sounded an awful lot like a woman's whisper threading through the wind.

I noticed it out of the corner of my eye first. A shifting, where things shouldn't have been shifting. I forced myself to stop, to focus on what was off.

Then I saw it. The shadows seemed to stretch, grow longer, wider...somehow darker. They slithered across the open spaces, melted into one another.

I stared at the thickening darkness, my legs locked in a familiar fear.

They weren't shadows...they moved, filled with something, or many things, fluttering and quivering, barely contained. And I knew what they wanted: to swallow the world.

Chapter Three

A low moan began, carried on the wind. It was echoed a hundred times over, the sound rising to wrap around me. A sound that had so often sent me screaming from my bed in the middle of the night as a child.

They were coming for me.

A whimper escaped my throat.

No. I would not just stand here and wait for them to suck me down into the dark. I had to do something.

But I didn't know if I could.

The thought was enough to send panic exploding through my body. I took off like demons from hell chased me...and maybe they did.

I pelted down the path, desperate to make it home, to make it to safety. Desperate to be out of the woods. Barely slowing, I threw open the gate at the wall, sprinted through, heard it bang as it closed behind me. I didn't stop. I pumped my arms and legs as hard as I could.

Suddenly I was ahead of my feet. I couldn't catch them up. I fell, just managing to turn enough to roll as I landed. I was back on my feet before I even felt anything, frozen, staring as hard as I could at the woods, my muscles trembling.

There was nothing there. Not a hint of anything strange. Only trees bending in the wind that gusted through, giving glimpses of the wall beyond.

What the hell?

I had to know. Slowly, every step full of tension, ready to run again at anything that felt off, I made my way back along the path to see if they still lurked. But there was nothing. Not even the sinister feeling crawling along my skin. Simply normal woods.

Had it all been my imagination?

It was like my bad dreams had jumped out of my head into the world around me. Was it possible to have a nightmare so strong it takes over your waking mind?

When I finally blew through the front door, the stillness inside was a relief.

I trailed down the hallway toward the flickering light in Sebastian's study. He sat in his chair by the crackling fireplace, reading an ancient, leather-bound book. He raised his head when I knocked, a smile crinkling his face.

"Hi, Evie. Come in, join me." He beckoned me deeper into the warm glow. The two of us had passed many long winters reading in here. "How was your day?" His smile faltered a little when he saw my face. "Come sit. I want to hear all about it."

I sank into the chair next to his and closed my eyes, hoping to avoid answering. I wouldn't even know where to start: hated at school, or hallucinations in the woods?

"Tell me what happened sweetie." He reached a long, lanky arm out, squeezed my hand. He probably still believed he could fix whatever was wrong, make it all better. For a moment, I stupidly wished he could.

"It's nothing. I'm just tired."

"Hmmm, I see."

"What are you reading now?" I asked to distract him.

"It's a recent find. A boring history."

I stood up, patted his arm. "Well, enjoy. I should go start my homework."

I paused near the door at the sound of his voice.

"We should have sent you to school a long time ago," Sebastian said softly. "I'm sorry you've had a lonely life here. And I'm sorry we haven't done as much as we should have to help."

I went back, kissed him on the forehead. "Don't worry about me. You did fine – I wouldn't have wanted it any other way." I didn't want him to think any of this was his fault. He hadn't made me the way I was.

But when I closed the door behind me, I saw him frown as he stared out the window, brooding over the life of his strange orphan.

If he only knew the truth…

*

I mastered my routine. I spent classes trying not to outdo the other kids. The in-between times were all about avoiding notice. Then my guard came down each day when I stepped through the gate in the wall. Nothing more happened in the woods.

Now, ahead of me were two blissful days I wouldn't

have to see anyone from school. The crows wheeled about happily, one of my favorites swooping down to perch on my shoulder.

"Hey, Stopha," I murmured.

The energy in the air was charged with the shifting season. Excitement fluttered in my heart as I felt the change.

My musings about mysterious possibilities brought me through the front door absently. I almost walked straight into Agnes, who hurried through the foyer.

"Good, you're back. We could use help with dinner."

"I'll be right there. I just need to put my stuff upstairs."

"Sebastian is in his study," Agnes said as she disappeared down the hall. "Do me a favor: pop in to say hi."

I dumped my things and scooted down to see Sebastian. I suspected they took turns spending time with me after school to make sure I wasn't going to crack up or anything.

The door was open. Sebastian sat sifting through files on his desk.

"Hey, Basher, I'm home." I put my hands on his shoulders, peeked over his head at the mess in front of him.

He patted my hand. "Evie, my dear. I'm glad you're back. The ladies could use your calming influence in the kitchen. How was your day?"

"Fine. Looking forward to the weekend, though. What's all the fuss about dinner?" I perched on his windowsill and gazed out at the lazy waves of the turning tide.

"Didn't I tell you?" Sebastian asked, his attention on the paper before him. "We're having guests for dinner. Some new neighbors I discovered who've recently moved into the cottage up the beach." My head snapped around. He couldn't be serious, could he? "I stopped by earlier in the week. There's an older woman and her grandson. You may have met at school, actually. I believe he's around your age."

My head spun while he went on about how the woman hadn't felt well when he visited, so they put dinner off until tonight.

"Which works out better actually, since it's not a school night for you kids. You'll be able to spend some time with us, right?"

I nodded, too distracted to really listen. Tristan couldn't possibly be coming here for dinner. Was my luck seriously that bad?

"Eva? Are you feeling all right?"

I looked up. Sebastian peered at me with concern.

"Yeah, sorry. I just, um, realized I might have left my math book at school."

"Oh dear. Well, have you met her grandson? He would also be new this year."

"I've seen him around." I forced myself to sound normal. It doesn't matter. Tristan wouldn't come. Not after what everyone told him. I was sure it would be just his grandmother. Which I could totally handle.

"Eva?"

I realized Sebastian had been speaking. "I'm sorry. What?"

"I said would you mind helping the ladies in the kitchen? We haven't had outside company in quite some time and I think they're a bit panicky about getting everything done nicely."

"Of course. Yes. I'll go help. Right now." I tried not to feel panicky myself. I hurried to the door, knocked my shin on a stool piled with books.

"You okay?" Sebastian called after me.

"I'm fine. Don't worry." I escaped down the hall, my leg throbbing. Okay, don't freak out.

In the kitchen Mary scurried about, her cheeks flushed, trying to do three things at once. Agnes hurriedly chopped vegetables, chucking them into a simmering pot on the stove. Even Helen, usually the most steady of the three, looked harried as she tossed a salad together, wisps of dark hair escaping her bun to curl around her face.

"Em," Agnes waived a carrot at Mary as she swiped peels out of her way, "those rolls are going to burn if you leave them in the oven any longer."

"Don't you worry, I've got it all under control." Mary pulled the rolls out with one hand, added another pan with the other.

The walls of the kitchen were a homey yellow, the cabinets white. I would've found the warmth and bustle of the room a comfort if not for the anxiety gnawing away at my stomach.

"Everything smells great," I said, which drew relieved greetings from the women. "Anything I can do to help?"

"Absolutely, sweetie, thank you." Mary gave me a quick kiss on the cheek while she piled apples on the island counter in front of me. "Sebastian gave us very little notice about this dinner. Be a dear, please – peel and slice these for the pie."

I picked up a knife, my fingers moving automatically to peel a strip of red skin.

Okay, Tristan hadn't done anything out of the ordinary today. He'd ignored my existence as thoroughly as he had for the past couple of days. Obviously that meant he wasn't coming.

Why did I feel a thread of disappointment slip through me?

It would be so painfully awkward to have him here. But some treacherous part of me wanted him to see there was nothing sinister at Ragnarok. I wanted him to see me away from school, where I could be myself (well, maybe not totally myself).

I gripped the knife tighter, tried to think clearly. I pulled the blade through the apple, letting the peels fall away to the side.

The nasty rumors about me were the only reason he even knew who I was. The last thing I should do was daydream about how things might change if he came. Tristan wasn't any different from the rest of the kids.

A new, horrible thought dawned on me: if he did come and anything even remotely strange happened, on Monday he'd be spreading more stories about me. Everyone would want to hear details about what went on inside the abbey.

Holy hell, this would be a disaster.

"Ah…Eva?" Agnes interrupted my thoughts with a tight voice.

I looked up to find all three nuns staring not at me, but

just off to my left. My skin tingled as I turned to see what had them frozen. Hovering in the air next to me were long peels from the apples I'd gone through. While I had my meltdown, I must've made them float up from the counter. Now the strips of red, with their pale undersides, spun slowly in big loops through the air.

This was what I'd tried to avoid for years, tried not to let anyone see. The idea seemed to fill the room even as someone breathed the word: "Magic."

For a long moment everyone stared. I would've found the twirling streaks of red rather mesmerizing if not for the heavy stone sinking inside my chest.

Deep breath. Now concentrate. I realized how I was doing it, almost like finding a muscle clenched that you hadn't known you were using. I released my breath, the whistle of air past my lips and a bubbling pot on the stove the only sounds in the room, and I let the apple peels drop to the floor.

Afraid to look anyone in the eye, I bent down to collect them. They all knew what I could do, but since I'd grown old enough to control it, mostly it remained unmentioned, though never forgotten. It had been a long time since I'd slipped up in front of them.

Delicate, creamy skinned hands covered with freckles reached out to mine. "Let me take those." Agnes gathered the pile away with a crooked smile.

"Don't worry about it, dear. I thought it looked quite lovely," Mary said in a soft voice, patting me on the cheek.

Both nuns turned to look for Helen's reaction. I raised my eyes. I deserved whatever lecture she gave. The danger of losing control like that, of getting caught, in front of anyone else was something I could never afford to do. Ever.

Helen's severe gaze assessed me. After a long moment with the weight of my guilt growing, her frown disappeared.

"Perhaps, dear," she said with amusement, "it would be better if you helped by setting the table instead." She turned back to her work.

Relieved, I left the warmth of the kitchen for the large dining room. The long oak table in the center could hold far more people than we ever had with us, so usually we clustered at one end. The room was all dark wood, with stained glass patterning the edges of the windows that faced the ocean. It was beautiful, though more formal than comfortable.

I pulled nice china pieces out of the cabinet, but paused, uncertain of how many places I should set. One for Tristan, just in case, but there were also currently three other nuns with us: Catherine, a visiting nun I rarely saw, and Sisters Claire and Margaret.

Helen came through the door as I set down plates.

"None of the other sisters will join us for dinner, Eva. Seven settings will do."

"Okay, thanks."

She smiled at the relief in my voice. "I believe Father Sebastian strongly discouraged Sister Claire from gracing us with her presence. And Sister Margaret followed as she always does." Her voice was mild, but I knew her dislike of the two nuns ran deep.

I'd just placed the heavy iron candlesticks in the center of the table when Agnes walked in.

"Eva, what are you still doing in here? It's almost time for our guests to arrive. You need to run upstairs to get cleaned up."

As I left, I heard her muttering about how they should have bought me some decent dress clothes. I began to resent how the impending visit made everyone feel.

I hurried upstairs to wash my face. I inspected my reflection in the bathroom mirror, keeping in mind who might be seeing me. My hair hung down my back, all long black waves, and for a bright second, I thought I looked pretty. Maybe this night wouldn't be so bad after all.

But a moment later, the feeling passed.

I pulled my hair loosely into a clip and went to see if there was anything more I could do to help.

When I reached the bottom of the stairs, the doorbell rang. My pulse kicked up. I forced myself to cross the foyer, open the door.

On the porch, rimmed with soft golden light from the setting sun, stood Tristan and his grandmother.

The woman was slim, with a long, iron gray braid draped over her shoulder. Her skin was lightly lined and a shade darker than Tristan's, as though she spent more time in the sun. I couldn't tell how old she was. There was an energy about her that made her seem young.

And then there were her eyes. I couldn't look away. A lighter green than his, they sparked with yellow flecks. I stared at her, mesmerized.

Time slowed. Petals had blown toward her from the hanging plants and swirled slowly now through the air, everything else gone still. I glimpsed something reflected deep in her gaze, something vast...something wild. I was drawn inexorably within, seeing nothing else.

Steps sounded behind me. Everything snapped back into place, the moment gone. I stood in the doorway. The woman looked beyond me, no hint anything strange had occurred, though Tristan studied me with a curious frown. What had he seen in my face?

After a beat, however, he turned his attention to Sebastian, leaving me unmoored.

I had to get a grip. Whatever freak-out my magic was having, it had to stop. Now.

"Welcome. It's so good of you to come," Sebastian said with enthusiasm, his hand on my shoulder. "We've looked forward to this all week."

Not at all liking Sebastian's "we," I kept my face blank, my eyes away from Tristan.

"We have as well," the woman said in a strong, steady voice. "It's very kind of you to invite us to your home."

"Of course. Please, do come in." He led us down the hall to the reading room. After settling our guests, he held out his hand. "You must be Tristan, it's good to meet you. I'm Sebastian Blackwell."

"It's a pleasure, Father. Thank you for having us."

"Mrs. McGrath, it's good to see you again. I'd like to introduce you to Eva."

Piercing eyes turned to me. Under her sharp gaze, I felt exposed.

"I'm delighted to finally meet you, Eva. I've heard so much about you." My eyes flickered to Tristan's, but his expression revealed nothing. "But please, call me Greta."

A thrill went through me knowing Tristan might've talked about me, but it turned icy when I thought about what he would've said. Steady now – I could handle this.

"Thank you. It's nice to meet you, too."

"And I assume you two know each other," Sebastian said.

I looked at Tristan, at a loss for what to say.

"We haven't been properly introduced," he said with a wry smile for me, "but we have a lot of classes together."

I nodded but couldn't help dropping my gaze, my jaw clenched. Of course he would be polite in front of the adults. Had I expected him to ignore me as usual?

Just as the silence started to feel awkward, the nuns came through the door at the other end of the room. New introductions were made.

Helen wore one of her nice black dresses that showed off her trim figure. She looked lovely as she gave me a reassuring smile.

"Dinner is ready," she said. "Why don't we all head into the dining room."

Everyone followed behind her. Tristan and I reached the door at the same time. I paused, waited for him to go ahead. But Tristan had stopped to let me go. I wasn't sure if I should keep waiting or go.

Tristan, his lips quirked in amusement, placed his hand on the small of my back and gently guided me through the door ahead of him. He dropped it as soon as I was through.

My skin tingled where he'd touched me.

I took the empty seat between Helen and Mary, feeling unsettled. The sensation of his fingers on my back lingered, and I looked up to see Tristan take the seat directly across from me. We locked eyes briefly before I looked away.

The serving plates were passed around, the smells of roasted chicken, vegetable soup, and fresh bread filling the room.

Before long, Greta turned her attention to me. "So, how do you find the school? I hear this is your first year there, as well."

"Some of the classes are interesting." If I had to tell an outright lie, it would only give Tristan another embarrassing story to share with the bloodsuckers at school.

"How about you, Tristan?" Mary asked. "Do you like your classes?"

"They're okay. The teachers all seem nice."

"Oh, that reminds me," Sebastian said. "Eva, didn't you say you left your math book at school? Maybe you could borrow Tristan's, if you're in the same class?"

It took a moment to remember what he was talking about.

My cheeks flushed. "Um, well, I…"

Tristan was watching me. Though his face was composed, there was amusement in his eyes. "I would be happy to loan you my book. I could bring it over tomorrow if you like."

"No! I mean, actually, it turns out I do have my book here," I replied, flustered, before adding hastily, "but thank you."

He shrugged. "No problem."

I was a fool to panic. If I'd let the lie go, I would've met with him again tomorrow. Just the two of us...

Okay, no. It was definitely better to avoid that.

"What about your other classes?" Greta asked. "Do you study a foreign language?"

"I take French. It's the only one they offer."

"And how is your French then?" She asked in perfect French.

"I enjoy the language," I answered, also in French, "but the class isn't very challenging."

Sebastian and the nuns looked on curiously.

"Good. I would expect you to be strong with languages, it's best to be prepared," she said before switching back to English. "My father was a big believer in education," she explained to the rest of the table. "I was fluent in six languages by the time I left home."

"Wow," Mary responded. "That's quite impressive. What about you Tristan? Do you take French with Eva?"

"Actually I don't. My grandmother is also quite dedicated to my education, so I already speak it fluently. The class would be a waste of time, as I'm sure it is for Eva, considering how well she speaks it."

Everyone turned to look at me.

"Well, sort of. Yes. But it was that or nothing." I shot an annoyed look at Tristan. I was constantly unbalanced tonight, but he, of course, appeared completely at ease.

"Unfortunately, that's one of the drawbacks of a small town," Helen said. "When Eva was younger, a nun who spoke French stayed with us for a...a while, and was able to teach Eva." Yeah, she stayed a month. That's how quickly I became fluent. "We had hoped she would have more opportunities to learn from visitors, but it just hasn't worked out."

Helen had been totally pleased about my quick mastery. Sister Claire, on the other hand, had seen it as further proof I was possessed of some devious kind of evil. On the heels of Helen's praise, Claire had whispered in my ear, "The devil, too, has a talent for the tongues of men." I'd been seven.

Greta cocked her head as she studied me. "Perhaps I could teach you another language. It would be good for your education and I could use a new project to keep me busy."

"That's very kind of you," I protested, "but you really don't have to do that."

"Nonsense. It would be my pleasure. In fact, I insist."

I looked at Helen for help, but she nodded in encouragement. "I think it's a wonderful idea. It would be a waste not to take advantage of such a kind offer."

"Well, then, that would be great. Thank you, Mrs. McGrath."

I caught a satisfied look pass between Sebastian and Helen.

"Good. But please, child, call me Greta."

The way she called me "child" made me suddenly tense. It was just like in my...dream, for lack of a better term. I stared at Greta, but she gave me a pleasant smile back.

The conversation picked up, turned to the history of Ragnarok. Apparently Greta's ancestors had lived in town when it was being built so she knew quite a bit about it. I barely heard any of it.

Uneasiness churned in my belly as I picked at my food. Echoes of Greta filtering into a dream was weird, but let's face it, it wasn't the first time I'd dreamt of someone I was soon to meet...not that I'd ever admit it. She'd unknowingly repeated the message about being prepared, though. I couldn't ignore the reminder. What I'd been told on the beach had been a warning, and I believed the danger spoken of was absolutely real.

Like this night wasn't crappy enough.

Finally, when everyone finished dessert and the conversation hit a lull, Greta declared it was getting late.

I looked up when Greta said my name in the foyer. "How would you like to come over Sunday afternoon to begin your lessons?"

"That's fine," I managed to say around a big, nervous knot.

"Is one o'clock okay? Good. That's settled then. I look forward to getting to know you better, Eva." She turned to Tristan, who draped her shawl around her shoulders.

Despite her protests, Sebastian insisted he drive them home, so after Tristan politely said goodbye, they all left. The foyer suddenly felt much emptier. Some of the tension eased from my shoulders.

"Whew," Mary sighed. "They are delightful, but it's a relief to be through that. How about we start on the cleanup?"

"Sounds good," Helen said. "The three of us can work on the kitchen; Eva can clean up the table. Fair?"

Four trips later, the table was clear of everything but the still burning candlesticks. I glanced at the closed door to the kitchen as I weighed my next action. If I was going to take the warning from the other night seriously, I had to practice. At least in private, I couldn't keep pretending I was normal.

I focused on the flames that flickered on the candles. I concentrated, and with a thought, I snuffed the flames. Thin trails of smoke curled up. It was easy. I hadn't tried to manipulate fire since I'd shut the magic out as a kid, but it was still easy. The magic felt...eager, like an enthusiastic puppy...wanting to be played with.

Carefully, I brought new flames to life, one candle at a time, until they once again burned steadily. Mary came through the door and I jumped about a foot in the air, tried to pretend I hadn't.

"We're almost finished in the kitchen, dear. Why don't you head up to bed?"

"Are you sure there's nothing more I can do?" I quickly blew out the candles.

"Oh we'll be fine, dear, not to worry. Now off with you."

After all the stress, I was exhausted. I got into bed, dragged the covers over me and fell asleep immediately.

Dreaming claimed me quickly. Or at least, I assumed it was a dream – it wasn't exactly normal, even for me. I stood in the middle of a vast, barren desert, the night air dry and warm. Stars hung low all around, almost close enough to touch.

I took a step forward, but hesitated. Despite the brilliant light from each star, darkness thickened around me. The closest lights began to wink out. From behind, there was a sound of rustling feathers.

I wasn't alone.

I turned, moving slowly through the heavy air, and lifted my eyes to the man who stood there.

Black hair matched the large black wings spread wide behind him. He looked down at me with unsettling eyes. The outer edge of the iris was a deep golden color, but around the fathomless black of his pupil was a ring of yellow fire, like an eclipsed sun. I wanted to look away, but I couldn't move.

His brows drew down as he stared at me. His expression had the look of thunderclouds sweeping in, emotions I couldn't read flickering in the depths of his eyes.

"You." The word rolled through me as though his voice had substance to it, a heaviness that reverberated in my very bones.

Chapter Four

Fear shot through me, spurred me back a step. I couldn't name what I saw in his eyes, but whatever it was, it set my heart hammering in my chest.

Quicker than I could react, his hands shot out, grabbed my arms, pulled me closer to him. He searched my face. I felt a wave of magic flood over me, testing, scouring for...something, I didn't know what. It just slid off me, though, not catching, not hurting. But it was magic, magic so strong it made my breath catch and my skin itch.

I wanted to get the hell out of here. Now.

His eyes widened slightly when the last of his power trickled away. He suddenly let go of me. I stumbled back a step, watched his face as he struggled with whatever it was his magic picked up. But I didn't want to find out what burned inside this strange man. Or what he wanted with me.

His gaze sharpened on mine, and his hands reached for me again, as though he hadn't meant to let go in the first place. I spun around, slipped away from his grasp. Without even making the decision, I was already running.

Fear bubbled up the back of my throat, burning like acid. I had to get away. He was so strong. Too strong. I'd never felt anything like that before.

My eyes were wild. I searched ahead of me for anything: a place to hide, a way out, help…something. But the desert stretched away from me, uninterrupted sand disappearing into the darkness beyond, only the strange stars shooting past me while I ran.

My legs began to feel heavy. So heavy. Like I was running under water, the weight of the air pushing against me. Was he doing more magic on me? I ground my teeth, pushed myself as hard as I could.

I didn't know where he was, or what magic he might have unleashed on me. I darted a glance back at him, afraid of what I'd see…but there was no one there. Crap.

I whipped my head back around and screamed at the sight of him standing right in front of me. I veered off, kept my legs moving in a new direction. Distance. I just needed distance. But then what? There was nothing out here. I scanned the desert, hoping to find an answer, but when my gaze moved back, the winged man was there again. Right in front of me.

Another scream tried to burst out of my chest as I almost ran into him, but I just managed to push myself off into a new direction.

My legs ached. I couldn't keep this up.

It filtered into my head that he hadn't tried to reach for me again, though I'd been easily within his grasp.

Then he was there in front of me once more.

I slid to a stop. There was nowhere else for me to go,

anyway. If he could move that quickly but he didn't grab me...maybe I had a chance.

He stood there calmly, watching me while the blood pounded in my ears.

His words whispered around me, gentle this time. "I have searched the ages for you, little one."

Okay. That didn't sound good.

He waited for me to say something, or react in some way. His hand moved to reach out again and I flinched back. I couldn't even help it...I ran. He was too powerful. Whatever he wanted with me couldn't be good. I had to get out of here.

But in the next moment, there was a quick burst of light and an uncomfortable wrench in my belly. The desert and the winged man were gone.

I stood on the beach in front of the abbey, still breathing hard.

Tristan stood beside me. He reached over, rested his hand on my back, his fingers lightly fitted over the same spot he'd touched me before. My distress melted away as a feeling of safety spread from his hand.

I woke up then, lying alone in bed.

What the hell had that been?

My dreams had gotten a little too weird, even for me. I closed my eyes, tried not to see those strange eyes staring back at me. Eventually I fell into a deep, dreamless sleep.

*

Why had I agreed to do this?

I really did want to learn a new language, but it was hard to think past the idea of spending the afternoon at

Tristan's house. Growing up, I'd never gone over to anyone's house.

Once again I'd be thrown into Tristan's path. On Monday I'd have to face the consequences. Whether he told the truth or made things up about me didn't really matter in the end. It'd be more unwanted attention.

But first I had to make it through this afternoon. I straightened my shoulders, headed down to the kitchen where I found Helen finishing breakfast.

"Good morning, Sweetie. You're up early."

"I didn't feel much like sleeping in." I avoided her concerned look.

"Are you excited about this afternoon, Evie?" Sebastian asked as he came in, headed straight for the coffee.

On Sundays, Sebastian held mass in the small church in town, which all the nuns attended. I stopped going as soon as I was old enough to be on my own.

"Yeah, sure. It should be interesting." Out of the corner of my eye I saw Helen nudge him. I hid a smile.

"You aren't nervous, are you? I mean, it's okay if you are. Or if there's something else that's bothering you?" He tried to sound casual.

"All right, maybe I'm a little nervous about this afternoon," I admitted with a smile. "But I'll be fine. Don't worry."

They exchanged a look. I was sure the two of them could carry on entire conversations without actually speaking.

"Of course we worry," Helen said, but let it go. "I'm sure you'll have fun." She kissed me on the forehead.

"See you when you get back," said Sebastian, with a quick hug for me. Then the two of them left to get ready for mass while I headed up to my room to wait out the morning.

Though everybody slept on this floor, leaving the third floor entirely empty, there was still more than enough space. I was at the end of the hall, with empty rooms around me.

My bedroom, like the others, was a decent size but sparsely furnished. A bed, a wardrobe, a desk with a spider plant on it – that was about all I called my own. Hung on the wall was an old charcoal drawing of a ship at sea. In the winter the wood floor was always cold, though there was a red knitted rug in the middle, the only bit of color.

I paced around in circles as the knot of anxiety in my stomach grew. Weird dreams, creepy shadows, danger, and worst of all, Tristan.

I plopped down at the desk with a sigh. I noticed a brown discoloration creep along the leaves of my spider plant. It withered even while I watched, drooping as its energy was sucked away.

Great, another disturbing issue: I was losing control more often these days. I didn't want to admit it, but my magic seemed to be growing stronger.

Okay, deep breath.

I had to be more careful. I couldn't go around killing plants near me every time I was in a bad mood, like when I was little. Luckily the plant wasn't dead. I found out long ago that regardless of the extraordinarily weird things I could do, once something was dead it stayed dead.

I gathered myself together, concentrated on the plant, and directed my magic up through the roots, out along the leaves. Cells plumped; healthy green and white coloring spread to the tips, the wilt I caused erasing.

When it looked as good as before, I began to let go. A thought occurred to me though. I relaxed my grip on the trickle of magic and poured more of it into the plant, testing myself. The leaves spread thicker, longer. A new shoot stretched out, baby spider plants bursting along it.

I pulled back. It was lush and thick, with months of healthy growth gained.

Whatever threat I may face in the future, the ability to grow plants quickly probably wouldn't help much. But it seemed prudent now to figure out what I was capable of. And my limits.

When it was time to leave, I pulled on a button-down sweater, set out at a steady pace.

The crows perched on the roof swooped down around me, cawing their agitation in response to my tension.

"No, no, back to the abbey with you. You too, Stopha, I'm serious. I know you're worried, but I don't want Tristan to witness anything strange around me today."

After a walk that didn't take nearly long enough, I found their cottage, set a little ways back from the beach, nestled in the trees. It was the only house north of the abbey and had been abandoned for years.

It was a quaint little cottage that stood two stories high, its porch facing the water. The shingles were a weathered gray, with freshly painted white shutters to match the gingerbread trim trailing along the steeple roof. Vines and late blooming plants crept up the sides of the porch, twisting around the rails. It looked like it'd been plucked out of a fairytale. I'd always wanted to see inside.

I walked up the porch steps as my stomach tried to make a break for it by jumping out through my throat. Before I could knock, the door opened. Greta stood before me. She wore a light gray dress with a shawl draped over bony shoulders. I was only a couple of inches taller than her, and once again I found myself caught in her penetrating gaze.

After a moment she shifted her eyes to the sky. "Something's got the crows all worked up," she remarked in a grim tone. I followed her look and saw the disturbed crows flying circles above us. I tried to think of some excuse for their behavior but Greta continued, her attention back on me. "It's lovely to see you again, my dear. I'm glad you decided to come."

"I appreciate you taking the time to teach me."

"Oh, it's nothing. Come in, please. Would you like some tea?"

"Yes, thanks." I followed her in, looked around while she busied herself in the kitchen. The living room was neat and uncluttered, with elegant furniture. An entire wall was nothing but shelves filled with books. Candles were strewn along the mantle of a stone fireplace. Wooden floors, pale blue walls, and a large bay window gave it an airy feel.

"It's a bit bare, I know." Greta returned with a tray. "We have a big family house back home in Haverhill that's full of fancy old furniture and paintings and whatnot. It seemed like a waste to drag any of it out here, though. Besides, this is a bit more calming on the senses."

They certainly bothered to drag a whole lot of books with them. I approved.

I nodded with a polite smile, took the cup of tea. I wondered if they planned to stay here long but thought it would be rude to ask.

"Have a seat. If you don't mind, we can work here by the window. I love the view of the water."

We sat in rocking chairs and I glanced around, wondering if we were alone, before I noticed Greta eyeing me speculatively.

"I thought we might start with Italian," she said after a moment. "And don't worry, we won't be interrupted. Tristan is out for the afternoon."

Color crept up in my cheeks. "I've always wanted to learn Italian."

"Then let us begin."

Now this part, I actually looked forward to. There weren't any new or challenging subjects in school. This was it.

Greta opened with the basics. I had a good ear for pronunciation; the words seemed to flow out of her and into me. She wasted no time reviewing anything she'd already mentioned once.

"You've done quite well today," she said when I finished repeating a verb set.

I looked around only to find the light had begun to fade. "Oh no. I didn't realize it was so late. I'm sorry, I didn't mean to take up your entire afternoon."

Greta stared off at something outside. When she didn't respond immediately I wondered if I should repeat myself. "No need to apologize," she said suddenly. She refocused on me as I tried to see what had her attention. "I enjoyed myself. It's been a long time since I've met anyone quite so gifted with language."

I tried to smother a smile. Greta didn't seem like the kind of woman to give compliments out lightly. "Thanks. That's kind of you to say." I stood up, awkwardness catching hold of me.

"Will you come back next Sunday for another lesson?"

"I'd love to. One o'clock again?"

"That's perfect." Greta stood up with me.

"Well, I should get going. I don't want anyone to worry."

"Of course. Tristan will walk you home."

"No, please. That's really not necessary," I said, appalled at the idea of Greta forcing him to escort me. "I'd rather not wait for him. I need to get back."

"Don't worry. He's just gotten home." Greta glanced at the door just a moment before it opened. Tristan walked through.

My breath caught in my throat. His cheeks were flushed from the chill evening air. His bright eyes went straight to me.

"We're finished, dear, if you wouldn't mind walking Eva back?"

"Sure. I'm ready when you are."

"Honestly, I'll be fine on my own," I managed to mutter.

Greta put her hands on my shoulders, her expression hard. "I'm sure you can take care of yourself. But this world can be a dangerous place. It never hurts to be cautious." She released me and turned away, leaving a thread of disquiet. She continued in a lighter voice, "You kids should get going."

Tension crept up my shoulders as I followed Tristan out the door. The sun had almost completely set, the woods shadowy when we stepped onto the path. Just the two of us. Alone.

"Are you warm enough?" Tristan asked, startling me.

I glanced over at him but couldn't read his expression.

"Yeah, I'm fine." Okay, my sweater was thin — I was actually freezing, but I didn't want to admit it. Not to him. I could damn well tough it out for the walk home, even though the breeze that picked up sent icy fingers across my skin, making me shiver.

Tristan unbuttoned his coat and before I realized what he meant to do, he'd put it around my shoulders. I slowed down. "Really, you don't need to do that."

He stopped, turned to me. "You're cold, Eva. I'm not, don't worry. You'll be warmer if you put your arms through the sleeves."

It was strange to hear him say my name. I didn't want to examine the feeling it kindled too closely.

Tristan waited, his gaze intense as he watched me, so I slipped my arms into the coat and started to walk again. It was a thick, dark blue material with a high collar. I felt warmer immediately.

Guilt pushed at me. I looked over at him. He wore a

gray, cable-knit sweater over a long sleeve shirt, with worn jeans. He certainly didn't look cold.

I opened my mouth to start a conversation but snapped it closed before I did anything stupid. Just because he was polite now, outside of school, didn't mean we were friends. Come Monday, he could still throw me to the wolves.

Now that he was here, a silent presence beside me, it took so much longer to get back than my trip out had.

Finally, though, I started to catch glimpses of the abbey lights through the trees.

The view opened up. I wondered how imposing Ragnarok looked to outsiders. The slate gray roof sloped into turrets perched on the curved corners of the massive rectangular shape, rows of windows set against pale shingles. The stone chapel extended inland off the north side of the building, ivy climbing around the arched windows, a bell tower rising from its entrance. A fortress overlooking the sea.

I caught sight of Sebastian. He must have seen us come out of the woods because he angled toward us.

"Thank goodness you're back, I started to get worried."

"I'm sorry. I lost track of the time." I hoped any scolding would come after Tristan left.

"My grandmother wanted me to apologize," Tristan said. "She was having too much fun with the challenge of such a bright student to pay attention to the time."

I wished I could read his face better. It certainly sounded convincing, though Greta clearly had said nothing of the sort. If it kept me from getting into trouble, I supposed I was all for it.

"Tell your grandmother it's no problem. I really appreciate you walking Eva home."

"It was my pleasure."

Even that sounded sincere.

"I meant to tell you the other night," Sebastian said, quite pleased, "for school, if you take that path here to Ragnarok, there's another path that leads straight into town. It's much shorter than going along the road. Please feel free to cut through here to save yourself some time. I'm sure Eva would be happy to have company."

I couldn't believe it. There would be no end to these humiliations. I couldn't escape him.

"That's nice of you to offer. Thanks."

"Well, you have a good night. I'll see you inside, dear." Sebastian walked away. I wished he hadn't made it impossible for me to leave with him.

I could feel Tristan's gaze on me, but I had a hard time pulling my eyes from the woods to look back at him. I exhaled slowly. I'd at least be polite. "Thanks for walking me home. And for the coat." I pulled it off and handed it to him, the air so much colder after the warmth of it.

"You're welcome," he said with amusement.

I started to walk away.

"Eva." I turned back. The lights barely touched his face. "Goodnight," he said softly. Then he disappeared into the night.

For a long minute I stared into the darkness after him. I sighed, turned away. There was no point in wishing things were different.

Eventually, when I went to bed, I dreamt once again of

the strange night desert. As before, the winged man with the otherworldly eyes was with me. There was something subtly threatening about him, though he hadn't hurt me in any way. He seemed only to want to find me.

It was the fact that he wanted to find me outside of the dream, find me for real, that I found disconcerting.

I stood before him, trembling slightly, wondering if I should run, when a hand slipped into mine. I turned to see who it was, but there was a strong tug on my arm, a quick flare of light.

I was on the lawn in front of the abbey, the winged man gone.

Tristan stood beside me, his hand in mine.

"Go to sleep, Eva," he whispered.

The dream dissolved. I sighed, turned over, dreamt of nothing more.

Chapter Five

Mary put together a lunch while I tried to force down cereal at the kitchen table. My stomach wouldn't cooperate. There would be nothing good about this day except the fact that it would eventually have to end.

"Do you want an apple or an orange with your lunch?" Mary asked, good humor bubbling out of her even at such an early hour.

"You know I can make my own lunches, right?" I tried to rally.

"You're very capable, dear, I know. But I happen to want to do this. So what's it going to be?"

"Apple, please."

I managed a smile for her as she finished up. She kissed me on the cheek, wished me a good day, and went off to her own work.

I stared at the door.

There was no way to escape the inevitable, so I put on my coat, pulled the strap of my bag over my shoulder.

Thankfully, there was no sign of Tristan outside. Of course. Walking with me would give people the wrong idea.

So I left alone...one less ordeal to get through.

I had barely enough time to go to my locker before class. I'd discovered avoiding down time was key for surviving school. Most of the kids who stood around in the hallway ignored me, but a few stopped to stare as I passed.

Just keep calm – if I wanted to get through this, I had to learn not to care.

When the bell rang, I slipped into the flow of students, headed to class. As I sat down, I overheard the girls speculating about Tristan's absence. I was curious what might've happened since last night. Maybe my luck would continue...if no one heard about Tristan's weekend, it might even count as a good day.

Mr. Edwards ended the period with a quiz that was ridiculously easy. When he dismissed us, I followed Molly and Sarah out.

"This day totally sucks," Molly said, her pout clear even from behind.

"Seriously."

"Hey, guys, wait up." Katie caught up with them, breathless and flushed.

"Ugh, I do not want to know what you've been doing," Sarah said.

"What? No, I–"

"Not now, Katie," Molly said. "I need to borrow your notes. Mr. Edwards was completely unfair – he gave us a pop quiz. I can't fail the next one."

"Who cares about that? Way more importantly, I just saw Tristan come out of the office. He'll be with you in English."

"Really? That's awesome. Give me details, I want to know everything."

"Something about his grandmother keeping him up late. I think she didn't feel well or something. So he slept in."

I tuned them out as they chattered on about the encounter. I really didn't want to hear it. My legs somehow kept moving, despite my reluctance to get where I was headed. I filed into class behind the girls, saw Tristan at the head of my aisle talking to Lisbeth. Molly and Sarah joined them.

"I'm glad to hear your grandmother is all right," Lisbeth said.

"Yeah, me too," Molly added. She gave his arm a squeeze. "I was worried. We missed you this morning."

I slipped around them and then tried to disappear into my seat.

"Thank you. Both. That's very nice."

"You should know Mr. Edwards gave us a quiz. If you need help studying, I can tell you what was on it."

"Ah. Thanks for the offer, Molly, but I'll be fine. I'll stop by to see him later."

"So," she pressed, "what did you do this weekend? You didn't show up Friday night."

My whole body went rigid. I prepared myself for the looks of incredulity, the comments.

"Not much. Mostly I just spent time with my grand-mother."

I waited, held my breath.

"Oh, that's…nice. Maybe next weekend you can come hang out with us."

"Yeah, maybe," he said as the bell rang. I couldn't be-lieve it. Was that it?

Tristan walked toward the seat behind me, caught my eye. His mouth quirked in a little smile and then he passed me. I sagged with relief. Whatever his reasons, I could only be grateful.

I wasn't delusional – it's not like it was a declaration of friendship. But it seemed we had an understanding, of sorts.

At lunch, Tristan's group sat at the next table, as they had been every day. It got easier to shut them out, but at one point, when I heard his voice clearly, the details of my dream flooded back. I could almost feel his hand in mine.

Thank goodness he had no way of knowing about it. It was strange, though. There was nothing safe or reassuring about him in real life, why so in the dreams?

And he wasn't just in the dreams of the winged man, I had to admit. In almost every other regular dream I had now, Tristan was a steady presence, lurking in the back-ground, watching. My subconscious had a serious obsession with the guy.

Without meaning to, I raised my head, searched for the object of my thoughts. Tristan sat on the other side of the table, facing in my direction. Oliver told a story that had everyone laughing.

I studied Tristan's expression, curious. His green eyes were sharp as he watched the people at his table. He said very little himself. A trace of his smile lingered when he looked over at me unexpectedly. My heart skipped a beat and I dropped my eyes.

If I wasn't more careful, Tristan might just get the wrong idea. There was no way I wanted him to think I had a crush on him. I kept my eyes on my book for the rest of lunch while I tried to block out the image of his smile.

*

I dropped my bag on the grass near the garden, folded my legs beneath me, took a couple of deep breaths. Something bad was headed my way…I had to stop procrastinating. I had to start practicing magic every day, trying whatever came to mind.

Easy. Right?

I closed my eyes, reached out with my senses and caught the breeze as it brushed lightly against my skin. I pushed further, felt the wind that trailed through the trees, rustled the grass around me.

I drew on the air, spun it around me. When I opened my eyes, flower petals from the garden and fallen leaves were swept up. My hair blew against my face while I watched the small pieces of color whip past, urging it faster.

Beyond the whirlwind the trees still swayed gently in the light wind that had blown all afternoon. Nothing outside my little sphere was affected.

I let go. The leaves revolving around me slowly drifted to the ground.

Success.

I flopped back, stared at the sky, listened to the waves crash on the beach. It was no wonder the kids at school thought I was a freak. Magic wasn't supposed to exist. And yet, here I was, controlling the wind.

Magic. Something I'd forbidden myself from even thinking about for years now. How would Sebastian and Helen react if they found out I was playing around with it? I imagined trying to explain about the dreams, the un-known danger.

No, definitely better to keep them in the dark. They wouldn't understand. How could they? I didn't understand it myself.

A black shape floated across my vision. I sat up as Sto-pha swooped down to land on my bag.

"Hey, you," I said softly.

He cocked his head, opened his black beak to caw at me. A chorus of crows perched in the trees echoed him.

"I'm sorry, Mephistopheles. I didn't mean to make you nervous. I was just practicing." I stood up, stretched. "Don't worry, I'm done for now."

The abbey was quiet when I went downstairs later. I neared the kitchen and the sound of laughter escaped the closed door, echoing down the unlit hall. I paused, sud-denly reluctant. I didn't belong to the happy, uncomplicated world on the other side of the door.

Before I could shake the feeling that kept me rooted, the door opened, warm light spilling out.

"Oh my goodness!" Mary exclaimed, her hand on her heart. "Eva, why are you standing there in the dark? You nearly scared me to death!"

"Sorry. I was on my way to see about dinner."

"Well, you have good timing. I was just headed up to get you." Mary ushered me into the kitchen.

"We're having vegetable stew, and we'll eat in here. I hope that's okay," Agnes said, impatiently pushing back some long red hair that had escaped her braid.

"Sounds great, I'm starving. Where is everyone?" I began to set the table.

"Helen has a headache, and apparently–"

"Sebastian ate earlier."

"I have no idea where Catherine and the other two are."

My mood lightened while I ate, listening to the women talk about their day.

"So, my dear, Mary and I were chatting earlier and–"

"We wondered how things were at school?"

"They're fine. I did well on my math quiz today."

"That's excellent. But–"

"Aggie and I were actually more curious about the social situation."

"How that was shaping up."

"Specifically," Mary said, full of mischief, "we wanted to know about Tristan."

"Oh. We're not really friends." I knew where they would take this. Inwardly I groaned.

"But yesterday you spent all afternoon at his house," Agnes said.

"And Helen told us he walked you home."

"You don't have to tell us if you don't want to…but we'd love some details."

"You must think he's cute, at least," Mary said with a wink.

I couldn't help but laugh. "You two are impossible!"

"Well, you can't blame us. We just want you to have a little fun. Like we did when we were your age."

"What's this 'we' business, Em? You were the one who was boy crazy in school."

"Oh please! I certainly wasn't the only one. I seem to recall a certain boy you went to all the dances with."

"That's right! I forgot." Agnes laughed. "Oh, Ben was really sweet."

"Don't look so surprised, Eva, we weren't always nuns, you know."

"I know. It's fun to hear about it, though." I loved their stories – they'd been friends since first grade, knew everything there was to know about each other.

Mary sighed. "It was fun to live through."

"We just want you to have some good times like that," Agnes said. "Are you sure there's nothing you have to say about Tristan?"

"He did seem awfully nice," Mary said.

"Yes, he is nice, actually. But no, there's nothing to tell. Sorry."

"Okay. But you keep us updated if anything changes."

"You never know what might happen during a romantic stroll through the woods at night."

"Mary!" Agnes and I burst into giggles.

"There's no discouraging her, Eva."

*

School seemed more gloomy than usual, the students subdued. I stared out the window at the rain instead of paying attention...drifted from one class to the next, wishing I was curled up in Sebastian's study with a good book.

Tristan and I passed each other without any acknowledgement, though I was always aware of his presence.

School ended, and once I was outside, I didn't want to be cooped up again so soon. So instead, I wandered off on a side path in the woods to the small pond where my crows liked to gather.

I watched raindrops ripple across the surface while my thoughts strayed. After a time, the rain stopped, though the break wouldn't last. In the new stillness, the reflection on the water was crystal clear.

I crouched down to dip my finger in the water, swirling it idly.

I knew I should head home – with such dreary weather Helen might start worrying sooner rather than later.

The water shimmered oddly. I leaned over to look closer, and instead of my own reflection, I saw Helen.

Goosebumps broke out across my skin.

I concentrated on the image: Helen set a mug down on Sebastian's desk as he worked. I could see her lips move, but couldn't hear what she said. When she put her hand on Sebastian's arm, he smiled up at her.

I let the image of the tender moment fade. I wondered if I could see anyone like this, and unintentionally Tristan came to mind. Almost immediately a picture formed. He stood in the bookstore in town, searching along the shelves.

While I watched, he glanced around as though someone had called his name. I released my grip on the image, not wanting to see who might be there to meet up with him.

On a whim, I thought of Greta. She was on the beach, an umbrella against her shoulder, staring out at the water. Abruptly, she shifted her gaze – it seemed like she looked directly at me. A second later a drop of rain fell, disrupting the image, followed by a steady downpour.

I straightened up and hurried home, huddled under my umbrella. Okay, that was seriously unnerving. It was probably just a trick of perception. Of course, since I really didn't know what I was doing, anything was possible.

Inside, I crept down the hallway to Sebastian's study. He was there by himself, but the cup of tea was on the desk where Helen had left it.

All right then.

I didn't want to interrupt, so I went upstairs to distract myself with homework. Answering the questions correctly was easy. But making sure I got just enough wrong answers to keep from being singled out in class took more attention.

I went to bed late, listening to the patter of the rain against my windows. For the second night in a row, my dreams were nothing out of the ordinary, and when I woke up the next morning, I had an idea in mind for something I wanted to try.

The rain had passed. The sun was shining, the air crisp. The idea of working more magic was exciting...and a little terrifying. The more I used it, the greater the chances I'd be caught. I'd never purposefully done anything the nuns would disapprove of.

It also felt like the more I practiced magic, the closer I was inevitably drawn toward some unknown danger.

After school I grabbed a blanket, headed to the spot I'd used the other day. Because of the way the lawn curved out into the woods, any view from the abbey windows was blocked off. I spread the blanket out and sat down.

The realization had hit me that my best weapon would be fire. I really only knew how to light candles, though. I needed to learn how to handle fire without getting burned. After all, came the wry thought, I'd have to be able to defend myself in case the townsfolk ever came after me with torches.

I ignored the flutter in my stomach.

I held out my hand, concentrated on creating a flame just above my palm.

Nothing happened. Great.

There had to be something missing. I imagined lighting the candles in the dining room, managed to call up a spark...but it died immediately. Obviously it must be different without a wick to sustain it.

I grabbed a few leaves. I'd have to start with fuel, figure out how to work without it from there.

I held them out, focused intently. Suddenly they burst into flame, burning my hand. I yelped in surprise and dropped the leaves, which continued to burn.

Quickly, I grabbed the edge of the blanket, used it to smother the flames.

I sat back, looking at the scorch marks. I had to admit, that was an unbelievably stupid thing to do. My control apparently wasn't very steady. And clearly, I needed to learn how to not burn myself.

I lay back, discouraged. This would take a lot of practice and patience. I was totally up for it, but I did feel a little deflated after such a botched first attempt.

I stared at the edges of the clouds swirling against the blue sky, tried to work out a plan. After a few peaceful minutes, though, the stress of my mishap eased, and I let my eyes drift closed as my late night caught up with me.

A scream suddenly cut through the air. I whipped my head up, looked around. And what I saw was horrible.

The world was on fire.

Chapter Six

I stood in the middle of a village, under a deep night sky, in a time long since passed. Fire howled as it spread from building to building, catching quickly on the thatched roofs. People ran past me. Their cries tore at me. There was a loud crash when the beams in the roof of the house next to me collapsed, sparks flying.

Over the roar of the fires, a sound far different from the comforting crackle of a cozy fire in the fireplace, I heard the unmistakable sounds of battle. Men shouted. Steel clashed against steel. It came from the other end of the village, the direction everyone fled from.

Without meaning to, I moved toward the fight. I wanted to turn, get away, but I had no control over my legs. The air was hot; smoke stung my eyes. I stumbled over something, realized it was a body that lay broken in the dirt. Panic flooded through me as I began to run, fearing I would be too late.

Some part of my brain realized I was seeing the world

through someone else's eyes, feeling what he felt. I was only an observer here.

I rounded a corner. The scene made me want to retch. Dead bodies were scattered about, the ground slick with their blood. Flames ringed the small battlefield, nothing more left of the village. This was what Hell must look like.

A small group of men still stood. Three of the villagers fought against one man, who wielded his sword in a frenzy. I ran to help, but I slipped, fell to my knees, seeing nothing but red.

I raised my head just as the man killed the last of the village's defenders.

I struggled to stand, knowing already I was defeated, but unwilling to give up. He strode toward me. The part of me still aware of myself recognized him as the winged man from my dreams.

My arm rose on its own and I found I held a sword. I faced my death.

He came at me with a scream of rage, knocked the blade out of my hand almost immediately. He threw down his own sword, and his hands wrapped around my neck, his eyes mad with grief. I struggled, tried to pull his hands away. I couldn't scream. My fingers clawed at him, but it made no difference. The world shrank to nothing but his gaze burning into mine.

I closed my eyes to shut out the sight of his fury.

A long, panic-filled scream pierced the darkness. I struggled harder.

"Eva!"

I couldn't breathe. I couldn't get his hands off my throat.

"Eva, stop it! You have to calm down!"

Someone grabbed my wrists, kept me from fighting.

"Hold still. I'm trying to help you."

The familiar voice began to penetrate through my terror.

"It's just a dream. Wake up."

I came back to myself fully then and stopped screaming. I opened my eyes to find Tristan leaning over me, my hands pinned to his chest to keep me from moving.

"Eva?" he asked in a gentler voice.

I drew in a ragged breath, tried to calm down. He let go of my wrists and reached down to run his fingers across my forehead. He smoothed my hair back. I couldn't stop shaking, and to my embarrassment, I realized tears streamed down my face.

"You're okay. It's over."

I wiped my face and sat up. I had to pull myself together.

Tristan sat back, watching me with a small frown of concern.

"Sorry."

"You don't have to apologize. Are you all right?"

"Yeah. I fell asleep. I guess I…I had a bad dream."

He raised an eyebrow. "That's a bit of an understatement."

I couldn't get those images out of my head. I didn't mean to say anything, but the words started dragging out of me anyway. "It was horrible. It all felt so real." My voice trembled. I swallowed against the tears threatening again. I absolutely couldn't fall apart in front of him any more than I already had.

"Here, let me look at your throat. It looks like you scratched yourself." He scooted closer, but as he reached over, I flinched. "I'm not going to hurt you, Eva."

His green eyes were steady, reassuring. I could do this. I nodded and closed my eyes. Cool fingers touched my throat gently, a relief against the heat of my skin. He felt at a sore spot, and my eyes flew open as my breath hissed out.

"Sorry."

"You don't have to apologize," I repeated, copying his soft Scottish lilt.

He suppressed a chuckle.

I turned my head a little, watched him carefully inspect my neck. His fingers moved lightly over my skin. His face was close – so very close. When he lifted his gaze to meet mine, I felt a sudden flutter in my chest.

"You scratched yourself up a bit," he said, straightening, serious again. "And I'm not sure how, but you managed to bruise your neck, too." He frowned, picked up my hand, pulled back the sleeve. The skin on my wrist was a dark red. "I'm really sorry. I think that's from me."

"Don't worry – it's not your fault."

"You're a lot stronger than you look, you know." His eyes had a teasing glint.

I couldn't help but smile.

I was undoubtedly grateful he woke me from the nightmare, but as my fright faded, my humiliation grew. It was bad enough Tristan had heard stories about how strange I was, but I'd hoped he would never actually witness any of it himself.

This wasn't something that happened to normal girls.

My hand still rested in Tristan's as he stared at my bruises, thinking who knows what. My entire awareness shrank down to focus only on the feel of my hand in his. I had to distract myself.

"Tristan, what are you doing here?"

He lifted his eyes to mine. I pulled my hand away.

"I suppose I thought I was helping you," he said, rubbing his jaw.

"Yeah, I got that part." I smiled. "And I appreciate it. I wondered more how you came to find me?"

He stared off in the distance for a moment. When he answered, his voice sounded strained.

"I heard you screaming. I got here as quickly as I could."

"From your house?"

"No." He met my eyes again, his lips quirked in a smile. "I happened to be passing through on my way home. I stayed late at school to do extra credit for the math quiz I missed, used the shortcut through the abbey. It was just lucky timing."

I felt an odd stab of doubt. But as I stared at my hands, I whispered, "Thank you."

"Do you want to talk about it?"

When I looked up at him, I didn't know what to say. I wasn't ready to think about it yet, and if I tried to explain I'd probably start to cry again. Not to mention he'd think I was crazy. I shook my head.

"You have nightmares a lot."

"Yeah. But not usually that...intense."

"I see."

Tristan went quiet. He stared at the ground, lost in thought. I studied his face. His eyelashes were incredibly long. For some reason it made him look vulnerable.

His eyes narrowed. He looked up at me.

"Your blanket is burned."

My cheeks flushed. "I had a little accident."

"You should be more careful," he said with a funny look, probably thinking I was an idiot. "Fire can be tricky."

"I'll keep that in mind."

"Anyway—"

"I know. It's getting late." I stood up.

"No. Wait." He stood up with me. "I was just going to say – my grandmother knows a lot of old herbal remedies. She might have something to help you sleep without the bad dreams."

I didn't know what to say. I was already afraid of falling asleep again tonight.

"Why don't you come back with me and talk to her?"

My relief vanished. A tense walk over there, an uncomfortable explanation to Greta – it was too much for me. I still felt shaky...and I didn't want to take up more of Tristan's afternoon.

"Thanks for the offer. I'd rather just go home, though."

He sighed. "I understand." He cocked his head as he studied me. "You have something that'll cover your neck? I'm sure you'd rather avoid people asking questions."

"My coat should hide it until I can change."

Before I could object, Tristan picked up my coat, helped me into it. When I turned to face him, he adjusted the collar for me, his focus intent on his hands. He was close enough that his warm breath brushed against my cheek.

"Tristan?"

He raised his eyes to mine, his expression unreadable.

"I just...well, thanks. For being here. For helping."

"You're welcome."

He released his hold on my coat and turned away. I had to catch myself when I swayed forward. I hadn't even realized I'd leaned into him.

I gathered up the blanket, started back to the abbey, Tristan beside me. The crows all sat in the trees nearby, watching, drawn by my fear. They wouldn't come near me, though, as long as Tristan was here.

When we reached the point where his path diverged, we paused. I figured I had to know. Deep breath.

"Are you going to tell anyone at school about this?"

He reached toward me, but as soon as his fingers brushed my arm, he dropped his hand with a frown. He regarded me silently for a minute. "Eva, you don't have to worry about that. I won't say anything."

"Good. Then I guess I'll see you around."

"Are you sure you're okay? I really think I should take you to see my grandmother."

"I'll be fine. Honest." Just turn and walk away. The concern in his eyes was genuine enough to make me want to pull down my guard, let him comfort me. But I couldn't deceive myself that it meant more than it did.

When I got to the door, I looked back. Tristan still stood there, watching me. A cold gust of wind blew my hair about me and I glanced up to see dark clouds moving in. It wouldn't be long before it began to rain. I wondered if my reaction to the fire in the dream was the cause.

I raised my hand to Tristan. He waved back, continued on. I pulled the coat firmly around me and went inside. I heard voices in the reading room as I quietly closed the door, started toward the stairs.

"Evie? Is that you?" Mary called.

I stopped, feeling caught. "Just headed upstairs to do homework."

"Dinner will be ready around six."

"All right. Thanks." Relieved, I hurried up to the bathroom. I pulled off the coat to inspect my throat in the mirror.

There were long scratches from my nails. And the developing bruises were shaped suspiciously like hands. Had my body been so convinced the dream was real that finger marks showed up? How was that even possible?

I didn't want to think about how it might've ended if Tristan hadn't woken me up.

I changed into a turtleneck with a jumper dress over it. At least the colder weather wouldn't make covering my neck look odd.

Finished with that problem, I wasn't sure what to do with myself. I sat down at my desk, pulled out my homework. But all I did was stare out the window at the small stretch of beach, the miles of water.

I couldn't help but go in circles about why I had it — some vision of the past. Maybe trying to work magic with the fire triggered it. After all, fire had been everywhere. Or maybe my subconscious wanted to make up stories about the strange man who appeared so often in my dreams. Or maybe, in the end, the truth was simply that I was losing my mind. That would explain so much.

*

By six o'clock, I was barely halfway through my homework. I had to read everything three times before any meaning sank in. Plus, every time I heard a noise I jumped, my pulse racing.

I tried to compose myself for dinner. I couldn't let on anything was wrong. So, after nervously tugging my sleeves down over my wrists, I went into the kitchen with a smile on my face that quickly felt strained.

"I already got a start on sorting everything," Agnes said.

"Good," said Helen. "Sebastian wanted to make the trip to pick up the rest of the donations this weekend."

Must be the clothes donations they collected twice a year. All the local contributions, along with any from further north, came here. Then Sebastian drove south to where the clothes were distributed, making stops along the way to pick up more.

Most of my clothes came from these donations, anything I'd outgrown added back in. The nuns were always careful with their spending. I knew there was at least one private donation to Ragnarok Abbey every year that helped pay for everything, but they didn't indulge in luxuries.

"How was your day?" Mary asked as she passed me.

"Uh, good."

"Evie, the clothes are all in the reading room. If you have time before Saturday, please go through everything, see if there's anything you need." Helen turned back to what she stirred on the stove.

"And if there's anything you're throwing in, I'll do laundry tomorrow," Agnes added.

"Okay, I'll take a look."

"Helen, will you go with Sebastian?" Mary asked.

"I think so. If the weather's fair, it would be nice to go for a drive."

I tried to concentrate on the harmless conversation as a distraction. Thankfully, dinner was ready before long.

Rain began to fall soon after. I sensed it a few moments before I heard the pattering against the windowpanes.

It was difficult to sit still. My nerves felt raw, overly sensitive. I had no appetite.

My attention to the conversation slipped after a few minutes.

My mind wandered. The memory of the flames suddenly rose. I quickly turned my thoughts away, tried to block the sensation of heat.

I looked up, found Helen frowning at me.

"You look flushed, Eva. You feel okay?"

"Yeah, fine. It's just a little warm in here, that's all."

Helen looked doubtful, but I put everything I had into a bright smile. After I joined the conversation, she seemed satisfied enough to let it go.

The pretense was hard to keep up, so I was relieved when dinner finally ended. I went back to my room where I could let my guard down.

The relief didn't last.

Dinner had provided a distraction. My room was too quiet. It was harder to keep myself settled. I finished my homework, had the whole night ahead of me.

There was no way I could let myself fall asleep.

It was probably ridiculous to be afraid. It was just a nightmare. There was no reason to believe I'd have it again. But every time I closed my eyes, the image of that man striding toward me with his sword raised sent me into a panic.

Reading was no good. I could only sit still long enough to stare at the page, uncomprehending, for a couple of minutes before I couldn't stand it anymore.

So I paced. I went in a tight circle around and around the room. I would've gone elsewhere, but I didn't want anyone to wonder why I was still up – I wouldn't be able to come up with a good lie.

The night wore on. When I got tired I'd sit on the bed. But each time my eyes started to droop and I felt sleep coming on, fear shot through me, sent me back up to pace. Around. Around again. Unending.

What if I had the same dream again and Tristan wasn't there to wake me? Could I die in my sleep from the power of a dream? I wished I could recapture the calm Tristan had given me that afternoon.

Now that I was alone, with the silence of the abbey

pressed in around me, my sense of safety from the everyday world was gone. Night had stolen away reason, left me with nothing but my fears and the vivid memories of fiery scenes of death.

Chapter Seven

Dawn approached, and it was more than just the fear of sleep that drove me to keep moving. I felt feverish, the heat from the fires burned along my skin. I knew I should rest. But all that mattered was not dreaming again.

And what about all of the following nights? What the hell would I do then? I couldn't keep this up forever...but maybe the more distance I had from the nightmare when I eventually slept, the less likely it was I'd have it again.

I wasn't even sure that made sense. It was hard to concentrate. My thoughts skittered around my head. When I felt too hot, I opened all the windows to let in the cold air. But after a few minutes, I closed them again for reasons I couldn't remember by the time I finished.

Morning finally arrived, a slow creep of gray light showing the rain still fell. By now I was certain I was making it rain, but I couldn't seem to stop. I just wanted to dampen the fires. I was certain the distraction of school was all I needed.

When it was time, I pulled on the black turtleneck and a

skirt. I didn't bother with breakfast. There was nothing I could eat...and I didn't want to see anyone. I put on my coat, had trouble with the buttons – my hands wouldn't stop shaking.

It was a relief to finally be outside, the air cool on my skin. I clutched my umbrella, walked quickly.

By the time I got to school the jittery feeling had returned.

I passed through the hallway, all the faces blurred together. My own face felt flushed with heat. When I closed my eyes, flames licked up around me.

Somehow I found myself sitting in my first class, though I had no memory of how I got there. Mr. Edwards stood in front. But I couldn't seem to hear what he said.

I put my head on the desk, tried to breathe evenly, but it didn't help. Fire flickered at the edges of my vision. When I raised my head, I turned and found Tristan staring at me.

I had the vague thought he wasn't supposed to look at me. I tried to frown at him. People would notice if he didn't stop. The last thing I wanted right now was attention.

I turned my feverish gaze away.

Class was never going to end.

Just when I thought I couldn't stand to sit there any longer, the bell rang. By the time I stood up the class was empty.

Somehow I got to the door. When I stepped out, the hall was empty too. Someone grabbed my elbow, began to pull me along. I didn't resist. After a few steps I realized it was Tristan who led me. Though I tried to pull my arm out of his grip, he held on too tightly.

He was saying something. I tried to focus.

"...already called Sebastian. You need to go home, Eva."

When I looked up, we were in the office. Tristan helped me into a chair. The next moment he stood at the desk, the secretary giving him a pass. I wanted to say this was ridiculous – I didn't need his help. But I couldn't get the words out.

Tristan was in front of me again. I noticed the world going dark around the edges. He leaned down, spoke in a low voice.

"Just wait here, okay? Sebastian will be here soon. I...I'm sorry Eva, but I can't stay with you."

I felt fingers brush along my cheek.

Then he was gone.

"Not feeling well, hun?" Mrs. Tinsley, with her curly blonde hair and soft white sweater, patted my hand. "Don't you worry, your dad will be here real soon. Are you sure you don't want to go down to the nurse's office?"

I shook my head, tried to smile. It was difficult to focus on the woman's face.

"All right. I'll be just over here if you need me."

A candle burned on her desk. The flame filled my vision, flickered, flared up as I lost myself for a moment. Quickly, before the other woman saw anything, I snuffed it out.

I concentrated on my breath, willed myself to keep it together. Even though I had trouble forming clear thoughts, I had to be more careful. I could burn the place down if I didn't pay attention. And if anyone examined me, they'd find the marks on my neck. The fear of more freaky occurrences connected to me spurred a rigid control. All I needed to do was make it back to the abbey.

Time stretched out. How long had I sat there? It felt like hours, but it was probably no more than ten minutes.

I felt the sting of smoke in my eyes. At times I heard swords clash nearby. Sometimes the secretary sat across the office…sometimes I saw nothing but darkness.

"Evie?" Sebastian picked up my bag. "I'm here now. Let's get you home."

Just hold on.

I stood up. He helped me put my coat on – I was already too warm. Idly, I wondered how I managed to keep my bag and coat with me. I didn't remember picking them up in the classroom.

"How are you feeling?" He led me outside, held an umbrella to keep the rain off. It still came down steadily. I was sure if the water touched my skin it would sizzle and smoke, I was so hot.

"I just want to go home." It was hardly more than a whisper.

"Okay, sweetie. The car is right over here."

The next thing I knew, we'd pulled up to the abbey. The rain looked so cool. Inviting. All I wanted was to lie down on the ground, let it wash over me. I was so tired.

"Come on," Sebastian said. "Let's get you inside." He helped me out of the car, frowned at the tremors he felt move through me.

I struggled to keep walking toward the stairs, onto the porch. My skin blazed from the heat of the flames. I heard villagers running towards me.

"Eva? How is she, Sebastian?" Helen. Coming to meet us. "She's burning up!" She ushered us inside.

"I know. I think we should get her up to bed, then I'll see if I can get the doctor out here."

"He's gone to Ashland for a few days – some emergency. I saw his wife in town earlier this morning."

We were a few stairs up when the doorbell rang. The two of them exchanged a look above me. Sebastian went to answer it.

Greta stood in the doorway, a bag in her hand. Rain poured down behind her.

"Greta, I'm sorry, this isn't a good time," Sebastian said, glanced back at us.

"I know. Eva's sick. I'm here to help."

"How did you...?"

"Tristan called me. If you haven't already tried the doctor, don't bother. He's out of town. That's why I'm here."

Greta went on about medical training she'd had...I wandered elsewhere. It got hard to see again, a steady black fog spreading.

I heard the crows calling to me.

"She certainly does have a fever. Get her up to bed."

My feet moved, so much heavier than usual. I was lowered onto a mattress.

Pieces of my nightmare shifted in and out of focus. There was so much fire. I couldn't seem to get away from it.

"Get me a bowl of cold water with ice and a wash-cloth."

Helen hurried from the room.

"Is there anything I can do to help?" Sebastian held my hand. I heard a crash as the roof fell in next to me. I tried to jerk away – the fire would spread.

"Help me hold her head up. She needs to drink this."

I was lifted, something thick and sticky poured down my throat. I coughed, managed to choke it down. Placed back on the pillow. The trembling eased a little...though I still flickered between worlds.

"Sebastian, will you get some hot water to make tea in? Don't worry – she'll be okay. The mixture will begin to work soon."

He hesitated, left the room. Greta leaned over, whispered something strange in my ear. Not a language I understood.

The words swirled around me...the flames began to recede. Was the mixture working? Sleep pulled at me. So heavy. I struggled against it.

"Don't fight it, Eva," Greta murmured. "It'll be a deep sleep, I promise."

I let go, slipped into the cool darkness, unaware of anything else.

*

Low voices reached me from far away. I drifted in shadow, more asleep than awake.

"How am I supposed to help her if I can't–"

"No," a soft voice interrupted. "You know the reasons, the dangers. You must keep your distance and we'll do what we can until..." The voices faded out. What were they talking about? Was I dreaming? I couldn't quite grasp at it, and as I tried, I drifted away, deeper into sleep.

*

Soft morning light filtered in with the sound of whispered voices. Helen and Sebastian sat next to the bed, their heads bent together in a quiet conversation.

So it all really happened – the nightmare creeping up around me, the fever. I closed my eyes, relieved it hadn't sucked me down in the end.

"Welcome back, Eva," Greta's sturdy voice silenced the whispering. "How do you feel?"

I opened my eyes again. Greta stood at the foot of the bed. "Better, I guess. How long was I asleep?" My voice was hoarse, weak.

"About twenty-four hours," Helen said. She took my hand.

"You had us worried there," said Sebastian.

"What happened?"

"You had a high fever," Greta answered. "I'm not sure how you managed to get yourself to school yesterday, you must have felt terrible. Tristan noticed. He said you were quite out of it."

"How could no one else have noticed?" Helen muttered.

I avoided her eyes.

"Well, anyway, Tristan called Sebastian, got you down to the office. Apparently you were adamant about not going to the nurse."

I had no memory of telling him that. But it made sense.

When I remembered why, I pulled my hand out from under the blanket to feel my neck. I still wore the turtleneck, thankfully.

Greta watched me, one eyebrow raised. Tristan had told her? I looked into the anxious faces of Helen and Sebastian. Neither of them had slept much, if at all. They didn't need any more reasons to worry about me.

"Thanks for coming to help," I said. "And please thank Tristan for me."

"Of course. You'll feel just fine after a little more rest."

Helen stood, took Greta's hands in her own. "How can we ever thank you enough?"

"Think nothing of it. I was happy to be able to help. Now I think I will excuse myself and head home."

"Let me give you a ride."

"I appreciate the offer, Sebastian, but I'd rather walk. It would be good to get some blood flowing in these old legs. You," she turned to me, "stay in bed for the rest of the day. I don't want you to do anything too difficult for the next couple of days – you need your sleep. Make sure you drink enough fluids, too. I'll check in on you later, dear."

Sebastian walked Greta downstairs. Helen sat back down next to the bed, stroked my hair.

"Mary and Agnes have been in and out all night, as much as Greta would allow. Everybody's been very anxious."

"I'm sorry."

"Don't be sorry, you silly girl. It's not your fault."

"I know. I just didn't mean to worry you."

"Eva, why didn't you tell me you felt sick?"

I shrugged. "It didn't seem that bad."

"I'm sure it was hard to think straight. You were pretty lost by the time you got home." Helen bit her lip. "It just seems like you keep a lot to yourself these days."

My throat pinched. But what was I supposed say? How was I supposed to confide to her all the strange things happening? Especially when she wouldn't approve of what I'd been doing lately.

Way more than any of that, I didn't want to scare her.

"Oh sweetie," Helen whispered. "It's okay. I only want you to know that when you're ready, you can tell me anything. We're all here for you. No matter what." She leaned over, kissed my forehead.

Exhaustion settled over me.

"Rest now," Helen murmured. She pulled the blanket up around my shoulders. Almost immediately, my heavy eyelids fell.

*

"I think she's waking up." Mary's excitement reached me as I shifted.

"Shhhh. Don't wake her before she's ready," hissed Agnes.

I smiled and opened my eyes to find the two nuns next to the bed, watching me.

"Oooh, you are awake! How do you feel?"

"Better. Thanks." I sat up.

"Here's another pillow." Agnes helped prop me up.

"Are you hungry? We've made soup, in case you are."

"Yeah. Actually, I'm starving."

"That's a good sign."

"I'll just pop down to get a bowl for you. Don't say too

much, I don't want to miss anything." Mary bounced out of the room.

"Even with hardly any sleep, that woman is full of energy," Agnes remarked.

"I know. It's impressive."

"I must say – you look much better. It took a while, but we finally managed to convince Helen to take a nap. She absolutely refused to leave your side earlier."

"I figured. What time is it? What day is it, I guess I should ask?"

"It's still Friday, early evening – you didn't miss much."

Mary returned with a bowl of chicken noodle soup and a glass of water.

Warmth spread from my belly as I swallowed it down greedily.

"Well," Mary said, "that was quite the night. Evie, dear, how did you even walk to school? Sebastian practically had to carry you up the stairs when you came back."

"I have no idea. I guess I thought I'd feel better when I got there."

"It's a good thing Tristan was there," Agnes said.

"That's right," Mary added, "and thankfully he called his grandmother. She was incredible."

"We really ought to have them over for dinner again–"

"To thank them properly, yes."

"Did Greta stay here all night?"

"She did," Agnes replied. "Even when it was clear the fever had passed. Tristan didn't leave until it was time to go to school this morning."

"What?" I sputtered, almost choking on the soup. "Tristan was here?"

They exchanged a look, both grinning. Mary explained. "He came over after school yesterday with some things for Greta. He stayed the whole night, helping her."

"Not that she needed extra helpers. But I think we got under foot a little too much for her taste."

"He looked quite worried about you, you know." Mary smirked.

"Are you sure there's nothing you want to talk to us about, dear?"

My insides squirmed at the thought of Tristan in my room while I was unconscious. This was unbelievable. And embarrassing. At least I'd been asleep. It occurred to me now to wonder what else I might have babbled to him in my fever while he dragged me down to the office, besides not wanting to go to the nurse.

"That was nice of him to stay to help his grandmother." I measured my words with care. "But don't read too much into it. He would do anything for her."

Mary looked like she was about to protest, but Agnes put a hand on her arm. "If you say so, Evie. We won't push it." She gave Mary a pointed look. "But let me just say, it was more than simple concern for his grandmother that brought him here yesterday."

I shrugged.

Okay, he probably was worried about me. After all, I showed up with a bad fever only a day after he found me in the grips of a violent nightmare. Frankly, I was lucky he was just a little concerned, not going around telling everyone what a freak I was.

"Well, we are under strict orders not to tire you out," Agnes said.

"That's right. You should rest more."

"More? I just woke up. I've basically been asleep since yesterday morning." I moved to get out of bed.

"Oh no you don't." Helen marched into the room. "Greta said you were to stay in bed at least until tomorrow."

"Helen, I feel much better. I just want to stretch my legs a little, get out of this room. I promise I won't exhaust myself." She didn't look convinced. "Then I'll come right back to bed and stay here until tomorrow morning."

"Fine. Just a short walk. That fever took a lot out of you."

I shuffled down the hall, supervised closely by the three women. By the time I got back to the room, I had no argument against getting back into bed.

"You guys aren't going to sit around and watch me sleep, are you?"

Helen dropped her eyes.

"Seriously, I'll be fine. And you look at least as tired as I do."

"She's right, Helen," Agnes said. "You need your rest, too. You heard what Greta said: she's in the clear. So I insist. Everyone out. Eva will sleep better without an audience."

She shooed them out.

I changed into a nightgown, pulled another turtleneck over it. I wouldn't put it past Helen to check on me while I slept, and my neck still looked...scary.

When I awoke later to an oppressive, middle of the night silence, I felt restless. Recovered or not, there was only so much time I could spend in bed.

With a blanket around my shoulders, I crept downstairs, out to the porch that stretched along the back of the building.

My unruly thoughts turned to Tristan. In my bedroom. While I was unconscious.

I sighed. It was unhealthy to dwell on that subject. No good would come from daydreaming about him.

I tilted my head back, looked up at a sky thick with stars. Waves crashed on the beach as the tide came in. It was easy, sitting there, to believe everything had gone back to normal. There was no danger coming. It was all just a bad fever dream.

But who was I kidding? Life had never been normal. And lately, things were only getting worse.

The nightmare was triggered by the magic I tried — it was the only thing that made sense. So forget that. No more magic. I wouldn't risk it. I'd screwed around with things I didn't understand, and I could've hurt someone. Or been caught. I refused to go through that again.

I was done with it, mysterious warning be damned.

Chapter Eight

At breakfast later, Helen mentioned postponing Sebastian's trip to drop off the clothes donations.

"No way. It's a beautiful day for a drive. I'm much better, and it's not like you'll be gone over night."

"We can go anytime," Helen said.

"They're expecting you today."

Sebastian was on my side, of course. As I left the room, I heard her insist the nuns keep a close eye on me and call Greta if I so much as sneezed.

The clothes donations were set up in neat piles. I looked through them, pulled things out as I went – a pair of pants, a high collared shirt, a dark gray dress.

I spent the next couple of hours lying in the backyard, watching the leaves flutter in the breeze.

Mary and Agnes brought lunch out. To my surprise, Catherine, the visiting nun who rarely spent time with anyone outside of prayers, joined us. She'd heard I was ill, wanted to see how I felt.

Catherine was older, a wisp of a woman who always

seemed content to fade into the background. She didn't say much beyond how pleased she was that I was recovered. Still, the impromptu picnic was fun.

After the nuns went back inside, I moved to a rocking chair on the porch to read.

A faint buzz pricked at my skin — I wasn't alone.

I looked around, saw Greta step out of the woods.

She strode across the lawn, and at my invitation, sat in the chair next to mine. Under her sharp gaze, I pulled my knees to my chest, wrapped my arms around my legs.

"You look well enough. Still tired?"

"A little. Not as much as yesterday, though."

"That's to be expected." Greta measured me. "Anything else unusual since the fever?"

"No. Not at all." She specifically wasn't asking about the unusual occurrence *before* the fever, and we both knew it. Tristan must've told her what he'd interrupted.

"Good. Well, I wouldn't worry about it happening again. You're safe for now."

I stared at her. Safe from another fever? Or nightmare? And how could Greta know it wouldn't happen again? Unless she just wanted to be reassuring. Which her ominous choice of words certainly didn't achieve.

Greta pulled a small jar out of her bag. "Tristan mentioned you had some scrapes and bruises. Put some of this on, twice a day, they'll heal much faster."

"Thanks."

"Also," she said, pulled some papers out, "Tristan wanted me to give these to you."

Why hadn't he come to deliver them himself?

I kicked myself. Don't go there.

I looked down to see it was all the homework I'd missed. It was thoughtful of him.

"He's hanging out with his friends from school this afternoon – invited them over to the cottage. He's been planning this get-together all week."

I tried to tell myself I didn't care, but the sinking rock in my stomach made me realize just how much I'd begun to fool myself about him.

"That's nice," I forced out. Of course when Tristan helped me it didn't mean anything. He was still the same person who'd been rude to me in the hall that first morning. He was still friends with the jerks at school.

I looked up to find Greta's eyes on me. I got the unnerving sense again that she could see into my head. My cheeks flushed.

She didn't need to be a mind reader to figure me out. I cursed myself for being so damned obvious.

"Please thank him for collecting my assignments."

"I will." Greta stood up.

"Are you still free tomorrow to teach me Italian?"

She studied me for a moment. "Why don't I meet you here, instead? There's no need for you to tire yourself out on the walk."

"If it's all the same to you, I'd rather have an excuse to get out of here for the afternoon."

She still hesitated.

"Helen won't object if you say it's okay."

"Very well. I'll see you tomorrow."

"Thanks."

"Goodnight. Don't forget to put that on." She gestured to the jar.

Before I went to bed, I spread the ointment on my neck. It smelled sweet, like herbs and dried flowers. In case it actually worked, I also put some on my wrists.

The next morning everyone went into town for services…a good sign they didn't feel the need to monitor me so closely.

I checked my neck in the mirror when I got ready. Holy hell. The bruises had faded completely, the scratches almost unnoticeable. The marks on my wrist were gone as well.

I inspected the jar. Clearly homemade – no way of knowing what was in it. Unless I asked, of course. Right.

Whatever it was, I was impressed.

The sun was bright and warm as I walked to their cottage, the smell of the woods mixed with the salt on the sea breeze. Greta stood on her porch, waiting for me.

"Come on in, dear. Can I get you some tea?"

"Yes, please."

The kettle was already steaming. She poured two cups at the table by the window.

I didn't bother to look for Tristan.

"Have a seat, we have a lot to cover. I assume you'll speak up if you get tired."

"Sounds good."

Greta jumped in where she'd left off. It almost felt as though the whole long week never happened. As before, she went through an incredible amount of information. I found I was picking up Italian even faster than French. The afternoon flew by…it wasn't until Greta switched back to English that I noticed how late it was.

"Well, my dear, I would love to continue, but Helen won't appreciate it if I keep you here any later."

She stared out the window, at what I had no idea. But when Greta turned her gaze back, I saw something in her eyes. For just a moment, I caught sight of that strange glimmer I'd been drawn into when we first met.

Then she blinked and it was gone.

"Eva? Is something wrong?"

"No, sorry. I'm fine. I just…I didn't realize how late it had gotten."

Silence grew heavy between us as we regarded each other. I didn't understand what I'd seen. Now that it was gone, I couldn't be sure if my mind had played a trick on me.

The front door opened and Tristan walked in. He locked eyes with me for a long moment, then turned to his grandmother. "How'd the afternoon go?"

"Lovely, dear," Greta replied. She didn't look away from me. "We're finished for the day, if you would please walk Eva home."

"I'll be out on the porch when you're ready." Then he was gone again.

"So, Eva, can I expect you back again next week?" Greta dispelled the odd – and possibly imagined – tension with a smile, as though nothing had happened.

"Yes. I'd like that."

"Excellent, I'll see you then. Take care of yourself."

"I will, thank you."

The sun was falling. The changing light warmed everything with shades of orange. Tristan leaned against the porch rail, watching me. I met his eyes, thought about the last couple of times he'd seen me…unconscious, delirious with fever, screaming and hurting myself while lost in a nightmare.

My world was suddenly fragile. I didn't want anyone to witness such vulnerable moments. What could he possibly make of all this? And why did he keep helping me?

Tristan's gaze bore into me, brows drawn over brooding eyes. Was he troubled by the same things I was? He opened his mouth to say something, but hesitated. His eyes slid away from me, and he seemed to change his mind. Instead he said in a curt voice, "We should go."

I nodded and we headed out. After a few minutes of tense silence, I glanced over at him. He stared straight ahead with his jaw clamped shut, the muscles in his neck strained.

My stomach clenched when the realization hit: this week I'd done nothing but offer up proof of what the kids at school had said about me. And now I made it impossible for him to avoid me.

Maybe that was the real reason Greta suggested we hold the lesson at Ragnarok. Not for my sake but for his.

I kept my eyes on the path and picked up the pace, my annoyance towards him growing in time with my anger at myself. When he'd been kind last week, I believed we were at least sort of friends. An understanding, I thought with disgust. Of course that went away once he started to see who I really was. I was wrong to let myself hope he'd be different from the rest of them.

He never should have bothered being nice in the first place. He should've listened to what everyone said about me and stayed away.

He matched my determined pace, and we made it back quickly.

"Thank you for walking me home," I said when we reached the lawn, my eyes straight ahead, not slowing down. He fell back.

When I reached the door, I meant to walk straight inside without looking back. But I couldn't help it. I saw Tristan still standing at the edge of the woods, his gaze fixed on me.

I stared back, lifted my chin. If he hoped for some reassurance that I really was just an ordinary girl, he'd be disappointed. The stories people told about me were mostly wrong, but at their heart, they carried a piece of the truth: I was different from the rest of them.

I went inside. That was the last time I wanted to be alone with Tristan.

Loneliness was something you could handle if it was all you knew, I realized, but it became unbearable if you were constantly reminded of what you didn't have.

Chapter Nine

The Friday afternoon of the first week after my fever, I came home from school to find a note from Greta with her apologies. She had to cancel our Sunday lesson. She gave no explanation, but I was certain it was because of Tristan.

So I went into the next week feeling just a little worse about it all than I had before.

At school I never looked at Tristan…though occasionally I swore I felt his eyes on me.

By the following Thursday, my anxiety began to ease. I hadn't tried any magic – whether as a result or not, I also hadn't had a single disturbing dream. In fact, I woke up each morning not remembering any dreams at all. It was rather blissful.

As I walked into school that morning, I wondered, not for the first time, if Greta had given me something during the fever to make me stop dreaming. It sounded far-fetched, but Tristan had said she might have something to help. Her healing ointment was certainly effective.

"Oh my God!" Molly's irritating voice broke across my thoughts. "Do you see what Eva's wearing?"

I glanced up to see Molly point at me with a look of mock horror. "Isn't that your dress, Lissie?"

I looked down at what I wore: it was the gray dress I'd picked out from the clothes donations. A plain, heavy material that buttoned up in the back, it looked like it had hardly been worn. It had never once occurred to me I might wear clothes to school the girls would recognize they'd given away.

Oh, holy hell. I should've seen this coming. Molly would make this as painful as possible. I raised my eyes to Lisbeth's, saw the same uncomfortable realization on her face.

"No, I don't think it's my dress, Molly," she said.

The people around us had heard Molly's loud comment. Conversations stopped as everyone turned to watch.

"Yes it is, Lissie. I recognize it. It's the one you gave away to the poor. How appropriate that Eva's wearing it."

"Poor Forsaken freak," someone said into the quiet hallway. A few people giggled, my cheeks flamed. I wanted to walk away, but I couldn't seem to make my legs work with everyone staring at me.

"Molly, just let it go." Lisbeth tugged on her arm. But she wouldn't budge.

"I can't give my old clothes away any more if they go to the creepy girl nobody wanted. I mean, look at her. Clearly dressing like us doesn't help."

Everyone laughed, except for Lisbeth, who shot an apologetic look at me before she managed to pull Molly away. It wasn't exactly worth much, though.

I turned to get away from the crowd and caught sight of Tristan. Of course. Because this didn't suck enough already.

He watched me from where he leaned against the lockers, arms crossed, his expression shuttered. He paid no attention to the group he was with. I walked towards him, didn't take my eyes off his. Tristan's friends caused this – I wouldn't make it easy on him.

I could feel those green eyes burning into me, even once I was past him.

I had no choice but to go to class, act like I didn't care, though Helen had encouraged me to leave early if I ever wasn't feeling well. I had no intention of giving Molly the satisfaction.

While Mr. Edwards enthusiastically wrote equations on the board, I regarded Tristan. Much as I wanted to put him in the same category as everyone else here, there was something...different about him.

Was it simply affection for his grandmother that kept him from laughing at me like the rest of them? That afternoon on the abbey lawn, when he'd woken me, he'd seemed genuinely concerned. Things changed though, I supposed. And come on, could I really blame him for keeping his distance? Who'd want to be friends with the Forsaken freak?

Tristan turned to look back at me. I didn't even care that he'd caught me staring. After a moment he faced away again. Whatever lingering curiosity he might have, I told myself, it would pass.

I sat down in English a short time later, eyed the new

books piled on the table beside the doorway. When I noticed Molly outside the door as she tried to waylay Tristan, resentment burned through me.

She came in when the bell rang. The moment she passed the table, the books went sprawling. Everyone laughed and her face turned an ugly red.

"If you wouldn't mind picking those back up please, Molly," Ms. Chadwick said. "I'd like to get on with the lesson."

Flustered, she bent down, started to stack them.

Okay, I knew it was petty, but that was really funny to watch – she totally deserved it. I ignored the weird prickle on the back of my neck, refusing to entertain the possibility that I'd nudged the books with my magic without even realizing it.

At the end of the day I remembered I'd left something in my locker, so I circled back, took longer to get out than usual. I was nearing the main entrance when Tristan came out of the stairwell. He saw me and gave a start of surprise. But he held the door open, waited for me to go ahead of him.

I went through, my heart suddenly trying to run away without the rest of me.

I realized Tristan had stopped at the top of the steps behind me. I turned back to see why. There was an awkward discomfort plain in every line of his face.

"Sorry, I just remembered I have a meeting with Mr. Jamieson about my history paper."

"Oh, right. Okay."

He hesitated. "See you later, Eva."

"Sure."

He went back inside. I walked away.

We weren't in the same history class, but Mr. Jamieson had assigned a big paper to both sections. It was possible Tristan really did have to meet with him, the timing just a coincidence.

A minute later, though, I saw Mr. Jamieson walk out of the side entrance.

Not so different after all.

Gloom settled over me. At least it wasn't all in my head…he wanted nothing to do with me. Well fine. On Sunday, if the lesson wasn't canceled again, I would leave early enough to avoid forcing him to escort me.

Halfway home, the weather changed. Clouds billowed through, low and heavy, to join the fog that swept in off the ocean. It began to drizzle and I didn't care if I got wet.

I knew I should be more careful, but it happened without even a conscious thought about it. That look on Tristan's face when he lied just kept popping up in my head. The miserable feeling in the pit of my stomach was now matched by the weather I created. So be it.

I spent the afternoon in the reading room. I barely knew Tristan. So it shouldn't matter. Still, I found myself staring out at the waves that crashed on the beach, daydreaming of a life that would never be mine.

*

I climbed into bed, and just when I began to drift off, I heard someone call my name. I jerked myself up.

An eerie sensation crept across my skin. I turned, saw my body still on the bed. Same as before. Only this time, I was sure I'd heard my name called.

The hallway stretched out, silent and empty, as I slipped along, made my way outside. But part of me didn't want to go forward. Part of me just didn't want to learn any more. My feet dragged, then stalled out altogether.

I looked around, awed again by the beauty here. Everything glowed with silvery light. The intricate patterns shining out from the leaves rippled when the breeze swept through them.

I sighed. I couldn't stay in the dark just because I was scared. So…onward.

The sand felt cold beneath my feet. The beach looked empty. I stared out across an ocean so different than usual. After a moment, the air shifted around me. Company had arrived.

"I know you're frightened. But you can't let that get in the way of preparing for what approaches."

I considered the figure beside me. With the light and shadow changing from one moment to the next, my eyes couldn't focus.

"Who are you?"

"It doesn't matter. What does is that you learn what you need to."

"How am I supposed to do that? Last time I used magic it gave me a horrible dream that could've killed me."

"You didn't have that dream because you practiced magic. It's not a trigger. Somehow you accidentally tapped into some connection to the past, a vision of someone else's life. The chances of that happening again are quite small."

"Oh that's very reassuring."

No response. Okay, maybe the sarcasm wasn't appreciated.

"I don't know if I can do this by myself."

"You're being protected as much as possible."

"By who? And protected from what exactly?"

"I cannot tell you that...but you can sense it, can't you? You can feel the corruption as it draws nearer to you."

"Yes," I whispered.

"Then be careful. And continue to work. Learn what you can – it's important."

I took a deep breath. "I'll try. But can't you help me? Teach me what I need to know?"

Silence. Then, "I'm sorry. There are...dangers."

"I understand," I said, though I wasn't sure I did.

The figure drifted away, the light fading, but the voice whispered in my ears. "Don't be afraid. You are not as alone as you think you are."

Then it disappeared.

I shivered in the breeze. The silver light seemed colder, less inviting than before. If something or someone was searching for me, I didn't want to be found here, in a place where I didn't know the rules.

Back inside, I started toward the stairs, but was distracted by voices in Sebastian's study. Why was anyone still awake?

I stopped just beyond the light that spilled from his doorway. Everyone was in there. I felt guilty eavesdropping, but when I heard my name, I waited to see what it was about.

"We know we're not the only ones worried about Eva," Agnes said.

"Of course not. We've all noticed she hasn't been happy lately," Helen replied.

"That's our point," Mary said. "Ever since she started school she's been glum, kept to herself more. She's never been sick before, now all of a sudden she comes down with a fever like that. I just don't like it."

"Neither do I." Helen sounded tired. "Maybe you're right – maybe it was a mistake to send her to school. It breaks my heart to see how hard she tries to look happy for our sake."

"Perhaps we should take that into consideration," Sebastian said, followed by silence. "What I mean is that she is trying hard to make it work. Eva hasn't said anything to anyone about being unhappy there. She hasn't asked to be taken out."

"Do you think maybe she's afraid we won't agree to it? We could ask her if she wants to go back to homeschooling," Agnes said.

"That won't help her to be less isolated, though, which is one of the main reasons we wanted her to go in the first place," Helen said.

"We could give her more time," Mary suggested. "I suppose she's only been there for a handful of weeks."

Nobody said anything for a minute. I stood in the darkness, shame wriggling in my stomach. So I hadn't fooled anyone.

"Well," Sebastian said, "for now, I think someone should speak with her, get an idea of how she feels about it. Carefully, though. Helen?"

"I've already tried – she won't talk to me. You should do it, Sebastian. She'll listen to you."

"Very well, I'll see what I can do. You should all get some sleep."

I froze when Agnes appeared in the doorway next to me, glowing softly with an inner light. "Goodnight, everyone," she said as she walked right past me.

Everything felt so real I'd forgotten I was only in a dream. The others followed, passed within inches of me. It was creepy.

I made my way back to my bedroom. I had assumed this was a dream…maybe not a normal one, but still some kind of dream. If what I saw actually happened, then this wasn't all in my head.

I closed my eyes, came to abruptly in my bed. I curled up on my side, tried to relax, but my thoughts were all tangled up. My chest ached. Despite what the figure in the dream said, I felt more alone than ever.

*

The day passed in a blur. I paid little attention to anyone at school, though I did notice Tristan was absent.

I wondered where he might be.

Then I reminded myself I didn't care.

Uneasiness followed me. I couldn't shake it. I wandered about the abbey after school until I passed Sebastian's study and he called me in. He sat reading in one of the armchairs. He put down his book, motioned for me to sit.

"How was your day, Evie?"

"Good. How's the book?" I tucked my legs beneath me on the chair.

"It's quite curious, actually, very obscure. Greta lent it to me. It's a history of the town and Ragnarok Abbey. Apparently her family helped build it."

"No kidding? Why was it decided to build an abbey out in the middle of nowhere?"

"It wasn't. This was not, in fact, originally an abbey. The book is a little unclear about what they built it for, though. A lot of mystery surrounded the project, nobody seemed to like to explain anything to outsiders."

"Interesting. So why'd it get sold to the church?"

"I haven't gotten far enough to know how it became an abbey, or why, but I do know the church doesn't currently own it."

"Who does?"

"I don't know. I just know that it's privately owned. The use of it has been offered to the church for decades. It all happened long before my time here."

"I see. Well maybe Greta wouldn't mind if I read it after you."

"I'm sure she wouldn't, but there are plenty of books that would be far more interesting to a girl your age."

"Are you trying to discourage me from doing some good, educational reading?" I asked with a laugh.

"Absolutely," Sebastian said with mock sternness. "It's your teachers' duty to assign boring books. It's my job to encourage you to read fun books that have no redeeming value whatsoever."

"How very responsible of you."

"Yes, well, I take my job very seriously," he said, his eyes crinkling as he smiled.

"Still, you'll have to make an exception. Anyway, I'm going to see about dinner, maybe lend a hand if they'll let me."

"Oh they won't," he assured me. "Stay here, keep me company for a while. They've got everything under control in there."

I leaned my head back against the chair, relaxed in the warmth of the room. "If you say so."

"I do, actually. Now tell me about school. I've hardly gotten to hear anything about it. My fault, of course," he continued, as I began to feel suspicious. "I've been far too lenient…letting you get away with your evasive answers. I get so wrapped up in my own world I forget to push. Do you like any of your teachers?"

"Some of them are okay. My English teacher, Ms. Chadwick, is good. I like the history class."

"Wonderful. Are the rest of the teachers at least decent, even if their subjects are a little boring?"

"Yeah, they're fine, I guess I get a lot out of them."

Sebastian continued to ask questions about school, tactfully avoiding any mention of the other students. Questions that would have seemed harmless if not for last night.

For the most part, I told the truth. Even in the least interesting subjects, there were new things to learn. If that was all there was to high school, life would be peachy.

Well, peachier.

"Now that you've been there a little while, it seems like

a good time to reassess the decision to attend. You know, we weren't sure that school would be the right place for you." He watched me carefully as he talked, trying to gauge my reaction. "We miss having you around here during the day. Selfishly, we'd love it if you decided to go back to homeschooling. But the decision is yours. You've been there long enough to form an opinion. So, Evie, do you want to stay in school? Remember, we'll support you either way, we're proud of you."

I pulled on a smile. "Thanks, Sebastian." I wanted to reassure him…I just didn't know what to do. If I said I wanted to leave school, things would go back to the way they had been. I wouldn't ever have to see the kids from school. Any of them.

"Think about it as long as you need to. There's no hurry to make a decision."

Last night's dream crept into my thoughts. Even if I no longer had to face high school, my problems still wouldn't be solved. And Helen was right about how isolated I was. I couldn't spend the rest of my life hiding in the abbey.

"I appreciate the offer," I said finally, "but I think it would be better if I stayed in school." Sebastian's brows drew together and he opened his mouth to argue. I held up a hand. "I know I haven't seemed very…happy lately, but I do get a lot out of my classes. More than I would only learning from books here. It's just taking time to adjust."

"If you say so. But do me a favor?" I nodded. "Don't keep going if it makes you miserable merely because you think it's what we want. I know you're not one to complain, but we want what's best for you. That means we want you to be happy, okay?"

"Okay. I'll let you know if I change my mind. But for now, don't worry about me, Basher. I can handle school."

He smiled at the nickname from when I was little. "You can be awfully stubborn, you know."

"Yeah, I know."

"All right, what do you say we go check on dinner? I'm getting hungry." He stood up and stretched.

"Lead the way." I followed him out slowly, trying to get my thoughts in order.

That confirmed it. But if it hadn't been all in my head last night, if I hadn't been dreaming, then what had I been doing?

"Hello, ladies, we've come to interrupt," Sebastian said as we entered the kitchen.

I breathed in the tempting smells.

"You always manage to sense right when dinner is ready," Mary said, pulling rolls out of the oven.

"It's a gift."

"More like a keen sense of smell," Agnes retorted.

"Evie, can you set the table?" Helen said. "This is almost ready."

I caught a look pass between Helen and Sebastian. I left them to their silent communication.

I looked around the table while we ate. This was my family, the people who cared about me. Was this what the dream meant about not being alone?

That was what I originally thought, when it was just another peculiar dream. But the more I obsessed over it, the more I wondered if it meant something else. Knowing the conversation I overheard was real changed things. I tried not to get ahead of myself. There were a lot of possible interpretations, with no way to know which was true.

It was a crazy thought. But I couldn't get it out of my head.

You are not as alone as you think you are.

What if there were others out there like me?

Chapter Ten

The walls began to close in on me the next afternoon, so I went outside to walk. Trees showed hints of red and yellow leaves. I pulled my scarf tighter against the crisp air that helped clear my head, and I reminded myself I didn't know what the dream...*non-dream?*...*half-dream?*...really meant. The conversation I overheard had happened. I'd traveled outside my body.

So logically, if it wasn't just a dream, then maybe what happened on the beach wasn't merely something my magic constructed to tell me about the future. It made perfect sense. Right? Maybe someone really was out there, protecting me.

I was such an idiot.

I picked up a rock, chucked it into the woods as hard as I could. How ridiculous, I fumed, resuming my pacing. Another like me, just waiting out there, watching? Of course there wasn't.

It was only my subconscious telling me what I desperately wanted to believe.

So I managed to spy on the nuns in my sleep. It didn't mean everything else I saw was real. Things didn't glow with their own inner light, certainly. Dressing up the warning to be more of a comfort, well, that wasn't surprising – the threat I perceived scared me more than I wanted to admit. It made more sense than an unseen protector who refused to actually help me.

When the crow called out right next to my ear, I let out an embarrassing shriek. I'd been so wrapped up in my thoughts I hadn't even noticed him swoop in to perch on the fence post at my shoulder.

"How long have you been there?"

He ignored me. He hopped onto my shoulder and adjusted his wings, content where he was. I found the rest of the crows scattered about the lawn, on the garden fence, circling slowly above. Well, I had some friends at least. They always came when I called, even when I wasn't aware I was calling.

After more fruitless pacing, I sent Stopha on his way, but when I began to walk back, I froze.

Claire stood on the porch, her long black dress swirling against her legs in the breeze. She watched me, her lips pressed together in a thin line, clutching her rosary tightly.

She'd seen the crows around me, further proof of my "unnaturalness," no doubt. The stony look in her eyes meant I'd have to come up with an explanation, listen to her hiss about the "wicked child plaguing God's house." Like I hadn't heard that enough from her growing up.

But when I moved towards her again, she turned and disappeared inside.

I saw no sign of Claire the rest of the night. Surprising, since she relished any opportunity to whisper about my unholy origins, always eager for reasons to discipline me.

But I had enough to worry about: the tension from avoiding practicing magic nagged at me. Even if the warning only came from my own subconscious — that was still worth listening to.

I had to prepare myself. I felt something coming, the same way I could sense an impending storm.

*

I knelt in the grass and placed three candles on a garden stone (I didn't want to accidentally burn down the abbey). I tried to still my jitters. This would be okay — practicing magic hadn't caused the fever or the vision. That, at least, I could trust to be true.

Right. So, after my last attempt, working on control seemed like a good idea. I called fire to one candle at a time, kept the flames small, and then snuffed them all out with a thought.

I carried on, made variations to test myself, shaped the flames in increasingly difficult designs. After a few hours of refinement, I felt confident about manipulating small fires with fuel. I was now totally prepared...in case of an attack by an army of cornhusk dolls.

Next step: figure out how to keep the fire burning without the wicks.

When it was time, I got my coat, left for the cottage. I reminded myself that long before sunset, I had to give excuses and run away...er, make my escape.

As I came up their porch steps, Greta opened the door.

"I've just poured the tea. Come, join me."

"How are you?"

Greta settled into her rocking chair, stirred sugar and milk into her mug. "I'm well, dear. And you? How has your health been?"

Maybe I was being paranoid, but I suddenly wondered just how much Greta heard about what went on at school. Something about the way she asked, the way she looked at me.

"I've been feeling all right."

"Good. Tell me, how does Sebastian like the book I lent him?"

"He's enjoying it. Actually I wondered if I could borrow it after him."

"I was going to suggest that myself. Ragnarok is an interesting place, though much of the inside story was left out of the book. There's probably a lot of history still tucked away in the building." Greta stared out the window, caught up for a moment in her thoughts. She gave herself a shake. "Anyway, it's still worth a read, I'd be happy if you took it next."

"I look forward to it."

"Excellent. Then we begin." She continued on in Italian. "Though I must say, it's almost time to move to a new language. You have this one quite nearly in hand, and so much faster than I expected."

Then the lesson started in earnest – more advanced sentence structure, a wider range of vocabulary. Our entire conversation now took place in Italian, and I didn't even have to think about it.

As planned, I kept an eye on the sun. Tristan obviously couldn't stand to be alone with the Forsaken freak, but Greta wouldn't let him out of walking me back once it grew close to dark. No matter how much he didn't want to.

And it would suck just as much for me.

That thought spurred me to vigilance.

"I'm sorry to do this," I said when she paused. "But I should get going, tonight I really must be home at a decent hour."

She studied me. "Of course, dear. I'm sure the nuns would appreciate having you back for dinner. And you have school work, no doubt."

"I do hate to leave early." Especially when I suspected Greta knew it was all a lie. "But thank you again for the lesson. This has been great."

"I'm enjoying it too." She stood up with me, but put a hand on my arm. "Before you go, I want you to take something for the week." She selected a book from the far corner of the neat but crowded bookshelves to hand to me. It was a thick book, written in Italian.

"Okay, sure." I itched to leave. Tristan usually came back around sunset. It would be easier if I didn't have to see him.

"Just read what you can. It's advanced, but you should be able to pick up most of it. It's important not to neglect reading with new languages. But that's all. I know you're anxious to get home." Greta smiled.

"Right, yes, I am. Well, this should be helpful – I'll take a look at it when I can."

I began to pull on my coat as I went out the door but stopped in surprise when I saw Tristan leaning against the porch rail, his arms crossed. He looked up, mischief flickering in his eyes.

"Leaving already?"

I realized I'd frozen in mid-motion and now stared stupidly at him.

Try to stay composed.

I went back to pulling on my coat. However, with the book in one hand, and Tristan watching me with amusement, I suddenly had trouble finding my other sleeve.

Before I knew it, he'd stepped over to me – he took the other end of the coat, held it up so I could get my arm through the sleeve. I definitely blushed, but I wasn't sure if it was because I was more embarrassed or annoyed.

"Thanks." I stared at the ground. It was a small piece of luck Greta had closed the door and missed witnessing this.

"You're quite welcome." Even without looking, I knew Tristan was smiling.

"I've gotta get going. See you later." I hurried down off the porch, but when Tristan followed, I stopped, turned to him with a frown. "What are you doing?"

"Walking you home."

"I have plenty of time before it gets dark. You really don't have to do that." He just looked at me with one eyebrow raised, not budging. "I'll be fine. Don't worry, your grandmother knows I'm walking home alone."

"First of all, my grandmother expects me to walk you home regardless of what time it is. You can't get out of it that easily, you know." A wry smile tugged at his lips.

Damn. Had he guessed that was why I left early? I tried to squash my guilt with a reminder of his lie to avoid me only a few days ago.

"And second of all," he said, the smile disappearing as he took a step closer so I had to look up a little to meet his eyes. "I promised Father Sebastian I'd walk you home any time you came here."

"When did you do that?"

"When you were sick."

"Oh." I couldn't think of anything else to say. There were questions I wanted to ask about that night, but I had trouble remembering what they were. His gaze was fastened on mine, drawing me in. It was hard to concentrate.

"Eva." He shifted fractionally closer. Without my permission, my heart started to race. "I'm sorry I..." He stopped, seemed to have trouble finishing the sentence.

I couldn't help fill in the blanks in my head: I'm sorry I watched my friends make fun of you and didn't stop them; I'm sorry I ignore you in school; I'm sorry I'm too freaked out by you to be your friend.

I took a step back.

It didn't really matter what he was sorry about. It didn't change anything that had happened. And when it came down to it, he was really only here now because of Greta and Sebastian.

"Well, anyway, I'm happy to walk you home."

"Don't bother. I'll tell Sebastian you did." I turned, headed to the path.

He followed me. "I *want* to walk you home," he said under his breath.

I looked over, but he kept his eyes ahead. I was sure I'd heard him correctly. But why?

He seemed determined to come though, so we continued in silence. I was desperate to ask why he troubled himself now, when he so clearly didn't want to have anything to do with me the rest of the time. And it would be the same as always at school tomorrow.

But I bit my tongue. If he had an answer, I wasn't sure I'd want to hear it.

When we reached the edge of the abbey lawn, I stopped. I wanted to say something. I wanted to demand he stop these random moments when he was nice to me. I wanted to tell him off.

But Tristan was staring at me.

I stared back, suddenly not sure I knew what was really going on. He didn't look away. He didn't say anything. For a long time we just stood there, neither of us making a move.

Finally Tristan smiled slightly, gave me a nod. He turned and walked away. I stood watching the spot where he disappeared, not knowing what any of it meant.

*

There was something depressing about facing an entire week at school, knowing at any minute things could go terribly wrong. It was like navigating a minefield.

The walk with Tristan last night didn't help my mood. I thought I knew how he felt about me. But then all he had to do was look at me like that and suddenly I didn't know which way was up. I swore I wouldn't get sucked in again by whatever power it was he held over me.

The early morning air was cold and frost covered the ground. On the path, the uncomfortable sensation that I wasn't alone crept over me, though I didn't see anyone. The birds still sang, uninterrupted, which wouldn't be the case if someone else were in the woods.

So...I was totally losing it.

I shrugged off the feeling and continued. This had happened a lot lately – just the feeling, though, nothing more – and I began to worry I was becoming delusional.

By the end of the day, I was so ready to escape. I'd caught Molly eyeing me, no telling what nasty schemes were going through her head. She could ambush me with new humiliations at any time.

As for Tristan, I kept myself from making eye contact, though I was less successful in keeping myself from thinking about him.

I relaxed as I walked into the library, another old brick building, but this one warm and welcoming. Sebastian had thought I was too studious and reserved as a kid, so he'd begun taking me to the library on Saturdays.

I'd always liked it here, a place filled with all the stories a lonely child could want. Adventure stories were my favorite – heroes trekking across the country in search of their destiny.

Originally it was the home of a wealthy shipwright, who donated it to the town. Inside, the dry smell of books permeated the rooms. Fireplaces had painted panels above large mantelpieces, the paintings all of the sea, with old ships tossing in the waves. One room had large oak tables for working, and this was where I set my things.

My history paper was about life in the early settlements of New England, and I found plenty of material. Eventually, I had a couple of books to take and a few pages of notes. But curiosity made me linger.

I looked up some local town history, wondering if I could find more information about the abbey being built, or even mention of Greta's family. I found articles about the church taking up residence, but none said what purpose the building served before that.

So I went back earlier, and that's where I began to find a lot of references to the McGrath family. Unsurprisingly, the impression I got was that they were a very wealthy family in Fairhaven. The first helpful articles were written in the late 1800s, around when the abbey was built. As it turned out, the McGraths not only helped build it, but they owned it at the time.

From what I could piece together, the family had a large home on the property, though it must have been a summer residence, because for a long time, they were rarely there. The property had been in their family since the town was first settled.

In the middle of one night in August of 1878, about a year after the family had taken up permanent residence there, a fire at the McGrath house was seen from town. When townsfolk arrived to help, the fire was too large to be stopped and the house was destroyed, though supposedly no one was hurt.

It was only too easy to imagine: panicked townspeople, afraid the fire might spread, running through the darkness to help their neighbors. Flames stretching into the black sky. I shuddered. Nobody died in that fire, I reminded myself, and it happened a long time ago.

A hand closed over my shoulder and I jumped.

"The library's closing, dear," said Mrs. Adams, the plump librarian who'd been working there since I was little. "Is there anything you'd like to check out?"

I handed her the books for my paper, quickly put the rest back. It was a lot later than I'd realized – the sun was already setting. No big deal. I just had to hurry. I thanked Mrs. Adams, shoved the books in my bag.

Outside, I headed toward the edge of town, and as the shadows deepened, I quickened my pace, my spine tingling with fear. My nightmares were too easy to call to mind, and the lingering spookiness from reading through the abbey history made me even more uneasy.

The wind picked up, fallen leaves swirled around the street. I swear there was something malevolent in the air. For the second time that day, I got the feeling I wasn't alone.

The houses grew farther apart. Soon I'd be off the street and in the woods, where the last of the sun's light wouldn't reach at all.

There was a noise behind me – something scraped against the ground. I whirled, afraid of what I might see. But no one was there. I stood still, my body tense, searching the street for movement. Nothing.

I turned, hurried on, increasing my pace as my fear irrationally grew. There was nothing behind me, nothing chasing me. But still, I couldn't shake the panic welling in my chest.

Then, out of the corner of my eye, I saw the shadows begin to shift.

Chapter Eleven

No, please. Not again. It was just a trick of the light, nothing more than my imagination wreaking havoc.

That light was fading fast as I neared the turn at the end of the street. Then it would be just a short distance down the road to the path...where I'd have to walk through the woods in the dark.

If I weren't so afraid of tripping, I might've broken into a dead run. As it was, I walked as fast as I could.

At the last house, I cut across the lawn to save time. I rounded the corner of the building and collided with someone, my heart jumping into my throat. A hand grabbed my arm tightly, and I sucked in a breath to scream. But another hand immediately clamped over my mouth.

"Wait. Calm down," an unmistakable voice said.

I stopped struggling, looked up, my pulse still hammering madly. I could just make out Tristan's features.

"Please don't scream." He slowly took his hand away from my mouth, though he still held onto my arm. "Sorry about that — but you'd probably have given some poor old biddy here a heart attack if you screamed bloody murder." I was still too taken aback to form any coherent thoughts. "You scared the hell out of me, you know. I didn't expect you to come charging around the corner like that."

As his soft voice calmed me down, I found my breath again. "Sorry, I wasn't expecting you either. Where did you come from?"

"I was walking home on Hazel Street, and I thought I saw you over here. I cut across to meet up with you." He shrugged. "I figured we could walk back together."

It was so unexpected I didn't know how to react. I found, a little to my dismay, that I was utterly relieved to have company, even if things had been tense between us. Though I was surprised Tristan bothered to make the effort.

"Okay. Yeah. That would be...good."

"So what were you in a big rush about?"

"It's nothing. I just got a little spooked." Now that Tristan was with me, I felt a bit silly. I concentrated for a moment to be sure, but I couldn't sense anything threatening out there. It really was only my imagination playing tricks on me.

Tristan peered behind me, frowning. "Are you sure? Do you want me to check?"

"No. Thanks for the offer, but there's nothing there."

"All right. Then we should go before it gets any later. I'm surprised you're walking home by yourself after dark."

Tristan finally let go of my arm, almost reluctantly, and we started to walk.

"Yeah, I'll probably be in trouble. Though it's not actually forbidden, Helen won't be happy."

"Then it's good we ran into each other. She'll be less angry if you have an escort."

"That's true," I said and found I couldn't help a smile. I hated to admit it, but even in the dark woods, I felt completely safe with Tristan next to me. Maybe it was just a holdover from the dreams I'd had about him. Yeah...I was sticking with that explanation.

We walked in silence, though I occasionally got the impression Tristan was about to say something before changing his mind.

All my earlier irritation with him was gone for the moment, replaced with an almost giddy relief that he'd found me. So as long as he was here, being nice, I might as well enjoy his company.

Even if it would make things harder later on.

"How's your history paper going?"

Tristan turned to look at me, but I couldn't see his face enough to judge his expression. He probably wasn't expecting idle conversation from me. "It's not bad – I'll finish it tomorrow. Yours?"

"I finished the research – it won't take long to write it."

"What did you think of his test last week?"

"I did okay, I guess. He's handing them back tomorrow, so we'll see."

"Somehow I doubt you have to worry about your grade."

Did he know how easy the class was for me? I couldn't

tell if he was teasing or not. I didn't know how to respond, so I kept silent.

"Eva," he said suddenly. "You're obviously a lot smarter than the rest of the kids at school, though you try to hide it. Why didn't you just keep getting homeschooled? You wouldn't have to deal with...with lame classes."

I knew what that pause meant. He wanted to know why I bothered going to a school where everyone hated me when I had an easy out. Good question. I sighed, wondering how to answer.

"I guess it would be easier to stay home, not have to deal with everything at school. But Helen thought having real teachers would be good for me – that I'd learn more."

"They didn't leave the choice up to you?"

"Well, yeah. If I wanted to leave, they'd let me."

"So why don't you?" He seemed genuinely curious, and I couldn't blame him. My choice barely made sense to me.

"I can't hide in the abbey forever." Crap, I couldn't believe I said that. I hadn't meant to be so honest, it just tumbled out. But somehow, in the dark, it was easy to talk to him, to let my guard down a little. Out here in the woods, it was easy to forget about everyone else.

"I get that," he said. "It's...brave."

I almost stumbled in my surprise, a rush of warmth flooding at his words. I hadn't thought of it that way.

Tristan thought I was brave. It brought a smile to my lips, and I was glad he couldn't see my reaction.

The lights of the abbey appeared ahead, safe and inviting. We were close to the edge of the lawn when he grasped my arm. "Wait a minute, Eva."

I could see his face a little better now with the light shining through the trees. His expression was serious as he studied me. It was late, and I knew everyone would be worried. But standing there with Tristan, I wanted the moment to last. I couldn't help it. Once we left the woods, things would go back to normal. I wasn't quite ready for that.

"I'm sorry about the way things are at school," he said, his voice soft. Then, more to himself, "I didn't know it would be like that."

I was barely breathing, caught by his words, confusion swirling through me.

"I can't change anything for you, and I know you don't understand that right now." Tristan took a hold of my other arm, too, which helped, since I felt unsteady suddenly. "But just...know that when you need me, I'll be there."

He stared at me for another long moment, then dropped his hands, started toward the abbey.

Holy hell.

The conversation had gone beyond my grasp. I couldn't catch up. "Wait, Tristan." He paused, turning his head so I saw a little of his profile. "What are you talking about?"

"Nothing. I shouldn't have said anything. Come on, I can see Sebastian. He looks upset." Tristan walked out of the woods, onto the lawn.

Sebastian had just stepped off the back porch with a lantern in his hand when he spotted Tristan. I hurried after him.

"Tristan," he called. "Have you seen...Oh, Eva. There you are!" He sounded so relieved that I immediately felt guilty. I made it to Tristan at the same time as Sebastian, my breathing uneven. "We were starting to get worried. I was about to head into town to look for you."

"I'm so sorry, Sebastian. I was at the library, working on my paper. I didn't realize how late it was." I knew my unhappiness was plain in my voice, but I couldn't stop it. It had been such a strange night to begin with, and after that conversation with Tristan, I felt adrift.

Sebastian looked from me to Tristan, whose face was set and unreadable. He seemed to pick up on the tension. "It's okay, sweetheart, I understand."

He held his arm out. I tucked myself under it, feeling Tristan's eyes on me.

"Were you working at the library, too?" Sebastian asked from above me.

"No, I was running errands for my grandmother. I'm sure Eva planned to call you when it got dark, but I happened to be passing by the library and I offered to walk her home."

"Of course. You've been great. It's a comfort knowing Eva can count on a friend like you. Can I give you a ride home?"

Tristan smiled. "No thank you. I prefer to walk."

"Very well then, have a good night."

"You too."

Sebastian took his arm off my shoulders and started back in. Tristan held my gaze for a long moment, his expression serious again. Then the corner of his mouth quirked up, and he winked at me. He turned, walked away before I had a chance to react.

I watched him disappear into the darkness, my heart skipping around my chest, until Sebastian called my name. I walked up to where he waited, watching me with a speculative look.

Much to my relief, though, Sebastian didn't say anything. It was one thing to have Agnes and Mary make comments about Tristan, but I definitely couldn't handle hearing it from Sebastian too.

Inside, I got a relieved hug from Helen.

"What were you doing out so late?"

"I was working at the library and I lost track of time."

"What a surprise – not paying attention to the time because you're lost in a book. Sounds just like someone else I know." She raised her eyebrow at Sebastian who managed to look abashed. "Well, anyway, dinner is just about ready."

All night my thoughts kept drifting back to Tristan, to everything he'd said. It didn't make any sense.

I sighed. Nothing would change at school. We'd be friends on his terms only, obviously, and I was entirely mixed up about that.

When I got into bed later, despite the buzzing of my thoughts, I fell asleep immediately. I had a sinking feeling as I looked around. The dark desert stretched away, small stars blazed all around.

I reached out to one of the light bursts, wondering if I could touch it. The star was bright but delicate. Occasionally a spark would shoot off, trail down to the ground. It was so beautiful it distracted me entirely from what else the dream held.

But as the darkness grew heavier, the lights began to blink out. I heard a whisper of movement, the shiver of his wings, and I spun slowly to face him.

It was difficult not to get lost in his strange eyes. The ring of yellow fire around his pupils burned in my vision. I saw planets being born, worlds destroyed. I saw magic in its most pure form.

Despite my fear, I was drawn to this man who searched for me still. Not once since that first dream had he done anything to me…maybe I'd been wrong about him.

His expression was utterly calm. He stared so deeply into my eyes I wondered if he saw everything I ever was.

He reached his hand out, inviting me to take it. For a long moment I wanted to. I wanted to know who he was, see what other glimpses of the universe he might offer.

But then another hand slid into mine. A strong, comfortable hand that felt familiar. I let myself be pulled away in the quick burst of light.

"Eva, please." Tristan stood beside me. "You have to be careful. Stay away from him."

"Who is he?"

"He's dangerous." He squeezed my hand, leaned closer to whisper in my ear, "Go to sleep now. I'll watch over you."

With my next breath, I woke up in bed. I had the sleepy thought that I really shouldn't have Tristan on my mind right before falling asleep. My subconscious needed no encouragement when it came to drawing up fantasies about him.

*

I left for school, pulled the hood of my coat up as the cold, damp air hit me. Tendrils of sea fog weaved their way onto shore. The day would stay wet and dreary.

I made my way through the woods, turning my thoughts to the real problem from last night: it was the first time I'd dreamt of the winged man since the fever. Had my defenses been down because I was so distracted by the walk home? Or maybe if Greta had given me something to keep me from dreaming, it had worn off.

The stranger held a fascination for me, there was no denying it. He scared me, and there was something unnatural about him...but at the same time, I sensed a deep sadness in him. I felt pulled towards him.

"It happened on Nathaniel's uncle's farm," Oliver said to the kid on the other side of him when I sat down in class.

"So what was it, really? I heard it was some weird sickness or something."

Molly joined them. "Are you talking about that animal thing in Willowbrook?"

"Yeah, I got all the details from Nathaniel," Oliver said. "Apparently they don't know what caused it. Nathaniel's uncle is really upset. I guess he went out yesterday morning and all the animals had dropped dead. The cows were on the ground in the pasture, every single chicken dead in the cages. Even the barn cats were dead."

"How can they not know how they died?" Molly asked.

"I don't know. They hadn't been sick, none of them looked injured. But I guess it's happened recently on two other farms farther inland. It's a mystery."

"It's definitely weird," she grumbled, "but I don't see why Nathaniel gets to miss school."

"His whole family went out there to see if they could help."

The bell rang. Molly went back to her seat as everyone filed in. Tristan came in last and sat down without looking over.

Willowbrook was a town far inland from us. I'd never heard of anything like that happening – all the animals dying at the same time. It left me with an uneasy feeling I tried to ignore as Mr. Edwards started lecturing.

Eventually, class ended and by the time I got to English, Tristan was there already, talking to Lisbeth. I suppressed a surge of hostility.

Lisbeth, or Lissie to her oh-so-honored friends, was well liked and rather pretty with her straight brown hair, soft brown eyes. She and Tristan frequently hung out together. I had completely legitimate reasons to hate her that had nothing to do with that, though. There was nothing wrong with holding a grudge about the rock-throwing incident.

Molly joined them, as she invariably did when given the chance, always vying for Tristan's attention. I passed them and sat down, wishing desperately that I didn't care.

Class started and soon Ms. Chadwick was calling on people who didn't raise their hands. I hated being called on. It was uncomfortable to dumb down my answers, or pretend I didn't know...though either was far better than showing up the other kids too much.

When she dismissed us, I left without looking back. History next – without Tristan, thankfully.

"Okay everyone," Mr. Jamieson said as the second bell rang. "Settle down."

He was a skinny man with a sharp nose that hooked slightly off center at the tip. He always wore old tweed suits. I liked him – he loved history and made it interesting.

"Your tests are all graded and I have to say, I'm disappointed. I thought I was clear about what this test would cover. I'm not sure if some of you even bothered to study. As I told you before, the test was graded on a curve. Many of you will be disappointed, you'll find."

He walked around the room, placing the tests face down on the desks.

"There was only one perfect score, though we had a very close second in the other section."

Oh crap. He stood next to my desk now, put my test down in front of me.

"Congratulations, Ms. Blackwell. You set the curve."

Mr. Jamieson moved on as every student in the room turned to glare at me. I put the test in my notebook without bothering to look at it. I must have been too distracted when I took the test to make sure I got some answers wrong.

This was a disaster. I glanced up inadvertently as Molly flipped her test over a couple rows in front of me. C-minus. Before I could look away, Molly turned and caught me. A look of pure loathing crossed her face.

Mr. Jamieson really hadn't done me any favors with

this. In fact, I thought bitterly, this would've been a good day to stay home pretending to be sick. If only I'd known.

The period went slowly, Mr. Jamieson reviewing the questions most of the students got wrong. I spent the time debating whether or not it would be safe to go to lunch. Molly'd make sure everyone in the other section knew I got the perfect score...and she'd make sure I suffered for it.

The whole point of staying in school, however, was to face up to the things that scared me. If I spent my lunches hiding in the bathroom, that point would be missed. Entirely. So I had physics to endure before I'd have to face whatever Molly pulled out of that venomous head of hers.

Everyone hung out in the hall between classes until the last possible minute, so it was crowded as I made my way through, and I quickened my pace when I saw the group from my class just ahead. My stomach twisted at the sight of Molly. She leaned against a locker with her arms crossed, staring at me with a sickly sweet smile on her face.

There was something mesmerizing about the nasty glint in her eyes. Trouble was brewing and it was clear what direction it would come from. I couldn't look away.

That was a mistake.

Chapter Twelve

I was so distracted by Molly that I didn't pay attention to anyone else around me. It was only too easy for Sarah to stick her foot out as I hurried by. Before I even knew what was happening, my foot caught. I tripped.

Everything I carried went flying and I landed hard on my hands and knees.

The conversations in the hallway stopped while everyone turned to look at me...and then they were all laughing.

I couldn't move. I was too horrified.

"Congratulations on your perfect score, Eva." Molly came to stand next to Sarah.

"Yeah, we just wanted to show our appreciation," Sarah said.

The skin on my palms and knees burned from hitting the floor so hard.

Very slowly, as I fought to gather myself, I sat back on my heels. Amidst the sea of unfriendly, laughing faces, I immediately caught Tristan's eyes. Of course.

He stared at me, a look of revulsion clear in his features. A quiet, detached part of my brain wondered idly if it was because Tristan also got a bad grade on the test and heard about my score. It didn't matter, though. It just made the humiliation a little more complete that he witnessed it.

I knew my face flamed bright red. More people gathered, pointing at me, laughing. Tristan had regained control over his expression — now his face had its usual calm, unrevealing set to it.

I lowered my head. My eyes stung, the weight of my misery squeezing me.

No. I damned well wouldn't give Molly the satisfaction of seeing me cry.

I had to gather my things, which meant crawling around on the floor...or I could simply walk out, leave everything. So much more tempting. But then she'd win. I had to pick everything up while the vultures watched, finish the day. Just me against the rest of them.

I took a deep breath. I could do this.

Then, all of a sudden, Tristan crouched down in front of me. I looked up into his face, wary of some new trick about to be played on me.

In a low voice, in Italian, he said, "I imagine homeschooling looks pretty good right now." I just stared as he picked up my papers. He switched to English, said in a casual voice for the others to hear, "So I take it you're the one who got the perfect score on the history test. Mr. Jamieson told me yesterday someone beat me by only two points. I'm impressed."

Tristan stood up, held a hand out to me, a hint of

amusement turning the corner of his mouth up. My brain stubbornly refused to make sense of what he was doing.

There didn't seem to be anything malicious or deceitful in his eyes, though, so I reached out, took his hand. It felt strong and comfortable, just as it was in my strange dreams. He pulled me up, handed me the pile he'd gathered.

"Um, thanks," I said, full of awkwardness. It was a little insufficient, but everyone still watched us.

"No problem." As he turned away, I heard him mutter to himself, "So much for not getting involved."

What did that mean? Why bother to help me if he didn't want to have anything to do with me at school?

The second bell rang, and I hurried to follow Tristan into physics, heading to the opposite side of the room from him. I was the only one without a lab partner, so I sat by myself, tried to keep as stoic as I could despite the jumble in my head.

I'd caught the expression on Molly's face. It was almost funny. She clearly didn't like having her revenge undone. It was a complete mystery to her why he'd bother with some-one like me. And, of course, that only made her hate me more.

Maybe it would've been better if he'd just left me alone...uncomfortable and painfully embarrassing, yeah, but at least it wouldn't have made an even fiercer enemy of Molly.

But when I thought over what happened, a thrill went through me. He was making a regular habit of saving me, this time in front of everyone at school. Why?

A truly awful thought occurred. What if Tristan kept

helping me, despite his obvious inclination to avoid me, because I forced him to? What if mind control was some new magic I was developing? That might make more sense than Tristan sporadically deciding, against his better judgment, to help me in my times of great need.

I started to panic. Controlling the weather was one thing, but controlling people was something else entirely. My brain spun and I was afraid I might puke.

Stop. Deep breath. I forced myself to think rationally, go over what happened, how I felt when I did magic. There was nothing. Not a hint of the feeling, that time or any other time he'd shown up.

That was such a relief. There was only so much weirdness I could handle. Of course, that brought me right back to wondering why he bothered. It certainly wasn't just for his grandmother's sake.

For the rest of the day I kept my head down and everyone ignored me, except for the occasional snide remark as I passed. Molly was strictly avoided.

When school let out, I took off without any thought of running into Tristan. Nothing could've compelled me to stay longer. I strode through the woods, my fists clenched as I thought about Molly standing over me, gloating. This wasn't over. Even more so now, she'd be determined to put me in my place.

If Tristan openly disapproved, though, I wondered if Molly would let it go. She obviously really wanted him to like her. It was so unbelievably frustrating, worrying about such petty things.

Why did they hate me so much?

But I already knew the answer to that. I looked down at my hands, thought about the potential power. It was undeniable: I was different.

I took all my frustration, my anger and humiliation, fed it into the space between my hands, into the spark I called up. The spark grew into a great ball of raging fire.

Instinctively I thrust the fire away, shot it in a long tongue of flame that stretched out in front of me before dying as suddenly as it had begun.

All my strength fled. I dropped to my knees in the mud. I didn't even know what I'd done — it just sort of happened, caught me completely by surprise. It took a lot out of me too. My hands shook. I was exhausted.

The stinging from the scrapes on my knees got worse as they pressed into the ground, penetrating through my shock. It was enough to get me up. Despite a heavy weariness, I tried to hurry. I was still outside the abbey property, and it was drizzling again. All I wanted to do was get dry and crawl into bed.

It didn't make any sense. Doing magic had never tired me. What had I done differently? I'd poured my emotions into the fire, poured my energy into it. Was that it? Using my own energy to fuel the fire drained me?

There had to be another way. None of my other magic had that effect.

Inside, I cleaned the cuts, put Greta's herbal mixture on my knees and palms. It was immediately soothing, and pulling on dry clothes made me feel better. When I eventually went down to dinner, everyone was there, including Sister Claire and Sister Margaret. Apparently it was going to be one of those days.

"Evie, sweetheart," Sebastian said as he dished out dinner, "tell us about your day."

"Well, I got a hundred on my history test."

"That's great," Helen said. "I used to run into Mr. Jamieson in town, and I always liked him. How is the class?"

"Good. He's actually a great teacher." Though admittedly, his telling everyone I'd gotten the highest grade dampened my enthusiasm. But I supposed he couldn't have known better.

"And how is my favorite neighbor, Tristan?" Mary asked.

"He's just fine."

"That reminds me," Helen said. "Eva, we were thinking we should have them over to dinner again. You know, to properly thank them for all their help."

"Oh. Okay. I guess that would be nice."

"Maybe tomorrow you could pass along the invitation to Tristan since you'll be seeing him anyway," Sebastian said.

"Right. Only, I'm not sure I'll necessarily run into him at school. I don't always see much of him there."

Sebastian raised an eyebrow at me. "I thought you had a few classes together."

I was cornered. Damn. I absolutely didn't want to talk to Tristan at school. Certainly not to invite him for dinner only a day after he stuck his neck out for me. "I guess I could make sure I see him to pass along the message. What night did you want them to come?"

Sebastian looked at Helen. She replied, "How about Friday? That worked well last time."

"Excellent," Sebastian said, a small smile playing on his lips. I couldn't help but suspect that after he found Tristan walking me home again last night, he'd joined Mary and Agnes in their scheming. They were all eager for me to have a friend my own age (and from the nuns' point of view it didn't hurt that he was cute). "Of course," he said, sobering, "Claire and Margaret, you both are welcome to join us."

"How kind of you," Claire said in a cool voice. She turned her gaze to me. "It would be nice to thank the woman who helped you when you were...unwell. We were so worried, we both prayed for you."

Okay. Something about the way Claire said it, in that eerily even tone, made it sound far less comforting than it might have otherwise.

And now I'd have to talk to Tristan at school tomorrow. Which he might not appreciate. In truth, I had absolutely no idea what he expected. He'd broken our unspoken rule about not interacting at school.

By the time dinner was over, I was exhausted again, my accidental magic having taken everything out of me. I went back to my room, crawled into bed, and fell asleep immediately. Once again I dreamt of the night desert. It was the same as all the others: as soon as the winged man appeared, Tristan pulled me away.

After settling back to sleep, I slipped into another

dream. I lay in bed while Tristan and Greta sat beside me, talking softly. I couldn't hear what they said. Why were they there?

My limbs were too heavy. There was a cold cloth across my forehead, bottles of powders and strange liquids on the desk – it was the night I was sick. The light was oddly dim so it was difficult to see their faces. I concentrated on their voices. Slowly the words became clearer.

Tristan leaned close to Greta, gesturing towards me. "How am I supposed to help her if I can't–"

"No," she interrupted, her voice low, intense. "You know the reasons, the dangers. You must keep your distance and we'll do what we can until..." Their voices faded.

I woke up, struggling to get my bearings. I'd forgotten that strange bit of conversation. I'd been almost unconscious, not entirely in my right mind between the fever and whatever medication Greta had given me.

Had it really happened? I sat up, turned on the lamp, pulled a blanket around me with my knees drawn. Assuming it actually happened (and I hadn't just imagined it, which was entirely possible), was there a logical explanation?

Of course there was. Greta could've been arguing with him about keeping his distance from me while I was sick. If she'd been worried I was contagious, the conversation made complete sense.

So that was it. That was perfectly reasonable. Right? At another time, I'd have accepted the obvious answer. But as I sat with the shadows gathered in the corners of the room, it didn't rest easy.

I thought back over the cryptic things Tristan had said recently, about not getting involved, not being able to change things for me. Was this all connected to that conversation he had with Greta? Why wouldn't she want him to help me? What dangers could there be in that? Or did Greta believe the rumors about me?

Why would he even want to help me?

I didn't have any answers. But if that conversation had taken place, and it was about more than just Greta's fear of Tristan getting sick, then there was something more going on that I was missing.

*

It was ridiculous to obsess about this. We'd spoken plenty of times. No big deal.

But as I walked to class, my heartbeat quickened. It wasn't like I wanted to spend time with Tristan; I'd have to make that clear. I'd say I had a message from Sebastian. Then he wouldn't get the wrong idea, I thought as I walked past Molly trying to flirt with him in the hall.

I fiddled with my notebook as I waited, pretending I didn't notice the slight tremors in my hands. The bell rang and everyone streamed in.

"Let's go," Ms. Chadwick said. "We've got a lot to cover today. Take your seats quickly please."

Tristan turned down the aisle and looked right at me. I opened my mouth to say what I'd planned, but nothing came out. He was so striking: his hair was all disorderly, and under his brown sweater, the green plaid shirt he wore matched his eyes.

He raised his eyebrows in question as I closed my

mouth, blushing. It was already too late – he was past me, the room quieting down.

So much for that plan. I was such a coward.

There was no way I could invite Tristan to the abbey within the hearing of anyone else, and he was always with at least one of the girls, if not the whole damned group. He caught my eye a few times, searched my face before he turned away again.

The obvious solution finally occurred to me as I left school: I could've just put a note in his locker. Yeah, I was an idiot. Unfortunately, I had no idea which one was his. I sighed. At least now I had a plan for the following day.

This silly business about dinner was so distracting that I was at the edge of the woods by the time I remembered I'd wanted to go to the library. There was plenty of material on Ragnarok to look at, and I was more curious than ever about the McGraths.

Well it didn't make sense to go back now. So I continued homeward.

Much to my surprise, when I got to the stone wall I saw Tristan leaning against a tree on the other side. And he'd been watching me, which made me entirely self-conscious.

Chapter Thirteen

Tristan came over, met me at the gate. Our fingers brushed as we both reached to open it. I looked up at him, at his deep green eyes framed with long, dark lashes. We hadn't spoken since the hall yesterday when I'd been tripped, and I couldn't help feeling flustered. Of course, at this point he'd seen me in enough embarrassing situations that it shouldn't matter so much anymore.

In an effort to sound more confident than I felt as I stepped through the gate, I decided to be direct. "Hey. What's up?"

He looked at me with amusement. "Nothing really. It seemed like you wanted to say something to me in English. I was curious, so I figured I'd wait for you."

"Oh. Really?"

Tristan merely shrugged, waiting.

"It's not...well, it's just that Sebastian wanted me to invite you and your grandmother over for dinner Friday night. They wanted to thank you for um, for helping out when I was sick and everything." I couldn't look at him – I felt like an idiot. Should I thank him for rescuing me from such a humiliating moment yesterday?

I glanced up at him, decided not. Even though that would be the gracious thing to do, I absolutely didn't want to bring it up. Ever.

"I'm sure my grandmother will be happy to come over, though really, no thanks are necessary." He put particular emphasis on that last part, making me wonder if he also had yesterday on his mind. "But I should double check with her for an official answer. Can I let you know tomorrow?"

"Yes. Of course."

"Good. You're walking home, I assume?"

I nodded and we started down the path, everything muted from the gray cast of the mist coming off the water. I peeked over at him as we walked. He was lost in his own thoughts, his gaze off in the distance. I considered my dream. What had the rest of that conversation been? I wanted to ask.

And had I been a bolder person I might have.

"How have you been sleeping?" He said out of nowhere, taking me by surprise. He met my eyes briefly before he glanced away.

"Fine, I guess." I figured he was concerned about my nightmares. Well, okay, I'd started to have those dreams again with the winged man (and Tristan, for that matter). But he didn't need to know about those.

He stopped walking, watched me as I came back to where he stood. His voice was mild, but the look in his eyes was completely serious. "No more deeply disturbing, violent nightmares?"

"Nothing like the one I had that afternoon, no."

He searched my face, as if evaluating what he saw in my eyes more than what I said.

"Good. That's good to hear."

"Tristan," I began with a sigh. I was tired of these confusing displays of concern – I wanted answers. I'd just ask him straight out, repeating Greta's words from the dream deliberately to see his reaction. "Why don't you keep your distance from me like you're supposed to?" His gaze sharpened on me, but he remained silent. I couldn't help adding, "Everybody else does."

He regarded me intently for a long minute before answering.

"I tried," he said quietly.

We stared at each other in silence.

Part of me fluttered around inside, barely containing a giddy smile. But part of me, the rational part, couldn't let go of the uncertainty snaking around in the back of my head.

A mischievous grin stole across his face. "But that wouldn't be very neighborly of me, now would it?"

Damn it, I couldn't help but smile back, his was so infectious. "Well, we certainly couldn't have that, now could we?"

With the serious mood broken I decided to let it go for the time being. We continued in companionable silence until the abbey, where Tristan said goodbye.

I was too restless to stay inside, so I went down to the beach.

With the fog over the water, everything took on a ghostly appearance – all subdued grays, greens and blues.

Smoke from a chimney fire threaded the salty air. It was a cozy, dry smell, and it brought to mind comfortable memories.

My crows flew over, swooped down around me, circling and calling out. Stopha glided in to take his usual perch on my shoulder, and I absently stroked his feathers as I stared out at the crashing waves.

I needed to know whether or not my magic had somehow changed, or maybe been affected by what I did yesterday with the fire. The beach was deserted and I couldn't see anyone up at the abbey, so I searched for a suitable experiment.

"You don't have to stay, but I want to try something."

The crow cocked his head at the warning but remained on my shoulder.

I concentrated on the sand in front of me, floated a few handfuls into the air. Slowly, I swirled the sand around in small rings. I fed more sand into the lazy whirlwind, spreading it wider as I did.

When I had enough, I froze everything in midair. Each grain of sand hung separately, strung along in motionless circles. I didn't feel any different than I normally did – this didn't take anything out of me.

A gust of wind picked up, and I let go of the sand, watched it blow back to the ground. So that answered one question. Now I just needed answers to the hundreds of others troubling me.

Later, I practiced more magic in my bedroom. I kept it simple. I drifted soft breezes through the room, called bright flames to life on candles. There was no way to know if any of this would be helpful, but it was better than doing nothing.

*

I'd dreamt again of the desert with the strange winged man. It was the same as all the others, so it was hardly worth thinking about. My only concern was that I now had the dream every night.

I twitched my shoulders at the uneasiness that settled with that thought. But there was nothing I could do about it, and there didn't seem to be any harm in the dreams.

When I opened my locker, a piece of paper fell out. It was a note from Tristan. In neat handwriting he'd written:

E –

She said she would be delighted. We'll come by tomorrow at six o'clock if that's okay.

– T

So that was that. I guess I didn't need to worry about talking to him at school again. It wasn't exactly a relief, though I had to admit, it was kind of fun to get a note in my locker from him.

I concentrated on keeping a low profile and let out a sigh of relief when the last bell rang. Another day down without anything bad happening: that was something to appreciate.

This time I remembered to turn down the street to the library. I said hello to Mrs. Adams, who asked a few friendly questions about school that I answered politely, if a little dishonestly.

I gathered a pile of sources, settled at one of the tables. I was interested in the time when the McGraths lived at the residence, so I'd skipped over the later articles and journals from after they left town.

The library faded.

Rumors spread quickly but quietly after the fire about how it started. Since the McGraths had only been full-time residents for about a year at that point, the townsfolk hadn't had much of a chance to warm up to the outsiders. The official newspaper articles made vague references, carefully stepped around accusations...but the private accounts were a little more forthright. It seemed that after the fire, suspicions they'd secretly harbored about the strange family became more pronounced.

Some speculated that a member of the family started the fire on purpose. Others thought it was started by accident during a fight. A local priest claimed privately that God himself had sent the fire to punish the family for their wicked sins, though just what those were he didn't say.

As far as I could tell, the townsfolk didn't trust the McGraths because the family tended to keep to itself and had come and gone without explanations for years. In the small, superstitious town back then, that kind of thing didn't go over well.

Despite the mistrust and whispers, no one dared voice any of this in the hearing of the McGrath family. For reasons not mentioned in the papers, the townspeople seemed to fear them. I wondered if it was because they were so rich. Other articles mentioned money they'd donated, important properties they held. If the McGraths withdrew their support of the town, people would face some serious difficulties.

Another possible explanation was that the head of the family appeared to be a formidable, aristocratic type. If Greta's ancestor was anything like her, I could see why the townspeople might find him intimidating.

So, whatever the reasons, the rumors were kept quiet. In the end, no one outside of the family knew for sure what happened the night of the fire. They took up a temporary residence in town and began to work on plans for rebuilding.

I sat back, rubbed my neck. It took a lot of sifting through articles and accounts that weren't relevant, but it was so fascinating it was hard to stop. I craned my neck, checked the clock on the wall. There was still a lot left to look through, but I didn't want to lose track again, get stuck walking home late.

Greta's ancestors seemed just as mysterious as her. What had brought her to Fairhaven, anyway? Was it simply to see the place her ancestors built? Tristan said she wanted to be near the sea, so I supposed it made sense to return to a place her family used to call home.

Was it coincidence that around the same time Greta showed up in my life things began to take a decidedly strange turn? Of course, nothing had ever been normal around me. But certainly in recent times the nightmares, weird occurrences, and especially my magic, had all begun to change.

I shook my head and kicked a pebble as I walked, watched it skitter out in front of me. Then there was Tristan. I'd given up on being embarrassed that he was in my dreams every night. Well, mostly given up. If Tristan ever found out, I might not show my face at school again. Scratch that. I'd crawl into a hole until he left Fairhaven for good.

When I walked into the abbey, I was surprised to find Mary sweeping the wood floor in the foyer, Helen dusting picture frames in the hallway. The two women greeted me cheerfully and continued on with their work as they asked about my day.

"Tristan said he and Greta will come by tomorrow at six."

"Perfect," said Helen. "We'll have plenty of time to get everything ready by then."

Agnes came in carrying a stepladder that she set in the center of the room.

"They've already been inside," I pointed out. "I don't think they're going to notice or care about dust on top of the chandelier."

"Nonsense," Mary said, trying to sweep around the ladder. "Just because we didn't have a chance to do a proper cleaning last time doesn't mean we shouldn't still try to put our best foot forward. At least this time Sebastian didn't forget until the day of the dinner to tell us about it."

"Besides," Agnes said, straining to reach the highest lights on the chandelier, "Greta is the kind of woman who notices everything. Of course she's too polite to remark on it, but trust me – she sees it all."

I had to agree with that. "So what can I do to help?"

"Don't you have homework?" Helen asked.

"Not much. I can do it after dinner, no problem."

Helen studied me, but they all knew I could breeze through my assignments. "Okay then, only for a little while. Why don't you pull out the nice silverware in the dining room for polishing?"

"Okay."

"The polish is in the drawer underneath the silverware," she called after me as I headed down the hallway.

Doing repetitive, mindless tasks all afternoon gave me more time to brood about Greta.

Of course the woman had never said anything particularly illuminating, but going back, she'd been unusual from the start. As I swept out the corners of the reading room, one particular conversation with her gave me an idea.

She'd mentioned there was probably still a lot of history tucked away in the abbey. It had been a long time since I'd been up in the attic, but there were plenty of things up there from previous inhabitants. There was at least a chance that some belongings of the original McGraths had been kept.

An exploration through the attic was just what I needed. Unfortunately, it was going to have to wait. There was a long list of things the nuns wanted cleaned, dusted, polished, and organized.

Besides, I'd rather the nuns not find out. The attic was technically off limits. Once, when I was younger, Helen had gotten cross when she found me playing up there. I'd never wanted to repeat the experience. I'd assumed it was because it was dark and dusty, and I could've gotten hurt, but if the church didn't actually own Ragnarok, it was possible Helen hadn't wanted me going through the real owner's property.

Well, if not tonight, soon.

After dinner and homework, I spent the rest of the evening trying to figure out how to keep a fire going without any fuel, and without exhausting myself.

I was unsuccessful, yet again. If I had to defend myself, I would fail. And there was no doubt – something was creeping nearer. There were times when, if I wasn't focused on anything, I would suddenly sense it. I would feel it along every nerve as it closed in on me.

I tried not to let those moments happen often; I tried to keep my guard up. Those times left me feeling exposed, vulnerable. If I were just able to make more headway with learning magic, it would help. But this trial and error method seemed futile.

Eventually, when I drifted off to sleep, it was to the place I visited every night now. Small details varied, but mostly it remained the same – a pattern I repeated night after night. Was his approach what I sensed?

After I dreamt of Tristan and me leaving the desert, I faded in and out of a restless sleep. By the time Friday morning came, I'd barely slept at all. I dragged myself out of bed blearily, cursed myself for not being able to shut my brain off long enough to get any rest. I already had a nervous knot in my stomach about dinner tonight.

After a slow start, I just made it to class in time. The rest of the day followed in much the same way – with me barely avoiding disasters. In math, I fell asleep, though if Mr. Edwards noticed, he didn't say anything. Ms. Chadwick had to say my name twice before I realized she was calling on me, and since I'd been in a bit of a daze, she then had to repeat the question. Luckily, I was at least able to answer correctly.

School ended with only one more mishap. I walked down the hall, not paying attention and bumped into someone. I looked up to say sorry and my stomach clenched. It was Lisbeth. I apologized quickly, but she smiled.

"Don't worry about it."

I watched her walk away. That day when we were little, when she and Molly saw me with the crows, Lisbeth had been the vocal one. But since I started school, she hadn't once been mean to me. I wondered if it was possible she'd changed.

When I got home, I went up to the back porch, sank into one of the rocking chairs. I just needed to relax for a few minutes. I wasn't quite ready to go inside and join with the preparations.

Though the sun was shining, I drew my coat tighter around me, pulled the hood up. I watched the big, puffy clouds moving quickly across the sky, my tired brain focused on nothing more than the shifting shapes. Before long, my eyes closed. I fell asleep.

The sound of shouting woke me.

I pushed up off the rocking chair, looked around, my heart hammering.

The house I was in was unfamiliar. Dim candlelight showed simple wood furniture, a basket on the floor that held old clothes, some sewing needles and thread.

The yelling outside took on an edge of panic. A feeling of dread gripped me. I knew what was happening: I was in someone else's head, someone else's experience in the past. I guessed it was maybe the 1600s, but I wasn't sure and I didn't have time to look around. As before, I had no control. I grabbed up an old rifle, ran out into the night, my long skirt swirling around my legs.

Chapter Fourteen

The dark sky was lit with an orange glow. Some of the houses must already be burning, I thought, my alarm spurring me faster. I ran around the corner towards the center of town and a man knocked into me.

"The defenses have been breached," he said, breathless, grabbing my arm. "The most powerful have already fallen. There's nothing left to be done but to flee and save ourselves."

I pushed him off, kept moving. He'd have to lead the survivors to safety without me. I couldn't leave those still fighting.

In the town square, everything was chaos. Buildings burned. Some of the people had stayed to put out the flames, but with little success. A few horses kicked their way out of their barns and pounded down the lane, whinnying in fright.

A rifle shot sounded somewhere ahead. I ran towards the sound, my arm over my mouth, trying not to breathe in the smoke. I made my way across the square, ignoring the calls for help from the people struggling with the fires. The buildings were already lost, they just hadn't accepted it yet. I rushed on. I needed to go where I might still make a difference.

In the clearing out past the courthouse, I saw what remained of the townsfolk fighting against a lone man. They fought with all the weapons they had left.

I skidded to a halt, dropped down on one knee, and raised the rifle to sight along the barrel.

The man I aimed at was the same man from my dreams, dressed in dark clothes of the time. But I didn't have a chance to wonder about him. He grabbed a rifle out of someone's hand, flipped it around, struck his attacker in the head with it.

Suddenly flames rose up around him, burning bright enough and tall enough to hide him from view. A few long seconds later, though, he stepped out of the fire, unharmed, and the flames flickered out. In that moment, as he stood alone, I fired a shot. It kicked back hard into my shoulder, but I was already up and running.

The bullet disappeared before it even reached him.

I threw the rifle aside – I didn't have time to reload. I grabbed up a sword from someone lying dazed on the ground, charged on towards the man as he knocked one of my neighbors to the ground.

"No!" I cried, almost upon him.

He turned his fierce gaze on me.

He held up a hand, said, "Wait."

But I needed to kill him. With everything I had, I struck

at him with the sword, screaming my fury. He ducked. I swung again, and kept swinging as he evaded me with ease.

I couldn't give up. I feinted one way, tried to catch him off guard, but he slipped around the blade, seized my arm. He drew back his other hand and punched me, the powerful blow catching my temple.

I fell, hit the floorboards hard, still screaming. Hands closed around my arms, tried to hold me still. Now there were others shouting. As I struggled, I heard another voice chanting.

"*In nomine Patris exorcizo daemonas ex hac puella. Adsit ei Spiritus Sanctus iudicium subeunti flammarum.*"

It was Sister Claire's voice.

I realized I was on the porch. I stopped screaming, went slack in the arms that held me. My heart still raced, my breath came out like a sob. I lifted my head to look around.

Just off the porch, my crows flew about, cawing frantically. Helen dropped to her knees in front of me, tears streaming down her face. It disturbed me more than the vision. I'd never seen Helen cry.

"Eva? Oh my goodness, Eva, are you okay?"

Mary and Agnes stood behind her, clutching each other's hands for support, uncertain of what to do. Claire stood off to the side, holding her rosary before her, still reciting in Latin what I suspected was some sort of exorcism prayer.

"Claire, shut up," Sebastian cut her off, surprising me with his harsh tone. He was the one who'd been trying to hold me down. I was now slumped back against him, too weak and shaky to push myself off. "Evie?" he asked. He gently sat me up so he could look at me.

I sent a reassuring thought to the crows, and they quickly settled down. As I pushed my hair back from my face, trying to pull myself together, I thought I saw Tristan standing at the edge of the woods. But when I looked again, there was no sign of him.

"What happened sweetie?"

"Isn't it clear? That child has the Devil's hand upon her."

"Thank you, Sister Claire." Sebastian bit out the words, putting a hand on Helen's arm to silence her own furious reply. "We can handle this from here."

Claire was incensed, but she was too proud to argue such an obvious dismissal. She made the sign of the cross, a grim figure in her long black dress, and swept inside.

"Eva?" Sebastian prompted me.

"It was just a nightmare." I sounded hoarse and trembly.

"That must have been some nightmare," Helen murmured.

Mary and Agnes crouched down next to Helen.

"I saw you out here through the window," Agnes said. "I came to get you, but you wouldn't wake up. Then you started screaming. It was the scariest sound I've ever heard."

"We thought something terrible must be happening," said Mary. "We ran out here and you were..."

"What? What was I doing?"

But Mary dropped her eyes, pressed her lips together.

Sebastian took my hand. "You were thrashing around on the rocking chair. I was afraid you'd hurt yourself. We tried to call to you, but you wouldn't wake up. We couldn't get you to stop screaming or struggling, either. Then you sort of threw yourself to the ground. That's when I grabbed you. But after a moment you just went limp. Will you tell us what happened?"

"I didn't sleep much last night. When I came home from school I sat down, just to rest for a couple of minutes before going in. I fell asleep and then...then when I woke up, I was on the floor." I couldn't handle going through the details of the dream for them; it was too upsetting. Besides, I didn't want to worry them.

Though from the looks on their faces I was way past that.

"This wasn't like your other nightmares, Eva," Helen said.

I was completely thrown. How did she know about the other dreams? But then I realized — Helen was talking about my childhood nightmares. When I was little, the nuns had taken turns helping me back to sleep after my bad dreams. As I grew older, the nightmares had continued, but I stopped talking about them. Endless dreams of being chased by those shadow terrors...dreams that felt like warnings.

Of course Helen hadn't forgotten. And she was right: this was different.

"No, I guess not. But it's really not a big deal, it was just a very vivid nightmare. I'm sorry I scared you, but I'm okay now." I had to reassure them, even if I was freaked out.

The last time I had a vision of the past, it was followed by the fever that had felt so awful.

"Oh dear, Evie," Mary said. "You've got a big bruise forming. You must have hit your head on the floor when you fell."

Gingerly I felt along my temple. It was tender where the man had punched me, and as I moved, I noticed my right shoulder was sore from the rifle's recoil. My hands began to shake, my breath caught. What if the injuries in the vision had been worse? I was lucky he only hit me.

"It's okay sweetheart," Helen said, putting her arm around me, assuming my new distress was from the pain of the bruise. "Let's get you inside."

A sudden flash of lightning made me jerk, followed a second later by a crack of thunder. I looked out, saw heavy, dark clouds had rolled in.

There was no doubt I called up the storm.

We all stood. No one said anything as we stared out over the rough sea, a curtain of rain sweeping toward us. The trees bent and waved in the icy wind that blew in off the water.

I sighed. It wasn't surprising, I supposed. Storms had been off the coast for the past couple of days anyway. This one would blow itself out eventually, without any more help from me. I hoped that would be the only repercussion of the vision.

"Come on Evie, you need to get some rest." Helen guided me through the porch door.

"I don't need any more rest, Helen. I'd rather help with

getting everything ready." She started to disagree, but I stopped her. "Really. I'd just like to keep busy."

She didn't look happy, but she certainly couldn't argue with that. "Why don't you set the table then? And I suppose the rest of us should get back to the kitchen."

Sebastian had brought in my bag, so I went upstairs to put it away. From the look that passed between Helen and him, I guessed there would be more concerned conversations about me. Great. Exactly what I didn't need.

I walked into my room to find a dress laid out on my bed. It had a note resting on top.

Evie,

We thought you could use a nice dress for special occasions. Hope you like it.

Love,

Helen, Agnes and Mary

It was a simple, sleeveless design with an empire waist and a flowing skirt. It was a shimmery, gray-blue that matched my eyes. The dress looked new, and it was far prettier than anything else I owned. The nuns must have found it in town, splurged on it so I'd have something special to wear.

With the vision still so fresh and all the upsetting things that happened during the week wearing on me, the thoughtful gesture came close to pushing me over the edge.

After a few deep breaths, I reined myself in. I couldn't fall apart. The nuns needed to see me unaffected. I'd already have to work extra hard to ease their worries. Not to mention that Tristan would be here before I knew it. Just thinking about it put the nervous flutters back in my stomach.

I gently picked up the dress to hang it. The fabric was soft and silky. I couldn't help but feel a thrill at the thought of wearing it.

Downstairs, everything was polished and clean. Even the stained glass windows had been washed, though the light coming through was a subdued gray.

I arranged settings for everyone but Sister Catherine, who was in the middle of a self-imposed few weeks of silence. No avoiding Claire and Margaret unfortunately.

Once everything was set nicely, I headed to the kitchen to see what else needed to be done. Just outside the door I heard Mary say my name and Tristan's name, but I didn't catch the rest of the sentence. I pushed through the door.

The women looked over at me with guilty expressions.

"Evie, sweetheart, did you need anything?" Mary asked, recovering first, suddenly all innocence.

"What are you three up to?"

"Up to?" Agnes asked, turning back to the stove. "I don't know what you're talking about."

"We're just getting everything ready."

"Right. Well, I wanted to thank you for the dress. It's so beautiful, you really didn't need to do that."

"Oh dear," said Helen. She came over, squeezed my hand. "I completely forgot. I was so distracted by...well this afternoon has simply been so hectic. But I'm glad you like it." She tucked my hair behind my ear with a warm smile.

"You deserve a treat," Agnes added.

"You do work hard, sweetie, and you never complain." Mary pulled me in for a hug, all softness and comfort, and smelling faintly of sugar.

I kept smiling. Hard. "Thank you. It was really thoughtful."

"Nonsense. We should have done this a while ago," Helen said. "Mary, dear, that sauce is going to burn."

Mary rushed over to the stove to turn it down, while the other two went back to their own tasks.

"What else can I do to help?"

"I think we have everything under control in here for now, Eva, but I didn't have a chance to wipe down the tables in the reading room. Unless you have homework you need to do?"

"No, I have all weekend. I'll go work on the tables." I left them, wondering what they were really talking about before I interrupted.

But I had other things to worry about, things in the vision I had trouble accepting. The fire that sprang up around the winged man wasn't natural. Someone there had used magic to defend the people. Equally as strange, I hadn't sensed any surprise from the woman I experienced it through.

The thought set my heart racing.

Okay, calm down. Just because another like me existed some three hundred years ago, didn't mean there were others out there today.

And who was this man I saw in my dreams every night now? Did he not age? I knew he searched for me still...knew he was getting closer. So why did I see him in the past? Why was I connected to him?

Too many questions. I poured my frustration into the tasks at hand, scrubbing determinedly, relieved to at least be productive.

After a while I was called back to the kitchen to help with the odds and ends getting away from the nuns. It was warm and pleasant, though I had to pretend not to notice a few worried glances from Helen. I kept a smile on my face, tried not to let my darker thoughts show.

As six o'clock came closer, the nuns took turns disappearing to change and freshen up. Finally Agnes kicked me out, insisting it was more important for me to get ready.

I brushed my hair out, left it falling loosely down my back. After checking my reflection, I carefully put some of Greta's healing ointment on the bruise. It was already a dark, bluish-purple color, but I hoped my hair would at least partially hide it.

I pulled off my school clothes, slipped into the new dress. It was a perfect fit, hugging my small frame snugly, making me look elegant. It fell just below my knees and swished softly when I walked. My insides squirmed at the thought of Tristan seeing me wear something different for a change.

As much as I tried over and over again to convince myself I didn't care what he thought of me, I really couldn't change the way I felt about him. Even if I didn't have a chance with him compared to any one of the girls he was friends with at school.

Downstairs, I paced. The nuns wouldn't let me return to the kitchen. So back and forth I went until the clock chimed, announcing the hour.

The doorbell rang.

Chapter Fifteen

For a long moment I hesitated, suddenly wishing I could spend the evening alone, curled up with a book. But that wasn't an option, so I took the few steps forward, opened the door.

Greta and Tristan stood on the porch, the rain coming down heavily behind them. Both wore solemn expressions.

"Please, come in." I stepped aside, holding the door. "May I take your coats?"

Greta handed me her shawl, and I took Tristan's coat without meeting his eyes. Their somber presence filled the room, made me feel shy and uncomfortable.

I was relieved when Sebastian came down the hall. He was full of good humor, and the atmosphere relaxed as I hung up their things.

"Hello, welcome back. We're so happy you could make it."

"Thank you," Greta said with a smile. "It's a good evening to spend with friends."

"I couldn't agree more. Tristan, how are you?" The two men shook hands.

"I'm doing well, thanks. And you?"

"Wonderful. The ladies have all been cooking up a storm. Why don't we sit in the reading room while we wait? It shouldn't be long now."

We followed Sebastian down the hall, and as we settled into chairs, he asked Greta about some herb or other he was thinking of planting next spring. I turned to Tristan with a tentative smile, but he met my eyes with a frown. He seemed worried as he searched my face. When he caught sight of the bruise, his expression tightened.

Odd – he seemed almost to expect it. Maybe I hadn't imagined seeing him when I woke from the vision. I'd been screaming loudly, after all. It wasn't out of the question that he'd been close enough to hear and came to investigate.

We sat staring at each other. I suddenly felt defensive. I wanted to explain, tell him it wasn't a big deal...but I didn't want to say anything in front of the other two. I wondered at my bad luck: Tristan always caught me in moments that proved how different I was from everyone else.

Yet here he was, his green eyes studying me, no noticeable judgment in them.

"So Tristan," Sebastian said, drawing his attention away from me. "How is school going for you?"

"It's been well."

"That's good to hear. I know Eva's been working on a big history paper this week, what about you?"

The two of them discussed Tristan's topic. While

Sebastian talked, I saw Tristan give Greta a look. Greta's attention immediately focused on me, her expression troubled.

What was that? If Tristan had seen me this afternoon, he would've told his grandmother what happened. And she knew what followed the last time.

Despite how shaken I still felt from the vision, though, I didn't feel nearly as terrible as I had after the first one. Instead of feverish panic, I just felt raw, wrung out. Maybe I was getting used to it. It hadn't been the same shock to my system.

Helen came in, interrupting the conversation and my distracted thoughts. I stood to join the others as they said their hellos.

"I'm sorry it took us so long to have you back," she said. "We wanted to let you know how much we appreciate everything you've done for Eva."

"Nonsense," Greta replied. "She's been great company. I look forward to her Sunday visits."

"Well, just about everything is on the table, and Mary is getting the other Sisters, so we're ready to eat."

As they made their way into the dining room ahead of us, Tristan took a hold of my hand and pulled me aside. I looked up at him, totally aware of my hand in his.

"Eva," he said, his voice soft. "Are you all right?"

His concern made something inside me ache. "So you saw me this afternoon?"

"Yeah. It was the same as before?"

I shrugged, offered up a weak smile. "More or less."

He opened his mouth to say something else, but Helen

called my name from the next room. I'd almost forgotten where we were.

Tristan squeezed my hand before letting go, and we went in to join the others. Mary was pointing Claire and Margaret to the two end chairs next to her on one side, Agnes on the other; everyone else was already seated. The only two chairs left were next to each other.

I sat down, Tristan settling next to me, and caught Mary's smug look. So that was what the nuns had schemed up – making sure the two of us sat side by side. I shook my head, smiling to myself. There really was no discouraging her.

I slowly relaxed as we ate. Sebastian and Greta shared funny stories about Fairhaven from the book she'd lent him. Helen, Agnes and Mary joined in, adding their own entertaining encounters with some of the more interesting residents over the years.

The pleasant conversation continued as it grew dark outside. The rain went on falling steadily. Tristan and I answered questions about our schoolwork, though neither of us was keen to elaborate much on the subject of life at school.

I was relieved when the focus turned to Greta and some of the incredible things she'd done in her life. In addition to traveling around the world, she'd studied thoroughly in a wide range of subjects.

We were all impressed with her stories from the time she spent working in a hospital in Prague.

"What a wonderful thing to do," Mary said. "And thank goodness you did, so you were able to help Eva when she came down with that fever. We'll always be grateful to you for that." The others chimed in with thanks, and Greta smiled at me, opening her mouth to say something.

"Are you sure it was just a fever?" Claire asked.

Everyone turned to look at her.

My heart dropped. Around the table the other nuns also tensed.

"Yes, it was definitely a fever," Greta said with a frown, glanced over at me. "Were there other concerns?"

"Of course not." Helen's voice was firm as she shot a warning look at Claire. "Eva is fine."

"Obviously that isn't true. You've denied the signs for years, Helen, but today's manifestation can't be ignored."

"Sister Claire, that is enough," Sebastian cut in.

"No. I won't pretend she's just an innocent child anymore. She has demons inside, working their wicked deeds through her. We all saw them possessing her today."

The silence that followed had a sharp quality. I held myself completely rigid, unbearably mortified that Greta and Tristan were here for this. I kept my eyes on the table, but out of the corner of my eye I could see Tristan's hand on his leg, his fist clenched so tightly his knuckles were white.

Greta cleared her throat, drawing everyone's attention. I held my breath. She raised an eyebrow and said in an icy tone, "That is one of the most ridiculous and mean spirited things I've ever heard. I would have expected better from a woman living in a house of God."

"You don't understand," said Claire, her thin mouth twisting down.

"Oh, I understand you better than you might think, and I assure you, you are mistaken."

I looked at Helen, panic welling inside me. I appreciated Greta defending me, but Claire had seen me do strange and inexplicable things when I was little. If Claire gave examples, if she shared my secret, reinforcing what Tristan had heard about me in school, there'd be no undoing the damage.

Tristan already knew I was weird, but I couldn't handle the idea of him finding out just how different I really was. No one could know.

Helen understood. She got up abruptly, knocking the fork off her plate in a clatter, deliberately interrupting whatever Claire was about to say next. "Well, it looks like everyone is finished with dinner. I think it's about time for dessert. Sister Claire, since you and Sister Margaret didn't help with the cooking I'm sure you'll be happy to help with the clearing. If you wouldn't mind."

Claire apparently wasn't up for further argument – unsurprising, since nobody disobeyed Helen when she used that tone of voice. Everyone handed their plates down the table, whether they were finished eating or not. Claire stacked them with help from Margaret, who shot apprehensive looks at Sebastian more than once.

When they took the plates into the kitchen, Helen followed. Agnes stood up, too, shaking her head slightly when Sebastian moved to stand. "If you'll excuse us, we'll just help them get the dessert ready."

Then it was nothing but uncomfortable silence.

I felt my skin flush with heat. I couldn't bring myself to

look at anyone else. It wasn't a surprise to hear Claire say those things. The fact that she said them not only in front of Sebastian, but also in front of guests, however, showed how utterly certain she was of her truth. And what if she was right, I thought, misery seeping through me. It wasn't like I had any proof against the accusations.

I sensed Tristan shift in his seat to turn and look at me. Even if he didn't completely believe Claire...would he believe he was better off keeping his distance again?

"You know it's a funny coincidence," Tristan said in a mild tone. "When I was younger, my aunt was convinced I was the devil's spawn."

Greta chuckled. "Well, no one could blame her. You were a little hellion."

"It sounds like you must have some great stories," Sebastian said, joining the effort to lighten the mood.

"Oh, I can definitely see you being a troublemaker. And I bet you were really good at charming your way out of it too," Mary said.

"Maybe at first," Tristan said, smiling. "But once my aunt caught on, there was no getting out of anything. In fact, even things that weren't my fault got blamed on me."

"I'd be willing to bet that most of the things that weren't directly your fault, could still be traced right back to you."

"See, even my own grandmother thought the worst of me."

"Something tells me she may in fact be right, though," said Sebastian.

Before Tristan could respond, Helen and Agnes came back through the door carrying the dessert and plates. Everyone seemed to hold their breaths.

Helen, appearing entirely calm and composed, set the cake down. "I'm so sorry, but it turns out Sister Claire isn't feeling well. Sister Margaret has gone with her to help her up to her room. They both send their regrets at leaving early."

You could almost hear the sigh whisper through the room as we all relaxed. I wondered about the scene that must've taken place in the kitchen. Helen could be ferocious when she needed to be, especially with Agnes to back her up.

Conversation picked up again as plates of pumpkin spice cake were passed around, cups of tea poured. We didn't quite recapture the easy mood of earlier, though. There were heavy silences. When we'd finished and there was a lull, Greta declared it was time to head home.

"Before you leave, I was wondering if we could speak to you about something," Helen said. "Perhaps the kids could wait in the reading room?"

"Sure," I murmured as Tristan nodded. I knew what Helen wanted to talk to her about. The question was would Greta tell them about my other violent nightmare? Or would she ease their worries?

I followed Tristan out of the room. I really didn't want to be alone with him after what happened, even if he had reacted better than I could've hoped for.

"Eva?"

Reluctance dragging at every inch of me, I turned to face him. His gaze fixed on mine, and once again, his brows drew together in worry.

He stepped closer to me, close enough that I could smell the fresh, faintly woodsy scent that always followed him. "My grandmother and I have to go out of town. I think she's going to want to leave as soon as possible."

Okay, that wasn't at all what I expected, but it was better than talking about what happened. "Where are you going?"

"Back to Haverhill, where we used to live. We have a lot of friends and family there she needs to see."

"Oh, well, that's nice. Have fun."

"Eva," he said in a soft voice. He gently moved the hair back from my forehead, his fingers brushing my skin, to inspect the bruise. My heartbeat quickened. His eyes shifted back to mine, though his hand stayed in my hair. "Promise me you'll be careful while we're gone."

I stared at him. Nothing else existed around us. "I promise," I whispered. I had no way of stopping the nightmares, but I promised anyway.

Greta called his name from the hallway. Tristan pulled his hand away, gave me another long, searching look before heading for the door.

"Oh, one more thing, Eva." He turned back to me, a smile tugging the corner of his mouth up. "You look lovely tonight." He disappeared into the hall.

After a stunned moment, I followed him out. I couldn't help smiling. Suddenly the rest of the terrible day didn't matter so much.

In the foyer, Tristan was draping Greta's shawl across her shoulders. When he finished, she came over while the others talked.

"Did Tristan tell you we have to go away?" I nodded. "Good. There are some people I need to see back home. I don't like leaving now, but I've put off this visit for far too long. Anyway, we're leaving tomorrow and we won't be back until at least the end of next week. So I'm sorry, but I have to cancel your Sunday lesson."

I wondered at the urgency I sensed in her. "Of course, don't worry about it. I hope you have a good trip."

She studied me carefully for a minute. "You seem to be holding up well after this afternoon."

Ah. That's what she was afraid of. This wasn't like the last time, though, I was certain of it. Despite the exhaustion, I knew I wasn't running a fever. "I don't know what Tristan told you, but I'm fine, really. Don't worry about me. Please."

Greta shook her head with a reluctant smile. "As surprising as that is, I do actually believe you, though of course I'll still worry."

I wasn't sure why she found it difficult to believe, but I appreciated not being pressed about it.

She leaned forward to hug me. "Take care of yourself, okay?" Then she murmured something, almost too low for me to hear, in a language I didn't understand.

I pulled back to look at her. The woman's eyes were oddly luminescent in the dim light of the foyer. "What was that?"

"Just an old prayer, dear, to keep the bad spirits away.

Be safe." Greta turned to nod at Tristan. "We very much enjoyed the dinner and the company. Goodnight everyone."

We watched from the doorway as the car drove off into the dark, rainy night. There was a long silence as everyone stared down the driveway.

"Oh, Eva. I'm so sorry I brought up your fever in front of Claire. I just never imagined she would say such a thing," said Mary, wringing her hands.

"It's not your fault."

"Eva's right," Helen said. She closed the door. "I have no doubt that if you hadn't given her the opening, Margaret was instructed to bring it up. Sebastian, those two are out of control."

"I know. It was way out of line. Clearly this has been brewing for some time."

"It's been brewing ever since the night Eva arrived here, and you know it," Agnes said. "Something has to be done."

"Wouldn't it be nice if you could impose a vow of silence on Claire?" Mary mused.

"I'm certain it would do more good for her than for Sister Catherine. But don't worry, I'm going to speak to Claire and Margaret tomorrow. This will never happen again." Sebastian's voice had an edge to it I'd never heard before. He'd always had an unlimited supply of patience for me as I grew up, and for the first time I was really glad he'd never been angry with me.

"Whatever happens," Helen said, frowning at me, "I don't want you to worry about it. And don't you dare give a second thought to what she said tonight. She's just afraid of what she doesn't understand."

"I know." But it was going to be hard to forget. I felt a heavy weariness pulling at me – I was sure I could sleep for days.

Helen and Sebastian traded a look. "Well, it's been a long day," Sebastian said. "I think we all could use some rest."

"Definitely. We'll handle the cleanup, you go up to bed," Helen said to me.

"No argument," added Agnes.

So while the others went off to take care of cleaning, I plodded up the stairs, barely able to keep my eyes open. Once in bed, I was asleep immediately.

It was a deep and heavy sleep, empty of any dreams.

*

Downstairs, I found Helen putting together sandwiches while Mary baked muffins. The kitchen smelled wonderful.

"What are your plans for the day, Evie?"

"I've gotta do homework, then maybe I'll take a walk."

"Don't go too far, okay?" Helen's voice was strained.

I was lucky I wasn't in full lockdown.

"I'll stay close, I promise."

I spent the clear, chilly afternoon on the beach with my crows. When the sun began to set, I went inside, where Sebastian and I spent the evening snug in our chairs in front of the fireplace. The fire was soothing, with only the occasional sound of Sebastian turning a page in his book next to me. More than once my eyes drifted closed. Eventually I gave in.

I stood up, kissed Sebastian on the cheek.

"Goodnight, sweetheart. See you tomorrow."

The hallway was dark and chilly after the warm glow of his study. I hurried up the stairs, went straight to my bed, crawled under the covers and fell asleep.

I slipped into the dream, looked around the desert. I was getting used to this. It felt so real here, like it was a place you might find in the waking world if you just opened the right door. The stars shimmered in the desert night, and I wondered if they orbited this world. If I looked down from a great height, would I see the lights slowly spinning?

I watched the night thicken around me, spreading to extinguish the stars nearby.

He was here.

I turned to see the man behind me, his wings a deeper black than the dark of the night that surrounded him. He stood watching me, holding utterly still. I waited.

Nothing happened.

I looked around; nothing had changed. No one else was there but the two of us. This wasn't how the dream usually went. I always had Tristan pull me away. He was the best part of the dream. But now the rules had apparently changed.

The man in front of me, without ever taking his eyes from mine, inclined his head slightly, acknowledging this was different. I wasn't going anywhere, and I sensed he'd been waiting for this.

Somewhere, deep down, I knew how to get out of this place, this dream. After all, I dreamt myself out with Tristan every night. But for whatever reason, I wasn't doing it now.

For the moment, neither of us made any threatening movement, each content to simply observe the other. Even beyond his incredible eyes, he was a striking man. He had a straight patrician nose, his bone structure strong, a little angular. His thick hair, which swept across his forehead and just covered his ears, was as intensely black as his wings.

He was tall and lean, though I knew he was incredibly strong, and there was a sharpness to him I couldn't define. He wore a simple black suit that fit him well. The practical, distracted part of my brain wondered how that worked with his wings.

I could make no guess at his age as I examined him. There was something about his features that reminded me of classical paintings from long ago, some sense of a different time period about him. But he looked young, fit. Had I seen him on the street in passing, I would've thought he was in his early thirties, though looking in his eyes now it was clear he was much, much older.

Very slowly, obviously trying not to alarm me, the man held his right hand out in front of him. When I glanced down, I saw a spark flare up and hover just above his palm.

My eyes flew back to his. He still gazed calmly at me, nothing menacing about the way he stood there. He tipped his head, drawing my attention back to his hand. As I watched, the spark flickered. It began to blaze bigger, brighter.

The fire grew, burning a strange, vivid blue, more like the color of a gas flame. He held it in his hand for a long moment, both of us watching the flames shift restlessly. Then he clenched his fist and the fire disappeared.

I looked up at him, wary of what it all meant. Why had he shown me this?

The man reached his other hand towards me, very slowly. He brought his index finger to the middle of my forehead, just shy of touching my skin, and I heard something whispered in my mind in some ancient language.

Then he stepped back, raised his right hand as he had before. He wanted me to keep watching. I tried to, but I had to rub at my eyes. Something was wrong with my vision. The man motioned more adamantly, though, so I looked again.

Strange wisps of light flowed around his palm. They came together as he called up the spark. The flame grew a stronger, brighter blue, while more trails of glimmering light melted into it.

I glanced up at him in surprise. I realized what I was seeing: they were lines of energy he used to keep the fire going, drawing them from the world around him. He nodded, catching my understanding. Whatever he'd done to me, it allowed me to see the currents of energy his magic pulled in to fuel the flames. I had used my own energy the other day when I accidentally called up the fire, but he was showing me another way.

I just didn't understand why.

Nor did I understand how he knew about my problem in the first place.

He gestured to me. It was clear what he wanted: I was supposed to try now. No reason not to, I figured.

I stared at him for a long moment, studying the patterns I saw in the air in front of him, the barrier he kept between his palm and the flame. I held out my own hand, called on my magic to tug the energy in as I caught up the spark. Carefully, I fed the fire so it grew larger, flickering above my palm. Unlike his blue fire, mine was a white-hot flame, almost too bright to look at.

I had done it. Pleased with myself, I looked up into the man's unfathomable eyes. He watched me with an intense expression on his face, and suddenly, I felt uncertain.

My fire flared up in response. I jerked back, catching my breath, only to find myself lying in bed, my heart racing. I sat up quickly and looked around, half expecting to see him standing in the corner. Of course, no one was there. It was just a dream. Right?

The problem was it had become more difficult to draw a clear line between my dreams and reality.

What would happen when I tried the trick with the fire? If it worked...I started to breathe faster, feeling a bit panicked. If it worked, it would mean what just happened in the dream had happened for real. How that could be possible, I wasn't sure. But there was no way I could convince myself I subconsciously figured out the secret and used the dream to show myself. Neither explanation seemed at all possible.

It was late, and I didn't want to risk trying anything inside. I'd wait until tomorrow when everyone was at church. And maybe it wouldn't work. It would turn out to be nothing more than a weird dream. I lay back down, forced myself to breathe slowly.

Would I get pulled back into that strange, starlit world? After a week straight of the same dream, last night there had been nothing. A prayer to keep the bad spirits away? It was an odd coincidence.

An equally disturbing observation was that the recurring dream changed as soon as the McGrath's were out of town. Why? A subconscious alteration on my part? Or did I really think Greta was capable of affecting me like that? I rubbed my temples. My uncertainties about the woman had been growing, but was my imagination getting away from me?

I mean, yeah, it was far-fetched. But then again, so was everything else in my life. If my theories about Greta were even close, it would change everything.

Chapter Sixteen

For whatever reason, the rest of the night carried nothing more for me in dreams.

I went down to breakfast once everyone else left for services in town. Everything I did was slow and deliberate. I washed up, pulled on a pair of pants, a long sleeve shirt, a sweater...then I couldn't think of anything else to put off what I needed to try.

First I sat on the steps to the back porch, but I was too jittery and nervous to sit still. Fine, on with the pacing. I just needed to build up my courage.

Deep breath.

I squeezed my eyes shut, visualized what I'd seen. Every detail was clear. I opened my eyes, held my hand out, and concentrated on drawing the energy around me to my palm. Almost like lighting a match, I called up a spark and fed the energy into it.

Without any effort, I pulled more fuel into the point of light, expanded it until the flames burned strong and steady,

licking up a foot high above my palm. It was the same painfully bright, white fire as the night before.

I watched the flames. There was nothing to it. And it
was familiar – I felt almost as if I'd been doing this all my
life. Just as the strange man had done in the dream, I closed
my fist around the fire, extinguishing it.

So that was it. I hadn't merely had a dream about a man
I didn't know. He had somehow entered into my dream.
There was no other explanation I could think of for having
learned this. He had either been crossing over into my
dreams or, I realized, he was somehow pulling me into his.

I started to feel lightheaded and I had to sit down. This
was too much. It was all just too damned much. What the
hell was I supposed to do with this?

I'd assumed I was catching glimpses of this man in my
dreams because he was out there looking for me. Like it
was some sort of alarm system in my subconscious – he
was a threat so my magic showed him to me. But it was
clear now that wasn't true.

And why had he shown me how to manipulate the energies for the fire? All this time, I'd feared the dark tide
rushing towards me, had feared this man coming for me.
My other dreams had been warnings about him. So why
would this supposed enemy want to help me learn magic?

I sat on the ground for a long time. There were still too
many missing pieces...I only came up with more questions.
Not any damned answers. Okay, so I did understand better
how my magic worked, how I had to manipulate the energy
from the world around me to fuel a fire, instead of pulling
it from myself – which, obviously, wasn't the better option.

The crows had all flown in and settled around me, a silent support.

I wished I could talk to Helen and Sebastian about this.

But, of course, that was out of the question. They were worried enough. It wouldn't be fair to lay more of a burden at their feet, even if it would be a big relief just to hand over the responsibility.

Back inside, I wandered around, unable to sit still, until Mary came home early. The excuse she gave was weak (she was a terrible liar), and I was sure everyone had decided I shouldn't be left on my own for too long. So we spent the rest of the afternoon in the kitchen baking.

As the evening wore on, my agitation increased. Would I dream again tonight? Would he show me other things? I knew I wasn't supposed to trust him, but still...there was something about him that intrigued me, once my original fear subsided a little. I was drawn to him for reasons I couldn't explain.

It seemed too early when Agnes declared her eyes were tired and the nuns headed off to bed, so I went to see Sebastian. In his study, I found Helen draping a blanket over him where he'd fallen asleep in his chair. She'd already taken off his glasses, and when she had the blanket arranged comfortably, she smoothed the hair back from his forehead.

I walked away quietly, not wanting to intrude.

It was late when I finally turned the light out. I'd given up guessing. As I lay there, sleep beginning to tickle the edges of my thoughts, I heard a strange sound. I shot out of bed, full of tension. Whatever it was, something about it put me on edge.

And it had happened again: I stood over my own body, the quality of the night somehow different.

At least I wasn't back in the desert, I thought with a sigh.

I dithered, going back and forth about what I should do. Then I heard the sound again. It was a low whistle, like when a strong wind blew through a crack in a building.

I swore I heard my name whispered over it.

Okay, now I really didn't know what to do. It definitely came from outside, but I wasn't sure if it would be a good idea to investigate.

Curiosity got the best of me.

Besides, I figured, if there was something dangerous, better to meet it out there than force it to come inside after me. Right? So down the stairs I went, out the side door to the lawn.

Everything around me was luminous. The living world pulsed with its own soft, silvery light, and my breath caught at the beauty of it. It was as though I were able to see the inner spirit of the earth, I thought wistfully. For all I knew, maybe I was.

I glanced towards the beach, but the eerie whistling picked up again, and as I reoriented on it, I realized it came from the woods. With a deep breath, I headed into the forest.

The sound faded away entirely. But I didn't need it. There was something out there...I could sense it. I made my way unerringly through the trees, the pale silver light shining out around me, shifting with every breath of air that stirred.

I was deep in the woods now. It wouldn't be long before I reached the stone wall that ran along the edge of the property, but I could feel I was getting close.

I came to a large tree with roots sticking out of the ground. I picked my way carefully over them, wondering if I tripped if I'd awaken later to find real injuries on my body. It seemed likely. When I was clear of the roots I looked up, stopped in surprise. The wall was in front of me. Standing on the other side was the strange man who plagued my dreams.

He stood still, his head bowed, wearing the same suit as before. His wings were nothing more than smoky shadows. A darkness grew around him; the silvery light withered, fading as the black stain spread across the ground at his feet.

A breeze picked up, ruffled his hair. As it died out, everything went quiet. He looked subdued standing there, without any brightness shining out from him like it did from everything else. Unconsciously, I took a step closer, uncertain of why he was here.

Slowly, the man across the wall raised his head until he met my eyes. He gazed at me for a long time, and I felt a growing sense of melancholy in him.

"Eva Harroway," he said in a voice that was soft but powerful. I felt it echoing in my head.

I frowned at him in confusion. My last name was Blackwell.

"Eva Harroway," he said again. "I have been waiting for you."

"But why?" I asked, finding my voice. "What do you want with me?"

"Come with me." He held his hand out. "Come with me, little one, and I will show you everything. I will give you all the answers you seek."

I took another step forward. He offered exactly what I wanted. All I had ever wanted. If he could tell me who I was, where I came from, why I was the way I was…then wouldn't it be worth the risk? After all, how could I know for sure he was a danger to me? I had no actual proof, nothing more than a whisper in a dream.

Another step and I could almost touch the wall.

Before I was able to reach out, I heard my name. It was faint, coming from far away. But there was no mistaking Tristan's voice, or the urgency in it.

"Don't cross the wall, Eva!"

The man in front of me turned his head towards the sound. He'd heard it too, and the rage suddenly rolling off him was palpable. It scared me.

I backed up a step, unsure of what I wanted. I heard Tristan call my name again. The fear in his voice took root in my chest. I backed away further, and the man watched, his face etched in stone, as I stumbled over the roots.

When I caught myself, I looked back up. He was gone. I didn't wait any longer. I turned, ran as fast as I could through the woods back to the abbey. Relief filled me when I finally caught a glimpse of the massive building between the trees, but I didn't slow down until I was all the way back in my room. As I slid to a stop, I pulled in a deep breath, found myself lying in bed.

Everything was changing.

*

I curled up under the covers, seriously considering claiming I was sick and had to stay home.

After I'd woken back up last night, I hadn't slept much…partially out of fear of where I might end up in my dreams, but also because I had too much tumbling around my head.

I'd always accepted there were things in this world that operated outside of what people considered the normal rules. I was one of them, after all. But the things I'd been seeing lately went beyond what even I'd imagined. It was hard to come to terms with.

And what about Tristan? For the hundredth time since I woke up, I went over it again. I definitely heard his voice. The winged man heard it too. I was afraid to think about what that meant. How was I supposed to know what was really happening in these half-dreams, and what was just the dream part?

It took only a few more minutes of brooding to convince me that I'd go crazy cooped up in my room all day. So I threw the covers off, got dressed, and left.

Math was easy, if boring. It was a review for a test and I knew the material. When the bell rang I went to English, tried to ignore the conversations about what everyone had done over the weekend. At least no one ever asked me. It wasn't until I heard Sarah happily call out Tristan's name that I looked up.

Molly and Sarah converged on him as he walked through the doorway. But he didn't pay any attention to them. His eyes went straight to where I sat. When he saw me, a look of relief came over his face. His whole body seemed to lose its tension. After looking me over thoroughly, he turned his focus to the two girls chatting away at him about what he'd missed that weekend. He looked exhausted.

What was he doing here anyway? Greta said they'd be out of town until at least the end of the week. And the way he'd looked at me...like he'd been worried I wouldn't be here, or wouldn't be all right. It was eerie.

It seemed impossible Tristan could've known what happened when I stepped out of my body in the half-dream. But something had brought him rushing back to Fairhaven. If the winged man was really there last night and could move through these half-dreams as he pleased, then it followed that someone else could as well.

That thought shook me to my core.

The bell rang. I kept my eyes on Tristan as he walked across the room and turned down the aisle towards me. He met my gaze squarely, the shadows under his eyes giving him a haunted look. But if I expected to find answers, I was disappointed: his expression revealed nothing.

Maybe for the first time, I truly began to believe Tristan and Greta weren't who they said they were. Certainly I'd speculated, with all of the strangeness that surrounded them. But I'd always thought I was being ridiculous and over-imaginative, sure there had to be a reasonable explanation for everything.

Until now.

For the rest of English, I was on edge. It was uncomfortable having Tristan behind me where I couldn't see him.

When class ended, I got my things together slowly. Unlike usual, Tristan didn't beat me out of the room. He shuffled his things together, stalling. For what purpose, I wasn't sure. He didn't even look up.

There wasn't anything to say, though, so I hurried out. How exactly was I supposed to get to the bottom of all this? Spying on Tristan and his grandmother didn't seem like the best idea, and neither did confronting them. I didn't even know what I'd be accusing them of.

Until I figured out a better plan, the best I could come up with was researching their family more at the library. It couldn't hurt. And I was definitely going up to the attic as soon as the time was right.

Admittedly, neither course of action was likely to lead to anything useful, but still, it would be something. I was way too in the dark about everything happening around me.

Classes went by in a blur. I went where I needed to, answered questions when asked. But the whole time, I was going over every detail I could remember of the last few weeks.

At lunch I sat at my usual table with a book in hand, but it was impossible to read. The few times I looked over, Tristan was paying little attention to their conversation, his eyes frequently seeking mine.

My heart still skipped every time I made eye contact with him, but I really wished he'd stop. The last thing I needed, on top of everything else, was for one of the girls at his table to notice his preoccupation with me.

And what was I going to say the next time we ended up

alone together? I wasn't sure if I should be alone with him, if I should trust him, until I knew more.

I snuck another glance. Even the tired smile he gave Oliver was irresistible. It was irritating.

I had a headache by the time I left the gym.

When the last bell rang, I had two options: I could either go to the library to read more McGrath history...or I could go look around the woods. I pulled on my coat, decided it would be best to try to find the place I went in my half-dream. I needed to see it. The library would have to wait.

I slung my bag over my shoulder, walked out the front doors and started down the steps. By the time I got to the bottom, Tristan had slid into place next to me, matching my stride.

Chapter Seventeen

Tristan and I walked in silence. I wondered if he realized I now questioned everything he and Greta had told me. I looked over at him, but he kept his eyes ahead.

From the beginning, I'd assumed the man from my dreams was the one to be feared. But so far, all he'd really done was show me how to work some magic and offer to give me all the answers I was seeking. Whereas Tristan...well he was another story altogether.

What if I had it backwards?

It occurred to me now that Tristan had appeared in my life the very day after my dream first warned me of an approaching danger.

Another quick glance at him and I sighed. Even with all my suspicions, with my new reluctance to trust him, I couldn't help but feel a pull towards Tristan.

"How was your trip?" I asked, trying to sound casual, watching him out of the corner of my eye. I wanted to know if he planned to keep up his normal act. Not that walking me home from school was normal.

"It was fine, I guess."

"I thought you weren't coming back until the end of the week."

"That was the plan, yeah."

He was trying to be as vague as possible. Normally, I'd have backed off out of politeness. But…"So what happened?"

Tristan glanced over at me and for a minute, I didn't think he was going to answer.

"We finished everything up quicker than planned. As my grandmother has grown fond of the town here, she didn't feel any need to linger."

"I see."

What secrets was he keeping?

We walked the rest of the way to the abbey in a charged silence. Surprisingly, Tristan walked me all the way up to the door. I reached for the doorknob, wondering what to say, when he asked, full of awkwardness, "So do you have any plans for this afternoon?"

I turned to face him. He shoved his hands in his pockets, hunching his shoulders a little, but he met my eyes resolutely.

"Not really. I have a lot of homework to get done. I guess that's it."

"Oh. Well, good luck with it."

"Um, thanks." I had no idea what to make of this sudden attempt at conversation.

"Right, well I should get going."

"Okay." I opened the door.

"Eva?" I looked back and he opened his mouth to say something, but then seemed to change his mind with a little shake of his head. "I'll see you tomorrow."

Tristan headed down the stairs as I went in. What the hell? Usually I was the one off balance. How was this weirdness connected to what happened last night?

Once the coast was clear, I walked outside in the direction I'd gone the night before. I had worried I'd have trouble finding the way – everything looked so different in the dream. But I found I knew exactly where I was going.

After what seemed like a much longer walk than the one last night, I came across the ancient tree with its roots sticking up, the wall stretched out to either side behind it. Though the forest grew around and over it, the wall was still straight and strong, despite how old it must be. Cautiously, I stepped up to the stones to look at where the man had been, just on the other side.

My breath caught in my throat.

In a large, irregular circle surrounding the place he'd stood, everything was dead. The weeds, the low bushes, even the moss, were withered and brown.

The black fog I'd seen the night before, smothering the light of everything around him, must have killed it all. I leaned over the wall to look closer. I could see a few insects lying on the ground, not moving. I straightened back up, a cold feeling slipping down my spine. If there had been any doubt left in my mind that it had all been real, that was gone now.

There was nothing more I could do here. Hopefully,

nature would take its course and new growth would eventually fill in the area. I turned around, headed back. I had to figure out my next step.

But I couldn't get the ominous image out of my head.

*

The abbey was quiet as I crept up to the third floor. Despite my sudden sense of urgency to explore the attic, I'd waited until everyone retired for the evening. I didn't want the nuns asking questions.

When I reached the top of the stairs, I held up a candle, lit the wick with a thought. All the doors down the hall beyond the circle of light were closed. We rarely came up here…it had been a long time since we had enough nuns visiting to need the rooms. I went to the first door on the left and opened it slowly, hoping it wouldn't squeak. Behind the door was a narrow staircase.

Almost every stair creaked loudly in the otherwise silent building.

When I got to the top, I sensed the large space I stood in, though I couldn't see much of it. The attic didn't have any lights. Handily, someone had left a candelabrum on a shelf just inside the doorway, and I quickly brought a flame up on each of the candles.

Old furniture, covered with sheets to keep the dust off, stood along either side. Along the cleared pathway, there were stacks of all kinds of things – long out-dated newspapers, magazines, empty bottles.

I went along, checking under covers, peeking in boxes as I went, not certain what exactly I was looking for. One box held charming wooden toys, one held ancient looking kitchen utensils. I opened another and my pulse jumped at the sight of books full of elegant handwriting. But when I flipped through them, I realized they were just recipes.

All the lost history was fascinating. Some of the pieces of furniture were hand-carved out of wood, made with elegant designs, and it seemed such a waste to have it all hidden away.

It was too bad I hadn't risked coming up here years earlier to explore. It would take a long time to really go through everything. As it was, I tried to keep myself from spending too much time on things that, while intriguing, held no information about the family that first resided here.

When I lifted the next sheet, it was to find a wooden trunk with gorgeously intricate carvings on its surfaces. It had a large, very old, padlock on it. Score.

After some deliberating and a frustrated failure at picking the lock, I decided to experiment. With magic. I knew the general idea behind the mechanics of locks – it seemed reasonable that if I could just shift the right pieces inside, I'd be able to unlock it.

Of course, it was easier said than done. But after concentrating, sensing along the parts inside, I finally found the right piece to move. With a satisfying click, the lock opened. I felt a strange shiver pass over me, but I dismissed it as I slipped the lock off and pulled the lid up.

It was filled with neat stacks of old leather-bound journals, papers, and other books. Eagerly, I opened the first one, hoping it was indeed a journal. After looking at the first page, I flipped through it quickly, picked up another. It was the same. They were all filled with entries written in a language I couldn't read.

So at the moment, they were useless.

I let out a frustrated sigh. It was entirely possible the journals held nothing more interesting than someone's accounts of their normal day-to-day struggles. I had a feeling, however, there was more to them than that. It would be a process getting them translated, though, especially without help.

On the inside of the covers, I did find the name McGrath etched neatly in gold. I was on the right track, at least. But for now there was nothing useful.

It was late and I needed to get to bed. I hadn't really expected a different outcome, but I was disappointed all the same.

Just as I was about to close the lid, a bit of bright color near the bottom of the trunk caught my eye. I shifted the other stuff aside, pulled up the book to examine the cover. Hand-painted, it was done with beautiful, if somewhat gloomy, detail. It was the deep red sky on the cover that had caught my eye, but it was the figure standing in the dreamy landscape that made my breath catch.

He had large, sweeping black wings.

I looked closely at the figure, but he was nothing more than a silhouette. I glanced around. It suddenly felt creepier up here. The soft candlelight flickered occasionally, while beyond it, the attic was still and dark. I turned my attention back to the book in my lap.

I opened it gingerly, looked through the pages. It

seemed to be some sort of dark, fanciful fairytale. The illustrations were vivid and bizarre, but lovely in an otherworldly kind of way.

It told the tale of winged creatures who walked the earth long before the dreams of men. They were the guardians of the old world, wardens of the gates to the Lost Lands. They lived in peace, cared for the land and nurtured the magic.

But things changed with the rise of humans.

Life shifted to make room, and the guardians tried to adapt. In a show of friendship, they shared some of their power with certain people, the ones they deemed receptive. The book illustrated an enchanted time, with new knowledge being passed along.

Then things began to go wrong. The winged creatures became jealous of the growing powers of the humans. Their anger and resentment swelled. One day, they slaughtered an entire village of people they'd been teaching their ways to, as a demonstration of their strength, a warning to the others.

The humans were forced to band together to fight against them. In a stroke of luck, an ally was discovered who shared the secret of how to kill the guardians. The tide of the war changed.

The humans killed off all of the winged betrayers they could find, and before long, the rest disappeared. It was not a lasting victory, however. The few surviving guardians began to appear out of nowhere to attack the innocents, only to fade back into the shadows each time. Vigilance would be forever imperative.

I closed the book feeling incredibly unsettled. It had seemed like a children's fairytale, but some of the illustrations were shockingly violent and disturbing. Not to mention, of course, the fabled characters bore a resemblance to the man who visited my dreams so often.

It must certainly be valuable: there was no date written, but it was clearly very old and painted with great care. It was no surprise it had been carefully locked away. For a moment, I felt a stab of guilt. The trunk surely belonged to one of Greta's ancestors...no doubt she'd find great worth in its contents.

I stood up, dusted myself off. I came to a resolution as I replaced the lock, took one last look around. Until I knew more about who Greta really was and why she was here, I would keep this discovery to myself.

*

I got dressed and washed up, my head full of distracted brooding. It wasn't until I was pulling my hair into a bun that I froze, realizing I hadn't dreamt at all last night. From the moment I closed my eyes to when I opened them this morning, there was nothing but a black hole. Slowly, as I let the thought settle, I continued getting ready.

I couldn't help the worrisome notion that it coincided with Greta and Tristan's return to town, though I still had trouble understanding how it could possibly be connected.

I pulled on my coat, grabbed my bag, and stepped out into the crisp morning air. My steps faltered when I caught sight of Tristan emerging from the woods. When he saw me, he angled towards me, his long legs covering the ground quickly. I watched his approach, filled with suspicion. Never once had we run into each other on the way to school, and now, after walking home with me yesterday he happened to show up just as I left? Right.

In fact, now that I thought about it, I wondered if his questioning my plans yesterday was an attempt to keep tabs on where I would be.

That was discomforting.

"Morning," he said, his smile guarded. "Mind if I walk with you?"

I eyed him a moment, but there was no easy way to avoid it.

"I guess not."

The trees along the path were all bright yellows, oranges and reds, autumn having firmly settled in. It would be a clear day too, though this far into the season it would remain chilly.

Tristan asked about some of our assignments. I replied. I was polite, but terse. After that, we remained silent. He clearly had no intention of giving me an explanation as to why he suddenly made an effort to accompany me, while I, in turn, wasn't going to ask.

Once we left the woods, I couldn't help but hunch my shoulders, scanning the street around us. Tristan seemed unconcerned with us being seen together – how nice for him – but I was not on board. People would take notice, and some of those people wouldn't be happy about it.

I'd be the one to suffer the consequences.

I drifted away from him as we neared the school, feeling more than a little stupid. Tristan glanced over at me, but he didn't comment, much to my relief. I so didn't want the embarrassment of explaining.

Inside, I turned down the hallway without a glance back at him. Focus. Whatever was going on outside of school, it was still important to keep my guard up here. Most days, everyone avoided me entirely, but I obviously couldn't count on that.

Once in a while, I caught Tristan watching me with a strange expression on his face. I totally didn't know what to make of it, so my brilliant way of dealing was to pretend it wasn't happening. Just ignore him. Which turned out to be difficult, though, as Tristan was constantly close. Every time I turned around in the hallway, he was there. He never walked with me, but he was always nearby.

Last bell was a relief, and I headed straight out for the library. I wanted to get more history filled in about Greta's ancestors. Next time I went through the trunk in the attic, I'd search for names to see if whoever owned the items was mentioned in the town papers.

My thoughts were so wrapped up in the contents of the trunk, it took a while to realize I had a shadow. Tristan walked down the other side of the street, headed in the same direction.

Unbelievable.

I stopped, debating what to do. This was getting ridiculous. It was impossible to ignore him…so I turned, hands on my hips, to stare at him. Tristan glanced over at me, his mouth quirking up in a smile. He gave me a small wave and continued to saunter along.

That was it. I wanted to know. Now.

I marched across the street, fell into step next to him. He looked over at me with raised eyebrows.

"What are you doing?" I demanded, keeping my voice low, controlled.

Now that I was actually walking next to him, I second-guessed this course of action. What if it was just a coincidence? Okay, of course it wasn't. But I still wasn't sure I should call attention to the fact that he was following me.

"I'm going to the library. What are you doing?" He seemed to find my irritation funny.

"I'm going to the library, too."

"Ah. I see. And you wanted to walk with me?"

I couldn't help it: I blushed. "No."

Tristan laughed. It was the first time I'd heard him do that. It was a nice, easy laugh, full of good humor.

"So you just came over here because it was imperative you know where I was headed?"

Yup, it looked ridiculous, I realized that. I was an idiot. But there was no way to go back and change it now.

I looked up at him. He watched me, his eyes bright with amusement. It was hard not to smile back at him. Damn.

"Never mind," I said, shaking my head at myself.

"If you say so."

We walked together the rest of the way in comfortable silence. And luckily, we didn't run into anyone from school.

Inside, Tristan stayed in the front to search through the shelves, while I went straight back to the room where the town's historical documents were kept, to find where I left off. Mrs. Adams said a quick hello, smiling cheerfully as she filed books away.

It didn't take long to be pulled back into the happenings of the town in the 1800s.

The McGraths were eager to get the rebuilding underway as soon as possible after the fire. They didn't seem keen on staying in town. Once the plans were settled, the townspeople were surprised to find the family wanted to bring in outsiders for all the construction work.

It was an odd decision. There seemed to be skilled builders in town, and it clearly wasn't a popular choice. But the McGraths insisted they had family connections with the people they brought in, which were important to honor.

Not long after complaints began about those strangers appearing, the McGraths put up the money to build a new town hall in the center of Fairhaven. All of that work was to be done by locals. It was certainly an expensive way for the head of the family, Tobias McGrath, to pacify the townsfolk.

I flipped through more accounts. It seemed that while the work was being done on Ragnarok Manor, the McGraths firmly discouraged people from visiting the location. The plans for the new building were kept under wraps, and the outsiders were closemouthed not just about the construction, but themselves as well. Even with the diversion of the town hall work, people were curious. They didn't take well to the mysterious happenings of strangers in their town.

I took note of any first names of the McGraths mentioned so I could check the trunk papers later. But mostly I was completely wrapped up in the townsfolk's impressions of the family.

Everyone had always been suspicious of the McGraths, sharing rumors behind closed doors. The late night fire hadn't helped. Now the secrecy surrounding the work at the new manor gave the imaginations of the superstitious people plenty of fuel. Tales spread about shady things going on at the site, in spite of the fact that no one would admit to actually having been out there.

I found only vague references to the two other wealthy families who came into town to stay with the McGraths to help with the construction. People seemed to find them equally as intimidating as their hosts.

Despite the rumored size of the new place, the family insisted when pressed that they weren't working on a hotel. There was some speculation their plan was to start a boarding school, but there was no confirmation of that either.

When Ragnarok Manor was finished, the McGraths moved in quickly. The two families who'd helped with the building joined them for a long-term stay and the whispers only increased. Whatever went on out at their home had the townsfolk on edge, though again, no one wanted to talk about anything specific they'd seen.

Time passed, the McGraths settled in. People grew bolder with their accusations. Naturally, this didn't happen until the town hall was completed and paid for. After a few strange incidents, the level of agitation in town grew. People began to murmur about unsavory dealings, even occult practices going on out there.

Things came to a head when a young man from one of the visiting families, the Moldovans, got into a scuffle with a local boy. The general assumption around town was that they fought over the affections of a young lady. But the reason was unimportant. The two came to blows and something happened during the fight that freaked the hell out of the kid from town.

The details were fuzzy as the kid refused to talk (ever again, it seemed), but the end result was a serious hostility towards the outsiders. Apparently the McGraths and the other visiting family, the Harroways, tried to step in to smooth things over, though to little effect.

I stared at the sentence I'd just read, my heart thudding in my chest. I closed my eyes, took a deep breath, looked back down at the page, assuming I'd misread the name. But there it was: Harroway. The other family staying with the McGraths when they were building Ragnarok.

It felt as though the room was falling away around me.

Chapter Eighteen

What could it possibly mean that the winged man had used the name Harroway, only for me to find out the McGraths had a connection to a family of the same name?

I didn't believe for one moment this was a coincidence.

Were Greta and Tristan somehow in league with my stranger? I didn't know if I could count Tristan's reaction to him in my half-dream as evidence, as it was, you know, still just a half-dream, and I didn't know what was real. But I didn't have much else to go on.

So who were the Harroways? Desperately, I read more, scanned the pages as quickly as I could.

The incident between the young men sparked more problems for the McGraths with the townsfolk, despite their efforts to make things right. People had observed too many things about the family that made them uncomfortable and come up with too many theories to explain their odd behavior, devil worship being the most popular.

Nothing more was mentioned of the Harroways. It was noted that, after a time, the guests left and things settled down a little. But it seemed the damage was done. After a few years the McGraths disappeared, leaving the building empty for a long time.

Eventually it was heard there was new ownership, though no one was ever spotted. People avoided the building, believing it to be haunted. At some point in the early 1900s the church moved in and began to use the property as an abbey.

I went back to search through every scrap of paper I could find about the construction of the building, but there wasn't any other mention of the Harroways by name.

Slowly, I gathered the papers, feeling numb. I totally didn't know what to do. What the hell was really going on here? And why did everyone else seem to know more than I did?

After a few minutes staring at the wall, I roused myself. I couldn't stay. Tristan was undoubtedly still skulking around here somewhere, and one thing I knew for certain was that I did not want to walk home with him. He was wrapped up in all of this, as surely as I was. I just didn't know how. I didn't even know what *this* was.

I put everything away as quietly as possible before pulling on my coat and bag. I tiptoed to the entrance of the room to peek around the corner. Tristan was in the front area reading, between the exit and me. I was certain if I went out that way, he would find some excuse to leave with me...and I couldn't have that.

Since the library used to be a house, there had to be other ways out. After checking around, avoiding squeaky spots on the floor, I found a door in the back marked for employees. It seemed like my best bet.

I held my breath, hoped Mrs. Adams remained in the front room, and eased the door open. The hallway beyond didn't get much light from its one window, but it was enough to see a door at the other end that opened out to the backyard.

I closed the first door behind me, tried to keep calm as I walked forward. I flipped the lock, opened the other door quietly, and relocked it so Mrs. Adams wouldn't notice anything amiss. Outside, I breathed a little easier.

Tristan would notice I was gone eventually, but I hoped I had enough time to make it back to the abbey. At this point, I just wanted to avoid talking to him. I needed to think.

I hurried down the street. He and his grandmother had always been friendly toward me (Tristan's ignoring me at school aside). But they were hiding things. There was no way to know for sure who they really were or what they wanted.

I couldn't help checking over my shoulder. I was lucky it wasn't dusk, or I'd have seen things lurking in every shadow. Despite the urge to run, I forced myself to keep steady. People in town thought I was weird enough already.

I started to feel better when I crossed through the iron gate in the wall that marked the property line. Home was close.

Soon enough, I made it onto the back porch, and as I opened the door, I turned to glance at the woods. It was just in time to see Tristan rush out onto the lawn. He froze the moment he saw me. The look on his face was a struggle between anger and relief.

Apparently my departure from the library had been noticed.

The moment stretched on as we stared at each other.

Eventually, I turned away from him, went inside. I was at a complete loss. I sat down, feeling cold inside. And that was where I stayed for a long time.

*

Sebastian sat at his desk doing paperwork, while I curled up in one of the chairs by the fireplace to read the book he had on the history of Fairhaven. I skimmed through it, looking for any mention of the other family, but I didn't find anything.

After a while, I just stared into the fire. The name Harroway kept echoing around in my head. I didn't know anything for sure, but the possibilities...no. Best not to go down that road.

Dinner was quiet, and afterwards, Helen pulled me aside to ask what troubled me. It was hard not to let everything spill out, but I managed a smile with an assurance I was only wrapped up in school things.

Helen had never been one to push, but from the look she gave me as she said goodnight, it wouldn't take much more before she started to demand answers. And I couldn't fault her.

I lay on my bed afterwards, staring at the ceiling. I needed a plan. Maybe I could try the attic again...but I wasn't likely to get any real, concrete answers. Which was what I desperately needed. Then there was my Sunday lesson to consider. I could cancel it, try to avoid Greta. Or I could use the time in their house to investigate.

Right, like the idea of snooping around while Greta was off in the kitchen wasn't entirely ridiculous. I sighed, pulled my pillow over my head in frustration. Something else had better present itself before the week was out.

Like the night before, my dreams remained shuttered. I woke up Wednesday not remembering anything. It was both relieving and disconcerting.

The day would be unseasonably warm and, as planned, I left for school forty-five minutes early to avoid Tristan. It was best if I kept my distance from him altogether.

I sat on the floor in front of my locker to read until first bell, and I supposed I wasn't overly surprised when Tristan walked by only a few minutes later. After yesterday afternoon had he suspected I'd try to evade him?

What the hell was the point of him tailing me anyway?

He didn't say anything as he passed, or even acknowledge my presence, but we were both aware of each other. He disappeared around the corner, though I sensed he remained close.

When the bell rang, I headed to math, Tristan right behind me.

That was how the day continued. I was hyper-aware of Tristan the whole time. He was my constant shadow. It felt like we were in our own secret dance, moving about the hallways from class to class, coming in close only to separate, no one else the wiser.

Lunch was a carefully maintained concentration: I kept

my attention on my book, ignoring any urge to look back when I felt his eyes on me. By the time I made it to French class, I wondered how I'd keep up the rest of the week like this. It was tiring keeping my eyes on what was in front of me, while my entire focus was really on Tristan.

I tried to pay attention in French, but I could've done the translations in my sleep. As my mind wandered, I felt something tug at my thoughts. After a moment, I let go, slipped away.

I found myself unexpectedly standing on a beach. Next to me stood the man who haunted my dreams. He appeared to be unaware of my presence, though, staring off at something with a look of fierce concentration. I turned to see what had his attention.

Ragnarok Abbey.

I went back to studying him. After a couple of moments, his gaze shifted, his eyes going to something I couldn't see, behind and a little above me. Surprise flickered across his face.

Something slammed on the floor, jolting me awake.

I looked around in confusion. One of the students leaned over to pick up the book that had fallen, but otherwise the class was focused on the teacher. No one had noticed me fall asleep, and I'd only been out for a minute. It was long enough.

Did he really stand out at Ragnarok this very moment? He certainly hadn't seemed to be doing anything harmful, simply watching. If there was even a possibility he was there, what did that mean for me?

Strangely, I'd gotten the sense he was preparing to leave

at the moment I'd woken up. But I was still on edge. Something wasn't right, I could feel it. The sensation itched all along my skin. There was nothing I could do about it now, though. Luckily I only had a couple more classes.

It was torture.

I wasn't sure if anything would be awaiting me, but I just couldn't shake the bad feeling. Which at least eased up my preoccupation with Tristan. I did inspect him carefully after class to see if he was aware anything had happened. But he looked exactly as he had all day: intent on sticking close to me.

The final bell rang, releasing us, and I knew my shadow would find me soon.

Sure enough, as I walked outside, Tristan came up alongside me, hesitation in his step. But I had to concentrate too hard on keeping myself together to deal with him. My whole body vibrated with tension. I didn't know why, though – I was absolutely certain the man was no longer on the beach.

His presence must have pulled me into the dream. On some level I'd sensed he was nearby. Now that he was gone, I needed to go down to the beach to check out where he'd been. I felt...drawn to it.

When I didn't say anything to Tristan, he gave me a curious look before turning ahead. If anyone saw us leave together, I was too wrapped up in my thoughts to notice. I certainly didn't care what he made of my silence. If he was here to keep an eye on me, and I assumed that had something to do with the man from the dreams, then I felt no compulsion to make small talk with him.

Okay, there was a small, scared part of me that wanted to bring him to the beach, just in case something was there. But I couldn't give in to the impulse. I had to keep reminding myself I didn't really know him.

When we got to the abbey, I muttered a goodbye, felt his eyes on my back until I was all the way inside. I waited at the window for him to disappear into the woods, thankful no one else was around. I didn't want anyone to delay me – I had to get down to the beach.

I walked across the lawn, started down the path. It was hard not to run. Whatever drew me out there filled me with an agitation, a sense of foreboding, which only got worse as I got closer. On the beach, I headed straight to where he'd been.

Something was terribly wrong. I could see now where he'd stood. Black shapes were strewn all about the sand.

Then I realized what I was seeing.

My crows.

They were all dead.

*

They lay in awkward angles, unmoving except for the occasional ruffle of feathers when the breeze picked up. I stepped closer, barely breathing. Slowly I knelt to examine one of the crows. I couldn't find anything physically wrong with him, but he was lost. There was absolutely nothing I could do.

Pressure built behind my eyes. They were dead. They were all dead. I couldn't stop repeating it; I wasn't capable of forming any other thoughts.

A solitary crow flew over from the woods and perched

on a piece of driftwood nearby, cawing to me. It was such a lonely sound.

I didn't know what to do. I just remained crouched at the edge of the madness, trying to understand. This was what had pulled me, what had felt so wrong.

There wasn't anything in my power I could do for them.

Thoughts flickered in and out. The crows were what had caught the man's attention, surprising him. Had they come because they, too, felt his presence, or had they somehow sensed me on the beach with him? Either way, it cost them their lives.

Was he responsible for the mysterious animal deaths happening in other towns? I'd already seen what happened to the life around him. Now it had happened again. To my crows.

Only Stopha remained. He cocked his head, called out again. He hadn't been with the rest of them – he'd been waiting by the school as he always did. Now the two of us sat staring out at the damage neither of us understood.

I had so many questions, but I wasn't sure if any of it mattered any more. It was such a senseless thing, killing the crows.

Tears began to slide down my cheeks. Then I couldn't stop crying. I shook with sobs, my arms wrapped around my body, trying to hold myself together. But there was no way to keep it in, and something inside me broke, everything that had happened since the beginning of school crashing over me.

All my heartache, all my disappointment and frustration, came rushing to the surface, released from wherever it was I'd tucked it away. It needed to get out.

I stood up slowly, closed my eyes. The pressure grew. A storm rose inside me, the power racing through my veins, crackling along my skin. I felt the energy building in the air as the wind picked up and the temperature dropped.

My hair blew against my face. I heard the surf pounding. All I had to do was free the storm and I could let loose my pain upon the world, if I chose.

The dead crows crowded about in my head as the magic blazed inside.

I released it with a scream, the energy snapping out into the world.

I opened my eyes. The sky darkened as heavy, seething clouds raced in. Lightning split the sky over the gray-green ocean, a crack of thunder reverberating through the air. I calmly held my arm out and Stopha flew over. He landed, climbed up to perch on my shoulder. I had made my decision. There was too much I didn't understand and I was tired of it. That all ended right now.

I turned away from the crows as the earth embraced their bodies, black shapes disappearing into gray graves. I made my way back up to the lawn. The trees whipped about in the wind and it wouldn't be long before the rain began.

There was only one place to go.

*

The woods enveloped me quickly. It was a ways to the McGrath's cottage, but I kept my steps even, steady. An eerie calm had settled over me...I would be the eye of this storm.

But the grip I had on my temper was fragile. It wouldn't take much to be swamped by the tempest raging around me.

On all sides, the woods were restless. Stopha called out uneasily. I reached up to put a soothing hand on him, murmured soft words. I caught a glimpse of the cottage through the trees. A thrill of fear shot through me about what I might walk into. But I reminded myself of the scene at the beach and pulled my resolve around me like an iron cloak.

I insisted Stopha wait in the woods. Just in case. He was reluctant, but after a minute of coaxing, he flew up to a branch to watch. The second I stepped out of the woods, Tristan burst out the door, ran down to me. He grabbed me by the shoulders, his eyes clouded with worry.

"Evie! What happened? What's wrong?"

I looked up into his eyes and I almost lost it. It would've been so easy to tell him, let him comfort me. But I didn't know what his reaction would be, if he was even on my side. I pulled myself in, reinforced my walls. Instead, the rain began to fall.

"Eva? Talk to me."

Behind him, Greta stepped out onto the porch, her eyes trained on me.

"Bring her inside, Tristan," she called down.

He turned to look back at his grandmother and then glanced up at the roiling clouds. When his eyes found mine again his expression was more guarded, uncertain.

He stepped aside. When I didn't move, he put a guiding hand on my back to urge me forward.

"It'll be all right, I promise," he said under his breath.

He followed along just behind me. Greta watched stoically from the porch. She ushered us through the door, casting her eyes around the woods before following us. As she closed the door, I caught a glimpse of Stopha swooping in to land on the porch railing.

For a long moment, Greta and Tristan stood surveying me in silence.

My pulse raced. I hadn't come here with a plan, just the belief that my suspicions about these two were right, and the desperate need to know what was happening to me.

Thunder rumbled above us. Greta glanced out the window with a sigh.

"Do you want to tell us what's wrong, Eva?" she asked softly.

If I began this, there would be no undoing it.

My gaze flickered back and forth between the two of them. Greta waited, her expression patient and polite, as detached as when she asked if I would join her for a cup of tea. But Tristan was full of tension. He nodded encouragingly to me, which should have been odd under the circumstance, but instead it helped steady me. What the hell was wrong with me?

I took a deep breath that seemed to go on for ages.

"My crows are dead." Now that I had to say it aloud, it was somehow worse. "I found them all lying on the beach."

Greta was staring at me, and I tensed as I saw the significance dawn on her. The air in the room suddenly vibrated with strained energy.

"I'm so sorry, my dear," she said. Then quietly to Tristan, a thread of urgency in her voice, "Go out and check the seals." He hurried to leave. Greta moved to a window, twitched the curtain aside to peer out. "What happened to them, Eva?" she asked with casual concern.

"Don't worry," I said evenly. "That man is already gone."

Greta froze. Tristan stopped where he was at the back door. The room was very still. The only noise was the howling of the wind outside.

Slowly Greta turned to me. "Is that so?"

"Yes, it is. Now I would like you to tell me who the Harroways are."

Whatever Greta had been expecting me to say, it wasn't that. She was shocked.

"How do you know that name?" she whispered.

"It doesn't matter. Tell me who you really are." My voice was cold. I had to concentrate on keeping myself closed off. I could feel my anger pushing at the edges.

She studied me. After a couple of moments, her shoulders relaxed and she nodded, gesturing for Tristan to come back. "Why don't we sit down?"

"I don't want to sit. I want to know what's happening to me."

"Are you really so certain you wish to know?" Greta asked, holding my gaze. "Knowledge like this comes at a price."

The moment expanded, her eyes boring into me.

"Tell me." I glanced over at Tristan. The look he gave me was full of pity.

It unsettled me more than Greta's words.

"Very well. But I'm sitting down, this may take a while." She sank down onto the couch. After an uncomfortable moment, Tristan sat next to his grandmother.

Fine. I took one of the chairs.

Greta stared at the cold fireplace, lost in thought. But I was out of patience. I'd start with something easy: one question, especially, had plagued me ever since this weekend when I'd begun to doubt everything about these two. I wanted it answered now.

"Is your last name really McGrath?" I asked, staying guarded. "Was anything you told me about yourselves the truth?"

"Eva," Tristan began to protest.

"No, Tristan," Greta interrupted. "She has a right to be mistrustful. In answer to your question: yes, we are who we said we were. But, as you guessed, there is much more to us than we let on. Just as there is with you, my dear."

So it was true. Greta wasn't just a kindly next-door neighbor. And she knew about me. I'd obviously had my suspicions, but to have Greta acknowledge it out loud still felt like a blow to my stomach. At least it wasn't all a lie. They were McGraths. For some reason it made me feel better.

She gestured toward the hearth. The logs ignited, fire springing up. I sucked in my breath. Okay, it was one thing to hear her admit to being different, but it was another thing entirely to see actual proof.

She met my eyes squarely.

"We are not so different, you and I," she said gently. "I know you have no reason to believe me right now, but try to trust me when I say I'm here to help you."

I stared at her, too many questions fighting to get out. "Then tell me. Tell me what's going on."

Greta sat back, stared into the fire. "Have you noticed your powers growing stronger lately?"

I hesitated, reluctant to reveal anything.

A small smile played on her lips. "It doesn't matter. I already know the answer, dear. It's part of the reason why I'm here at this point in time."

"It began a little before school started." The words slipped out, surprising me. I guess I'd kept all this inside, afraid to talk about it, for too long. "I've had more trouble controlling it, and I've been getting stronger."

Greta nodded. "That happens around your age; it's to be expected...though perhaps a little later than usual in your case."

She fell silent again.

"So," I prompted, "what does that have to do with you being here?"

She continued to stare into the flames as she answered. Her words gave me a shiver of unease. "As your magic grows stronger, it makes you something of a beacon...until you can learn to control it, hide it. You, in particular, are very powerful and that makes you shine out all the brighter."

She paused again, collected herself. I was just beginning to lose patience when her voice stopped me.

"We believed we weren't the only ones to take notice of you."

Even with the fire burning, the room suddenly felt colder. With a sick feeling in my stomach, I asked, "The winged man from my dreams?"

"Yes," Tristan answered. "He could sense you."

"How did you know that?"

He started to say something, but Greta spoke first. "There were portents. It became clear as your power matured that he was seeking you out."

"But why? What does he want with me?"

"That's not certain." Greta said it in a firm voice, her expression sincere. But when I glanced over at Tristan, he dropped his eyes, just a hint of discomfort about him. What were they hiding?

"So you...?"

"Tristan and I came here to watch over you."

"We've been trying to shield you," he said. "Make you harder to find."

"But it didn't work. He found me." I took a deep breath, shoving down a swell of panic.

"It would appear so," said Greta. "He shouldn't have been able to. He's more dangerous than we knew."

"Who is he exactly?" I wondered about my visions of him in the past. Was the strange storybook in the attic actually real? How did it all fit together?

"We don't know very much about him." Greta turned her attention back to the fire as she tried to explain. "So much has been lost over the years. The stories we do know...well, they're old stories. It's always been hard to know what to believe. But I've long suspected they're all true."

I waited for her to go on, but she was lost in her thoughts, so I turned to Tristan for answers. He met my gaze, not a trace of levity in his eyes. What they were telling me altered the significance of everything that had happened between the two of us since we'd met.

I was so utterly lost as I stared at him. How many of our conversations had been lies? Oh god…a new thought hit me, almost taking the wind out of me. How many of our moments together had been manipulated by him to get me to like him, to trust him? Had I been a fool to think any of that was real?

But before I had a chance to let that sink in, he began to speak.

"We know he's very old. The stories go back through the ages, some say to the very beginning. And, of course, he's extremely powerful." Tristan sighed, looked at me earnestly. "We didn't think he could come through to this world. It wasn't until Sunday night when he actually showed up, almost got you to cross the wall and go to him…." He shook his head, worry etched in his face. "If we had realized how close he was, we never would have left you here alone."

"What would've happened if I'd gone with him?"

He stared at me for a moment, fear shining out from his eyes. "I don't know."

"But I've seen him in my dreams for weeks," I said slowly, trying to figure out what had been happening. "Couldn't he have taken me any of those times?"

Tristan shook his head. "Sunday night he was actually here. You saw the mark his presence left on our world, I'm sure."

I thought about the discolored patch of dead things just beyond the wall and felt a chill at how close I'd come to taking his hand.

"You were there, too, you weren't dreaming. You'd left your body back at the abbey, but you'd cast your spirit out. It would've been all he needed. The other times were more like regular dreams, right?"

I nodded, entranced by the lilting of his voice and completely wrapped up in what he was saying. He could answer all the questions that had troubled me for so long.

"It's hard to explain exactly what was happening. When you fell asleep the other times, he drew your dreams into a different plane with him...it's what I call a slip-dream." Tristan seemed to struggle to find the right way to describe it. "Your interaction with him was real, it actually happened, but you could say you were traveling in a different manner than you were on Sunday. It was still only a dream. There was no connection to your body or spirit so there wasn't much danger of him hurting you."

Much danger? Was that supposed to reassure me?

"There was no way for us to safely know what his purpose was in bringing you there, though. We thought it was possible he was using that connection to find you. So that's why I monitored your dreams, pulling you out of them each time he showed up. We didn't want to risk anything." The meaning of his words clicked as Tristan's face was suddenly transformed by a mischievous smile. "I have to say, you're an incredibly active dreamer, very strong. It was exhausting trying to keep up with you."

But I didn't share in his amusement. A sick churning began in the pit of my stomach as his explanation sank in. I should have come to this conclusion so much earlier.

"So every time I dreamt about him, and you pulled me out, that was actually you. You were really there."

No. Please say no.

"Yes," he said, the smile still lingering.

Every time he held my hand. Every time he whispered in my ear, reassuring me back to sleep. It had all been real.

Damn it, couldn't I catch a break?

I felt heat rising in my cheeks. This was humiliating. All those mornings I'd gone to school relieved he hadn't known...

I realized out of everything they'd told me, it was ridiculous to get upset over this. But I couldn't help it.

Tristan watched as I tried to absorb this, tried to rearrange the truth. All those private moments when he'd comforted me, made me feel so safe – it wasn't something I'd just dreamt up. He had done it himself. My pulse hammered as I looked back at him, struggling to figure out why he'd been so tender with me. Everything I thought I understood about our friendship had shifted again. I was lost.

Greta cleared her throat.

My awareness of the rest of the room snapped back. I straightened up a little, realizing I'd been leaning forward. I turned my attention to Greta. She watched me with a trace of amusement in her eyes.

I blushed again, hating that I was so obvious.

"Tristan is very strong with dream magic. You're lucky, Eva, things could have been much worse. Though he certainly should have been masking his identity from you in the dreams." Greta raised an eyebrow at him, but he only shrugged.

I didn't feel particularly lucky. There were far more strange things going on around me than I'd suspected. Like these two, I thought, studying them. Greta and Tristan sat on the couch, neither one speaking, giving me time to think over what they'd revealed to me.

It was easy to see the family resemblance. They had the same captivating eyes, same strong bone structure, and they wore twin expressions of concern as they looked back at me. I could understand their fear that I wouldn't be able to handle all of this. But it was better to know; I'd been in the dark for too long.

And knowing they were like me was suddenly an immense relief.

I still had so many questions, though. Plus, not everything they told me added up. I didn't understand why the winged man had shown me how to manipulate the fire. It didn't make sense that he'd want to help me.

It was clear they were holding back, but I was certain they didn't know what happened that night in my dream. As I studied them, something told me I shouldn't share it either.

For now, I had other questions. Some of their behavior still puzzled me. I wanted to know more about them. However, the question I most desperately needed answered was what connection the name Harroway had to all of this. And, more importantly, what that had to do with me.

My pulse kicked up. I had to know. I kept my eyes on Greta's and began with caution. "Are there others out there like us?"

Greta took a deep breath. "Yes, there are."

"Tell me about them," I said quietly.

Greta exchanged a look with Tristan that I didn't understand. She turned back to me, resigned.

Just as she opened her mouth to speak, the crow outside cawed loudly, his panic going straight to my heart.

Something was wrong.

Chapter Nineteen

I stood up quickly, followed closely by Greta and Tristan.

"What is it Eva?" Greta asked in a hushed voice.

But before I could answer, Greta and Tristan both stiffened at the same moment.

"The seal," he said.

"I know."

Very faintly, I thought I heard the same low whistle I'd heard the other night, but it was hard to tell over the sound of the wind and rain. I strained to listen. Suddenly thunder crashed with a flash of lightning, making me jump.

"He's trying to come through, curse the gods," Greta said. "We don't have much time."

"Come through what?" Fear itched along my skin.

Greta hurried out of the room, saying over her shoulder, "Tell her."

The next thing I knew Tristan was beside me, speaking quickly. "It's the man from your dreams – he's trying to come through to this world again. Once he does, he'll know you're here. It won't take him long to break through our defenses. We have to get you back to Ragnarok."

"Why? What's at the abbey?"

Greta swept back into the room carrying a bag. "The abbey is much safer. We can explain the rest later. We have to move now."

She yanked open a desk drawer, grabbed a couple of papers and a few books, tossing them into her bag. Tristan had already moved to the door. He peered outside, tension in every line of his body.

Greta went over to him, whispered some quick instructions. She motioned me over.

"We have no choice — we have to risk leaving. We'll make a run for it. I'll go first, follow me closely. Don't look back. Tristan will be right behind you. We'll get you there safely, don't worry." She eased the door open a little further, closed her eyes, concentrating. "Run when I say to," she whispered.

I held still, anxiously staring over Greta's shoulder at my crow. He waited, wings half extended, unsettled by what he'd sensed.

A few seconds later Greta threw the door open the rest of the way.

"Now," she cried. She shot out the door ahead of me.

I ran. Stopha took wing the moment I moved. I didn't hear Tristan, but I knew he was close as I bolted down the porch steps onto the lawn.

Greta paused at the edge of the woods, turned back to the house. She said something in a low voice that I didn't catch. I felt a strange tingle sweep across my skin. Whatever magic she'd just done – it was incredibly strong.

I slowed unconsciously, but Tristan was right behind me.

"Keep going," he urged. "Don't stop for anything."

I accelerated as Greta spun, picking up her skirt, and raced into the woods. I couldn't believe how quickly the older woman moved. It was difficult to keep up. Stopha soared above, never straying more than a couple of feet higher than me. I kept as close as I could to Greta.

The rain pelted down. The ground was slippery. My muscles strained from trying to run as fast as I could while keeping my feet from sliding out from under me.

I felt it the moment he broke into this world and began to pursue us. My heart pounded so hard I thought it might burst out my chest. From the way Greta sped up even faster, I guessed the other two felt him on our heels as well.

Above the sound of the storm, I thought I heard the beating of large wings. I looked up but saw nothing more than my crow and the trees thrashing in the wind. Leaves ripped off, whirling through the air around us. A large branch somewhere to the right cracked, fell to the ground.

In the back of my mind, I realized there was still a strong part of me driving the storm, compelled along now by my panic.

I heard a pained screech somewhere behind. I couldn't help but glance over my shoulder to see what chased us. In that brief moment, I glimpsed only a deepening gloom of the woods. I saw nothing of the man.

I snapped my head back around, but my foot slipped,

shot out from under me. I went down hard on my knees, my hands slapping the mud as I landed. I scrambled to get to my feet. Then Tristan was at my side. He yanked me up as though I weighed nothing.

"Come on Eva, we're almost there."

I took off again, Tristan right behind me. Ahead, Greta hurled herself through the iron gate in the wall. A few moments later I followed. Tristan slammed the gate behind us.

Greta stopped running, turned to stare into the woods behind us. Tristan and I skidded to a halt near her. I didn't understand why we weren't still moving. He was so close…I could feel the wrongness of him.

My sides heaved as I tried to suck in more oxygen. My eyes ached from staring so hard at the woods. Even with the storm, it seemed unnaturally dark where we'd been just a few moments before.

Something black streaked down at me from the left and I sucked back a shriek. It was Stopha, swooping in to land on my shoulder.

"Why are we stopped?" I hissed at Greta.

"Don't worry. He can't cross the wall."

"Why not?"

"Now is not the time for explanations."

The seconds ticked by. My agitation increased. Besides the trees blowing in the wind, I couldn't see anything else out there.

Then, at the edge of my vision, I thought I saw something flicker, just a hint of movement. When I shifted my eyes, though, nothing was there.

It happened again. I opened myself, sent out my senses, my eyelids dropping as I concentrated. He was close. I could feel his frustration. And his anger. God...so much anger it almost hurt to touch it.

Greta whispered something furiously under her breath. As I strained to understand it, I realized Tristan had stepped up next to her and murmured along with her. The moment they stopped, he and Greta began to back up. I moved in step. Once we were further from the wall, Greta turned to face me.

"Go," she said.

Neither of us needed further urging. Tristan grabbed my hand, pulled me down the path. We ran for the abbey, my crow launching himself off my shoulder to soar above us.

I worried briefly about Greta behind us before I realized how ridiculous that was. She was obviously powerful enough to take care of herself. And she certainly wouldn't have trouble keeping up.

When I spotted Ragnarok through the trees, my heart lifted. Deep blue-gray clouds hung low over the building. It stood out grimly against the landscape, the colors darkened by the rain. Lightning flashed along the sky, burning the image in my eyes as thunder boomed.

We were so close. I could only hope we'd be safe once we reached the building. I picked up my speed. I wanted to make it there before anything else happened, but Tristan dragged against my hand.

"Wait, Eva," Greta called. "We need to talk for a moment."

Despite the fear that bubbled up in my chest, I slowed to a stop, tried to catch my breath. Greta came around me. Though her eyes warily scanned the woods behind Tristan and I, she seemed remarkably calm.

"Listen to me, Eva," she said, not the least bit out of breath. "We need to stay with you at Ragnarok Abbey. Whatever you do, it's imperative that you convince Sebastian and the nuns to invite us to stay the night as guests. Do you understand?"

"Yeah, of course. It shouldn't be difficult. But are you sure we'll be safe there? I don't want to put any of them in danger."

"I'm certain. You have to trust me on this."

I looked at her for a long moment, deliberating. Greta shifted her gaze from the woods, turned her full attention on me, her eyes hard, resolute.

If I couldn't trust her now, I wouldn't have anyone else to turn to. Besides, she was the key to finding all the answers I'd been searching for.

And I supposed, more importantly, I did actually believe she was on my side.

I took a deep breath, nodded. Her gaze lingered on mine. She seemed to understand what I felt.

"Good. We'll hurry the rest of the way, but there's no need to run. I don't want to alarm anyone. Will he be content to stay outside?"

I twisted my head to look at Stopha, who'd landed on my shoulder the moment I stopped again. I told him what I wanted. He took off.

"He'll do as I ask."

"Okay then, are you ready?"

"I guess so."

Greta turned, walked quickly down the path.

How much danger did I bring straight to my home? To my family?

But what choice did I have?

I vowed I would do whatever I had to in order to keep them safe. No matter what.

I realized I still gripped Tristan's hand tightly. Despite the strong need to follow Greta and get the hell out of the woods as fast as possible, I hesitated. I turned to look at him. His eyes burned into mine, scorching me to my core.

"I'm sorry, Eva," he whispered.

I pulled my hand out of his. "We need to go."

He looked like he wanted to say more, but he nodded. Without another word, the two of us hurried to catch up to Greta, who was halfway across the lawn.

"Should we go around front?" she asked, holding her shawl over her head to keep some of the rain off.

"No. Let's try the kitchen door. It's closest."

I caught a glimpse of my crow swooping in to land on the porch railing around the back. Just as we reached the bottom of the steps, the door was thrown open. Helen stood in the doorway, an anxious expression on her face as the wind whipped at her hair.

"What's happened? Where have you been?"

"It's okay, Helen. We're fine."

She ushered us inside. The wind caught the door, slammed it shut, made my breath catch. Mary and Agnes practically jumped up from the table at the sight of us, and

Sebastian stopped his pacing to collapse into a chair. Okay, maybe I underestimated how worried they'd be when I didn't show up after the storm began.

"My goodness, you're soaking wet," Agnes exclaimed.

"You'll all end up catching chills," Mary said.

"Eva, what on earth happened to you?" Agnes said.

Besides being drenched, I also had mud splattered all over me from my fall.

"I'm afraid we picked a very bad day for a walk," Greta said ruefully. "Tristan and I invited Eva to join us, and we got caught out in the storm. We just wanted to make sure she got back here all right."

"I slipped and fell in the mud," I explained when Helen raised her eyebrows at me. "I'm fine, though, really."

"Well, you should go straight upstairs to clean up and put on something dry," Helen said. "And as for you two, I'm sure we can find some clothes for you. There's no way you're walking back home in that storm."

"That's really very kind of you," Greta said. "Normally I wouldn't want to impose, but it's getting quite wild out there."

"Mary, if you could show them where they might wash up. Agnes can find you clothes."

"I'll help," Sebastian chimed in. "I'm sure I've got something that will fit you, Tristan."

"I appreciate that."

The five of them shuffled out of the kitchen, Greta making apologies about dripping all over the floor, and Mary cheerfully dismissing them.

Helen turned to me. "Are you sure you're all right, sweetheart? You look...I don't know, a little upset."

"I know, sorry. It was just a bit scary out there with the storm hitting so close."

"Well I'm glad you're back, safe and sound." Helen smoothed a piece of my hair back from my forehead. "Why don't you go up now? You'll feel better once you're warm and dry."

"Helen?" This was awkward, but there was no way around it.

"Yes? What is it?"

"I was just wondering...I mean, Greta mentioned they have problems with their house when it rains. I think the roof leaks and maybe a couple of other things, too." Helen looked at me shrewdly, but I stumbled on, wishing I sounded more off-handed. "I just thought maybe it would be a good idea if they stayed here tonight. We have plenty of room."

She studied me for a minute. Whatever she was thinking, Helen kept her expression carefully composed.

"Well, that is true," she said finally. "We do have plenty of room, and the best way to ward off the gloom of a storm is with company." She smiled. "If Greta doesn't object, they can certainly stay. I'll talk to Sebastian about it, then we'll ask her. How's that?"

With a relieved smile, I leaned over to kiss Helen on the cheek. "I think they'd really appreciate the gesture."

"Now you go upstairs before you catch a cold. I'll take care of it."

"Thanks, Helen."

I left the kitchen, my shoes squelching as I walked. Helen was probably just pleased I'd found people I liked enough to want to stay here. She still worried about my isolation. I hoped this would help ease that, even if it hardly counted the way she thought it did.

I made my way upstairs. There were four bathrooms on the second floor, so we could each take our time getting cleaned up. Mary pulled towels out of the linen closet, chatting all the while, and I gave Greta a quick nod as I passed.

Down the hall, Claire stood in her doorway. She watched the others with a stony look in her eyes. When she caught sight of me, she slipped into her room, closing the door without a word.

As the tub filled up, I undid my muddy shoes, awkwardly peeled off wet clothes. I finally slid into the hot water. Somewhere out there, the man who'd searched for me for so long prowled the woods, trying to find his way to me. Though it seemed Greta had been right: he couldn't cross the wall. How in the hell did that work?

And what was I supposed to do, stay in the abbey for the rest of my life? Along with the others? I saw no other way out – I was being drawn inexorably toward a confrontation with him.

The thought made my whole body tense with fear. It was different now that he was actually here. I'd seen what happened to people who went up against him. Would it be any different with the three of us?

I tried to distract myself, scrubbing at the mud.

All this time Greta and Tristan had been...watching over me.

Right, okay, totally appreciate it, but what did that mean?

I flushed as I remembered each time Tristan had appeared, drawing me out of the desert. Not to mention all the regular dreams he "monitored."

Nope. Better if I didn't think about that.

*

Once everyone was clean and warm and wearing dry clothes, we all congregated in the reading room.

We sat around, chatted about things like gardening and the benefits of living in a small town. The normality of it all grated on my nerves. Pretending nothing was happening when there was so much danger nearby. All I wanted to do was drag Greta into a room and force her to tell me the rest of their story, damn it.

Tristan nudged me with his elbow. I looked over to find him watching me, the sympathy easy to read in his eyes.

"Relax," he murmured. No one took notice of us as he bent his head a little closer to mine. "We're safe in the abbey, and there's nothing else we can do right now."

"I know. It just feels ridiculous to sit here, talking about nothing important."

"Be patient. We'll have time to talk later." Tristan gave me a small smile. "I promise."

So I had no choice but to wait. I tried not to fidget, but when I sat still, my awareness of the hostile presence outside sharpened. Which only made me edgier.

Dinner went by slowly. My impatience grew. But when I noticed Helen scrutinizing me, I kicked myself. I hoped she'd attribute my nerves to the fact that things had gone so wrong last time Greta and Tristan visited.

But I didn't need to worry about Claire, I realized, bemused. Greta and Tristan knew exactly why Claire had said what she did about me (which only made it slightly less embarrassing). She wouldn't come downstairs anyway, not after the warning Sebastian gave her about stepping out of line.

I shook my head. I had to revisit every conversation I'd had with Tristan and Greta.

In the middle of dinner, I felt a sudden release of tension; it was almost as though I stepped into a brighter room, able to breathe a little easier. The man had left. Wherever he came from, whatever door he used, he'd gone back through.

The three of us relaxed, Greta continuing to talk as though nothing had changed. He'd be back, but it was still a relief he wasn't out there now, stalking through the dark in the storm.

At last, the dinner broke up. Mary and Agnes showed our guests to the rooms made up for them. The nuns hovered as they said goodnight, making sure Greta and Tristan had everything they needed, which made it impossible for me to have a word with them.

When I walked into my room, though, I found a note on the bed. In elegant script, it read:

Wait in your bedroom tonight. Once everyone is settled and it's clear, Tristan and I will join you.

Finally. I changed into a nightgown, not wanting to explain why I was still dressed if Helen checked on me. Then

I sat on the bed, uncertain of what to do. I worried about them sneaking down here.

I waited.

Eventually, the building grew still. My door was open; the lamp barely touched the darkness beyond. Though I'd been staring at the opening, I didn't see Tristan until he was right in the doorway, the soft light falling on him. At my nod, he stepped in quietly, then stopped in the middle of the floor, uncertain.

Okay, I hadn't been prepared to be in my room alone with him. I suddenly had a hard time breathing quite right. His hair was disheveled, and though it was odd to see him in Sebastian's shirt and pajama pants, he was still striking. I couldn't look away.

His eyes were bright, his lips curved into a shy smile. He seemed as unsure as I was about what to do. Before either of us had a chance to say anything, though, Greta emerged from the hallway.

"Good," she said, closing the door, "you're already here." She pulled out the desk chair and sat down, which left Tristan no choice but to sit on the bed next to me.

This was incredibly surreal. But I realized with a start it wasn't the first time they'd been in my room in the middle of the night.

"So, Eva," Greta said. "I'm sorry about this afternoon. Though the end result is as good as I could hope for, I should have known better. I should have brought you here the moment you told us he'd been on the beach earlier. It's just that I...well you deserved an explanation. And in truth, I'm not sure I could have convinced you to leave the house without telling you at least part of it." She smiled wryly at me, and I couldn't help but smile back. She was right.

But that didn't matter now. My smile faded.

"Why can't he cross the wall?"

"Ah, yes, the wall. Well, you know my ancestors built Ragnarok?"

I nodded. It was one thing I had known.

"The original house here was a safe haven, a place to be kept as a carefully guarded secret. It was common for our ancestors to have many such places, scattered around the world. They were meant to hide us and protect us in our times of need."

As Greta spoke, I peeked at Tristan. He'd heard this before, clearly, so his focus was entirely on me.

"When the house burnt down, my ancestor, Tobias McGrath, decided to put a little extra into the new building. He brought in his most trusted – and very powerful – friends to help. This place," Greta looked around, not concealing her awe, "was built with ancient magics. Every piece that went into it was spelled for protection.

"It was an immense project. They sowed the spells into the land itself, created an absolutely impenetrable border along the property line, at the wall. But even if your winged man managed to break through that to cross the wall, this building was imbued with the magic of the most powerful people the world had seen in a long time. It's an unassailable sanctuary, all the more impressive because it's been kept such a secret all these years. The protective magic surrounding you here is part of the reason why it took him so long to find you, Eva."

I was astounded. All this time my beloved abbey had held such a secret. I guess back when it was being built the townsfolk's paranoia wasn't so unfounded after all.

I reached over, placed my fingers lightly on the wall at the head of my bed. I opened my senses, felt out past my fingers, and caught the sensation of magic surging through the wood. It was so strong it felt like it might burn me.

Without thinking, I opened myself further, became conscious of the entire building flowing with magic, almost as though it were alive. My focus sharpened. I felt the individual lives cocooned inside. Each person had a different quality to their essence; I found I could sense where each one was, who was asleep, who wasn't. When I turned my attention to Tristan and Greta, I could see they were different from the others. Like the building, they, too, pulsed with magic.

I pulled my awareness in, abruptly found myself back in the room with the other two staring at me. I couldn't exactly read their expressions, but I had the feeling I'd done something I wasn't supposed to.

"How did you learn to do that?" Tristan asked.

"I don't know – I just did it."

Greta shook her head, a small smile playing on her lips. "Well, I know I shouldn't be, but I'm surprised. It usually takes people a while to train their senses to be able to do that. And that's with guidance. But like I said, you're very powerful."

"Oh." I fiddled with my blanket, not knowing how to respond. I cast my mind back to what Greta had said and remembered my question. "So, with the abbey hiding me, how did you find me so much sooner than him?"

Greta leveled her gaze at me. "I already knew where to look."

Chapter Twenty

My heart began to beat faster. All the distractions were gone. Tension filled my body as I stared back at her, aching to hear the rest.

"How?" It was barely more than a whisper.

"I'll get to that part in a minute," she said with a sigh. "You asked earlier about others like us. I should explain. There are others out there. We tend to stick together, and for the most part, we prefer to live in isolated places. The countryside north of here has been home to many generations of some of our oldest, most powerful families.

"There were only a few old friends, friends I trusted, who knew I planned to come here to look after you." Greta chose her words with care now. "We decided it would be best if your presence here was kept secret from the others. At the time, it was uncertain just how much danger you were in. As Tristan said before, though we suspected that man would search you out, we didn't believe he was able to physically break through to this world."

I watched her, tried to absorb everything. All the while,

though, I wondered what Greta held back. It seemed she didn't necessarily trust all of her own people.

"As time went on, and he hunted you in your dreams, I began to worry he posed more of a threat than we guessed. But I kept arguing with myself that it couldn't be as bad as I feared. Then Tristan reported that you were slipping into that same dream every night, despite our precautions. It wasn't until you had the second vision of him in the past, though, that it became clear his connection to you had grown too dangerous. I had to warn the families."

"That's where we went over the weekend," Tristan's quiet words cut in. "If there was even the slightest chance he could come through, or even just come close enough to...hurt you, then the families needed to know."

That wasn't how Tristan had planned to finish his sentence, I was certain. Greta had given him a sharp look as he spoke. He seemed to edit himself mid-thought. What didn't they want me to know?

"So you went home to tell them?"

"Yes," Greta replied. "I thought it would be safe enough to leave you for a short while. The night before we left I wove a restraint around you, which kept you from dreaming. Unfortunately I think his pull on you was already too strong – clearly he found you. And certainly the restraint had no chance of working against you wandering the spirit plane on Sunday night, anyway."

"That prayer you whispered?"

She nodded.

"Luckily, I still tried to keep a watch on you," Tristan said, frowning at the memory. "I caught a glimpse of what was happening as you were about to reach out to him over the wall. From such a distance there wasn't much I could do. I just hoped you would hear me."

"I did hear you," I said with a hesitant smile at him. "So that is why you came rushing back?"

"Yes," Greta answered. "It wasn't ideal, to leave so abruptly. I needed more time there. The council is in an uproar." Her voice dropped as she spoke more to herself. "Our ancient enemy has returned and we've lost the knowledge of how to fight him. Even in his weakened state, the families aren't much of a match for him."

"What will they do?" I asked, interrupting Greta's broodings.

She sighed. "Now that they know he's back for sure, everyone is scared, so they're arguing. They haven't decided yet if they'll stand and fight, or go to ground."

"So no one will come to help us?"

"I'm afraid not, my dear. We are alone here."

I hadn't expected help anyway. I'd already moved on to other concerns. "Why didn't you tell me any of this sooner? Why didn't you warn me about him when you first came here? Maybe it would've made a difference if you taught me how to shield myself."

"It's complicated, Eva." Greta held up her hand as I started to object. "But I will try to explain. You see, those who knew the truth about why I came here, they agreed you should be protected. But their condition for helping me was that I not reveal my true nature to you. I wasn't to tell you what was happening or teach you any magic."

"But why? That doesn't make any sense."

Greta busied herself with smoothing her skirt over her legs as she answered. "From their point of view it did. You were an outsider, someone they knew nothing about. They were uneasy at the idea of me sharing our secrets with you. They thought it would be best if I simply came here to shield you, keep you from being found by him. Then you would be free to continue to live your life without being dragged into all of this."

I glanced at Tristan. He watched Greta, his brows drawn, his jaw set. Okay, maybe he wasn't a fan of these "friends." I turned back to her.

"But you didn't believe as they did? You thought they were wrong?" And then I remembered the strange night on the beach before I'd even met them. "Of course. You did warn me. You told me I had to prepare myself."

A mischievous grin spread across Greta's face, the resemblance to her grandson suddenly considerable.

"Well, I've never been very good at following rules. Much as I would have been happy to let you go on living your life without all the complications and the worries, I simply could not leave you so vulnerable. If I failed in my attempt to protect you, then you had to be aware of the potential danger – at the very least know whom your enemy was – and you had to have a way to fight. Besides, it's who you are."

"Will you be in trouble for telling me all of this now?"

Greta hesitated a moment before she relaxed into a reassuring smile.

"Don't worry about that, Eva, it doesn't matter anymore. With the return of our enemy, we all have far more to be concerned about. Besides, your being here is no longer a secret that can be kept from the families. We had to tell them when we warned them. And you could no longer be kept in the dark about us, either. So that's it. Now you know everything."

But that wasn't true. I'd allowed Greta to stall in getting to this point, partly because there was so much else I needed to know, but also because I was nervous about what she might say.

Now, so late in the night, with the storm raging outside, there was nothing left to distract me from the question that had burned away at my heart ever since I stood across the wall from that man and heard him say the name.

"Not quite," I said. "You still haven't told me who the Harroways are."

I matched Greta's stare, refused to drop my eyes.

"Are you sure, Eva? It's getting awfully late; you could use some sleep."

"I'm not tired." From the moment I found the crows dead on the beach I'd known there would be no turning back.

Greta looked at Tristan, who shrugged in answer to her unspoken question.

"Of course," she said. "You have a right to know. I shouldn't put this off any longer."

My blood quickened. I had to remind myself to breathe.

"The Harroways are a family as old and powerful as ours," she said, speaking softly. "When Tobias McGrath decided to build this place, the Harroways were one of the families he trusted enough to bring in to help him. They put a lot of work into making this building as strong as it is." I nodded impatiently at the old information. "You already knew that part?"

"I found the name listed in some of the old town records."

"Right. Your research at the library, I had forgotten. Well, through the years, our families have remained close. My oldest, dearest friend was a man named Reed Harroway. We grew up together, and we raised a lot of hell when we were younger. He was someone I trusted more than anyone. He was a brilliant man who, for a long time, led our council wisely.

"He was a great comfort to me during a hard time in my life. I, in turn, was there for him when he lost his wife. That was a very long time ago." Greta went still, lost in her memories. After a few breaths, she shook herself and continued. "They had a daughter he was very devoted to. She was a brilliant young woman, full of promise and power. Eventually she went abroad to study and see the world, something encouraged as part of our education. She had put it off longer than most to stay with her father."

Greta paused, set her piercing gaze on me, measuring me. I sat very still, my eyes wide as I waited for her to say what she'd been leading up to. Whatever Greta saw in my face convinced her to continue.

"When she came back home, she was pregnant."

I drew in a shallow breath. I couldn't look away from Greta, her sharp green eyes holding my own until nothing else existed but the story spinning out.

"Her homecoming was a big relief for Reed, who had

missed her desperately. And he was very excited at the idea of becoming a grandparent," she said with a wistful smile. "It was a wonderful gift to him that she decided to move back home to have the baby."

Greta's words swirled softly around me, her old memories coming to life.

"The pregnancy wasn't an easy one. She was often sick and in pain. It didn't help that as the time grew closer, portents about the baby's birth grew stronger. The baby would be very powerful, and that kind of news always makes the families nervous. They only made things harder for the poor girl, always plaguing her. It made her father furious.

"Reed asked me to stay with them near the end of the pregnancy to help. I've always been very strong with healing magic. So I moved in, tried to make her as comfortable as possible." Greta closed her eyes briefly against the memory. "The birth itself was quick. The baby was strong and healthy. But the mother was failing. The pregnancy had been hard on her and there were complications after the birth." Her voice dropped to a whisper, an agonizing look in her eyes as they met mine. "I tried everything. But I couldn't stop what was happening. She died not long after the child was born."

I saw it all: the birth, the panic, Greta trying desperately to stop the inevitable.

"For this, I could offer Reed no comfort. First his wife, then his beloved daughter. There's nothing so tragic as losing your child."

The room was quiet. Greta's words hung heavily in the air. Though I already knew how this story would end, I needed to hear it said out loud, or I was afraid I wouldn't believe it.

Despite my wish, however, nothing could compel me to intrude on her thoughts. I didn't know the specifics, but I remembered Tristan's story about his parents dying. Greta had known the same sorrow as Reed.

She looked over at Tristan now with a warm smile. "But you go on. You have others to live for." She shifted her gaze back to me. "Reed had a grandchild to look after, to protect. It was a dangerous time – the families were unbalanced, the council in an upheaval. With so much anxiety and alarm about the birth of one foretold to be so powerful, Reed feared for the baby's safety.

"He decided, and I agreed, that the child should be sent away in secrecy. It wouldn't be difficult to convince people the baby died with the mother. Reed and I would have time to bring the families to order, quell the growing trouble, search out the danger we knew threatened the child."

She leaned forward in her chair, kept her eyes locked on mine. "The decision almost tore him apart, but he believed it was for the best. So the day after the baby was born, Reed and I placed her in the care of my son, Keegan. He traveled for weeks, staying in different places, covering his trail. He was followed by storms from the moment he left us, called up by the child. Eventually, when we were certain it was safe, he brought the baby girl to our most guarded hideaway. In the middle of the night, he left her on the porch of Ragnarok. We knew about the priest who lived here, of course. We believed he would take her in, care for her as his own."

Greta went quiet, her story finished. A numbness had settled over me, beginning in my heart, spreading throughout my body. I'd heard that story, played it in my head so many times, just never from that perspective. Even though I knew it was the truth I'd searched for, I simply couldn't absorb it.

From the moment that man called me Eva Harroway, I'd understood the potential significance. But I hadn't allowed myself to openly think about the possibility in case I might be wrong – the disappointment would've been unbearable.

I had a family.

I had belonged to someone.

And my parents hadn't abandoned me because I was different.

Knowing that eased a pain that had hurt for so long I'd barely even been aware of it.

Without looking at Greta, I asked, "What was her name? My...what was the woman's name?" My voice sounded strange to my ears.

"Genevieve," she said softly. "Genevieve Harroway. You look just like her, you know." She stood up. "It's late. I think that's enough for tonight. You should try to get some rest."

"Wait." I held out a hand to stop her. There was just one more thing I couldn't bear not knowing. "What about my...my father?"

"I'm sorry Eva, I don't know who he is. If Genevieve told her father, Reed never said anything to me. She had given me the impression he would join her there at home

256

soon after the baby was born. But no one ever showed up. She was always a private woman. I'm sorry now I never pushed her for an answer."

I nodded. There was nothing else to say.

I had gained so much, and lost it all in the same moment.

Vaguely, I heard Greta and Tristan exchange a few words; the door opened and closed. Then there was nothing but silence. Just the cold, insensible silence of the abbey pushing in on me, what had once been a comfort suddenly becoming desolate and unbearable as my world turned upside down.

I didn't know how long I sat there, frozen, my mind blank, before I became aware of Tristan still sitting beside me. I'd assumed he left with Greta. I wondered idly why he was still there. I just didn't have enough energy left to ask.

A family. A mother. A grandfather.

They were suddenly real people. My mother hadn't chosen to leave me. My grandfather didn't want to give me up either. It made everything different. Soothed secret fears that had shaped me in ways I didn't want to admit.

A tear slipped down my cheek, but I didn't bother to wipe it away. Only Tristan was there to see it.

The day had been unbearable enough already. To have this added on top of it...I was dangerously close to breaking down and losing it. The mattress shifted. Tristan was close enough now that our legs touched. Without saying anything, he put his arm around my shoulders.

I held myself rigid for a long moment before I gave in, relaxed into him. I leaned my head on his shoulder, felt him press his cheek against my hair. We sat quietly and I could smell his faintly spiced, woodsy scent mingled with the smell of the abbey soap. It had become familiar, comforting.

What would life have been like if Reed had made a different choice all those years ago? An unfamiliar life spun out before my eyes. An adoring grandfather to raise me, teach me about magic. He would've reassured me, taught me not to be afraid of what I could do. I'd have always known who I was and where I belonged.

I would've grown up with others like me, had friends who didn't think I was a freak.

But there'd have been danger as well. Whatever my grandfather had been so afraid of, maybe it would've constantly loomed over us, made him always apprehensive and uneasy. And from the way Greta spoke of him, I would have ended up losing him eventually, too.

Strangest of all, I never would've known Sebastian and Helen. I wouldn't have grown up with Agnes and Mary and their quirky ways. My life here would've never happened. I did have a family. I had grown up loved. Would I trade everything I had here for a life I didn't know?

Helen had been the one to comfort me when strange things happened. It was Sebastian who'd cleaned up my scraped knees. Mary and Agnes had always been there to make me laugh.

How could I want another life when I wouldn't want to change anything about the life I had? I felt like I betrayed everyone by wishing, even for a moment, for a life with strangers. It was too confusing. When I realized I wouldn't even be able to tell them about any of this, my breath hitched, more tears slid down my cheeks.

Tristan gently rubbed my back, his touch soft, reassuring. After a while, some of my tension slowly eased. I felt safe with him, in the warmth of his embrace.

I must've drifted off...I became vaguely aware of Tristan lowering me onto the bed, pulling the blanket over me. I kept my eyes closed, felt his fingers softly brush the hair back from my forehead. He was my only comforting thought as I slipped back into sleep.

Chapter Twenty-One

I woke abruptly, springing up to stand beside the bed, vibrating with tension.

It took a moment to realize what shocked me out of sleep so late in the night. I heard the low whistle at the same moment I registered the fact that my body still lay in bed.

What had Greta called it? The spirit plane? Why the hell had I pulled myself out of my body again? Did it have something to do with that noise? The only other time I was sure I'd heard it was when the winged man had waited for me outside. Maybe it was some type of warning system or something.

So he was back – awesome.

But if he couldn't cross the wall, I wouldn't be in any danger if I went outside to investigate. The inevitability of a clash against him weighed on me. If I went out there now, perhaps I could discover what he really wanted, find a way to avoid putting everyone else in danger.

It wasn't the worst plan ever.

The decision made, I slipped out the door, headed down the hallway. I hadn't gotten far when Greta stepped in front of me. It was eerie: no one was supposed to be able to see me, but it seemed like she stared straight at me.

"Just where do you think you're going, young lady?" She asked in a low voice.

I froze, surprised by the words.

She flicked her hand at me with a sharp, "Wake up."

The next thing I knew, I was in bed, gasping for air. I sat up quickly, looked around, confused.

A moment later, Greta stepped through the door. She sat down on my bed. "Sorry about that, dear. But I couldn't have you wandering around out there. It isn't a good time."

"You sent me back here? How?"

"A little trick I'll teach you sometime. It's easy really – it's just about pushing things back to where they naturally want to be."

"I heard that noise again. I think it woke me up. Do you know what it is?"

"A noise?" Greta cocked her head, closed her eyes. It had been fading in and out. When it started again, she opened her eyes, gave me a long look. "I believe that is the sound created when he tries to come through. The sound of an open doorway. Don't worry – he still won't be able to cross onto the property. It isn't easy to catch though; I can't hear it so much as feel it...you said it woke you? And you've heard it before?" I nodded. "I think your connection to him makes you more sensitive to his presence. You seem to be able to sense him better than I can."

"Why are we connected?"

"I'm not certain. Somehow, through the dreams, he managed to tie himself to you."

"Do you think he'll stay out there all night?"

"I doubt it. I think it takes a lot of energy for him to come through, and even more to maintain a stable presence here." She shrugged. "We'll see I guess."

"In the morning, what will we do about school? There's only so much Helen and Sebastian will believe. If he's not out there when we get up, maybe it would be safe enough to go."

"I'll think about it."

I sighed. Greta wouldn't be pushed into anything if she didn't feel it was safe.

"Get some sleep, Eva. We'll see how things stand in the morning."

*

Dawn hadn't even begun to lighten the sky over the ocean when I awoke. The storm had calmed down, but I could feel the agitation in the air. More bad weather would come.

I was too edgy to sleep. I got up, got dressed, pulled my hair back in a braid.

The realizations from the night before kept hitting me again at random moments, nearly taking my breath away. Kind of like getting punched in the stomach over and over again.

I had no idea what the day would hold, which was slightly terrifying. However, I still had to act normal around the nuns. Helen, in particular, had always been good at sensing my moods.

A soft knock interrupted my thoughts.

I opened the door to find Tristan standing there in an old pair of jeans and a flannel shirt of Sebastian's.

"Couldn't sleep?" he asked quietly as I closed the door behind him.

"Nope. What's going on?"

"Greta decided we'll be safe to go to school if there's no change by then. She doesn't think he'll try anything in such a public place, and after he came through so many times during the night, he'll be drained. Plus she wants to delay any suspicion from the nuns. So it'll be business as usual. Sort of. Greta will, of course, walk us there and back."

"How long will we keep hiding out in the abbey, pretending everything is normal?"

Tristan shrugged. "She's working on it. She'll think of something."

His faith in his grandmother was reassuring. Having seen some of the things Greta was capable of, I could almost believe him.

Now a long day stretched before me of not only worrying about a threat that had stepped straight out of my nightmares, but also being on edge about what the kids at school might come up with for their own amusements at my expense.

What a fantastic day, I thought sourly.

"So," Tristan said, drawing my eyes back to his. "Just because we're sure you'll be safe at school, doesn't mean there isn't any potential danger. Greta will guard you on the way, but I'll stay close during the day. We won't take any chances."

The meaning of his words sank in, and a heavy weight settled in my stomach.

"It's a small school, we have a lot of classes together," I said lightly. "You're never very far away."

"Well there's no need to keep my distance. It doesn't matter now. I'll walk with you to class, sit with you at lunch. Okay? I'd feel better if we stayed together."

"You really don't need to do that." I turned away to get my things together. On top of the complications it would cause with his friends, I didn't want him to act differently with me just because he thought it would be safer.

"Why are you making this difficult?"

This was so not a conversation I wanted to have.

"Sorry, I'm not trying to," I said, still not looking at him. "I just don't think it would make any difference if you stayed with your friends instead of suddenly changing and…hanging out with me."

Oh my god, I felt like such an idiot, trying not to sound pathetic.

"Eva?"

"What?"

He put his hands on my shoulders, turned me to face him, though I kept my eyes on his shirt. His voice was soft, patient. "It isn't like that – I don't even like most of them. I didn't have a choice in how things were at school. I know I owe you an explanation. Will you look at me please?" When I couldn't bring myself to meet his eyes, Tristan gently put his finger beneath my chin, tilted my head up. "I'm sorry. I know it couldn't have been easy on you. Will you let me explain?"

I nodded, trapped now by his gaze.

"Before we even came here, Greta decided it would be safest if I didn't interact with you at school. We had no idea if the council was suspicious of us. At our house, and at Ragnarok, we're hidden by protective magic; but if they watched us in public, they would've examined anyone we socialized with. If they paid attention, they might've figured out who you were.

"On top of that, we weren't sure how much that man from your dreams could see of you out in the world. Once I started to pull you out of his slip-dreams, he would've known someone was helping you, protecting you. If I were seen with you at school, I would've been the obvious target. Either way, it would've put one of us in danger. We needed to be vigilant about how much contact we had with you off the two properties.

"I didn't think it would be so difficult, though, to keep my distance. It wasn't until the first day at school that I realized how isolated you were. I was curious about you...then I saw what they put you through, heard their stories. I have to admit, I was impressed with your strength. And completely intrigued."

This wasn't at all what I'd expected. His perspective of that first day at lunch was completely different. All my assumptions had been wrong. As he went on, I stared at him, trying to adjust.

"I had to wait until we came here for dinner to talk to you, see you with your guard down a little, though you didn't seem overly pleased with my presence. It was hard not to like you," Tristan said with a smile. "Luckily, that first Sunday, my grandmother thought it'd be best if I walked you home alone. You were kind of stubborn about not taking my coat, even though you were clearly freezing…did you really not like me? I was afraid that might be the case considering who I fell in with at school."

He waited for me to answer, amusement crinkling his eyes. I was totally lost for what to say.

"It's not that. I just…didn't know what to make of you I guess."

"Well, anyway, you looked relieved the next day when I didn't say anything about you to Molly, so I hoped you might give me a chance after all." He sighed. His brows drew together as the laughter faded from his eyes. "But it got ridiculous trying to help you without being able to talk to you, especially when you got sick with that damned fever. First I hear you screaming out on the lawn, and I honestly thought someone was trying to kill you. Then you show up at school, almost entirely lost to the fever dreams. I can't tell you how terrifying it was to see you like that.

"Once it was clear you would make it through okay, I got into an argument with my grandmother about my…restricted interaction with you. I was afraid of what could happen to you because we were being too careful. But she knew the dangers were too great. She insisted it would be easier for both of us if I distanced myself from you."

Tristan shook his head. "So I did. It was supposed to be for the best, and I thought it might be better for you anyway. Sometimes you seemed…uncomfortable around me. It made sense, considering who I'm supposedly friends with – though you should know, Lissie's actually quite decent. But watching you in school was awful. You were so quiet; you seemed so far away all the time. And always so alone.

"Then there was that horrible Friday, when I told you I had a meeting with Mr. Jamieson. You knew it wasn't the truth. You remember?"

I nodded, my jaw clenched. Of course I remembered. What could have been better than to be humiliated by Molly that day, only to have Tristan lie to avoid walking with me later?

Not a fond memory.

"I couldn't keep going on like that anymore. I was sick of it."

His steady, green eyes bore into mine. I was unable to say anything. After that day he'd begun to act friendlier outside school again. I hadn't expected an explanation, certainly not one that made it sound like he'd never wanted to be distant in the first place.

All this had been going on when he'd passed me in school, acted like he wasn't aware of me.

"I made the excuse to my grandmother that if I didn't start behaving differently towards you, then you'd never trust me later if we had to tell you what was really going on. But the truth was I just couldn't stand back any more, pretend I didn't care."

I stared up at him, tried to keep myself anchored.

Okay, it was a big relief to hear all of this — it made everything that happened less painful. But I seriously had to remind myself not to get carried away, thinking ridiculous thoughts.

Damn it, I should never have let this crush on him get any worse.

"Thanks for telling me," I said with a wry smile. "It explains a lot."

"You aren't angry about all the deception?"

I studied his face for a moment, saw nothing but warmth in his gaze.

"I guess not. I understand why you did it. Can I ask you a question though?"

"Go ahead."

"Why were you so rude that first morning in the hallway? Was that really necessary?"

Tristan looked confused for a moment. Then his eyes lit up and he laughed softly.

"Bloody hell, Eva, that first morning when I ran into you, you were calling up a storm in the middle of the damned hallway. I thought about trying to block your magic, force you to stop, but I wasn't sure if you'd realize what I'd done. I couldn't take the risk, but I also couldn't let you keep going. What exactly were you planning to do, anyway?"

My cheeks flushed. Of course...I'd totally forgotten what his bumping into me interrupted. It made complete sense now. I was an idiot for not thinking it through.

"I didn't actually have a plan – I didn't even know what I was doing. It was probably good you stopped me. Even if it wasn't the best first impression you could've made."

"But you forgive me?"

It was hard not to when he looked at me with that irresistible smile.

I pulled back a little. We were just friends.

"Of course."

"Okay then."

"But you still can't sit with me at lunch, or act like we're suddenly friends at school," I said, back to business, my tone firm.

He frowned at me.

"Eva, don't you see it doesn't matter anymore? I don't need to pretend we're not connected. The families know about you now. And after the night you almost crossed the wall to go to the winged man, he knows who I am. When I called out to you, he traced me back, caught sight of me. So there's no more danger in us being seen together. I will sit with you."

"No, you won't," I said with a stubborn glare back up at him. "You'll be one table over from me like usual. Don't tell me that small amount of distance would make one bit of difference if he were to attack."

"Why don't you want people to know we're friends?" he asked softly.

I sighed, shook my head. He didn't understand how vindictive Molly would be, or how easily she could make my life miserable. But, of course, she tried to hide that side of herself from him. I'd admit it would be extremely satisfying to see Molly's face if Tristan sat with me...but it so wasn't worth the extra worry. At least not right now.

"Don't act like it's that easy."

"It is that easy, Eva. I don't care what any of them think."

"I don't care what they think about me either, but I

don't want to make things more complicated at school right now. I have enough to worry about without having to stress out about all of them." I pulled in a deep breath, forced myself to calm down. "Please."

He held my gaze for a long moment. "Okay. If that's how you want it to be."

"It is. Thank you."

"Now can I ask you something?" His lips quirked up in a smile.

"I feel like I will regret saying yes, but go ahead."

As I finished the reply, a knock sounded at the door. I froze. How would I explain why Tristan was in my room?

"It's just my grandmother," he said. He walked over to let her in.

"Good morning," Greta said. She gave me a measuring look. "Did you get enough sleep?"

I shrugged. "More than I thought I would."

"Tristan told you about school? Good. After I walk you two there, I'll go back to the cottage to get some of our things together. Luckily he left our place undisturbed – if he'd breached the protection spells, I would have felt it. I have some old records there I want to go through, and I'll get you some clothes, Tristan. We'll have to tell Sebastian there's enough water damage and such that we can't go back there yet. Do you think he'll invite us to stay here longer, Eva?"

"Yes, of course. Though I should warn you, I wouldn't put it past Sebastian to insist he check your house to see if there's anything he can do to help."

Greta smiled, her eyes sparkling with mischief.

"That shouldn't be a problem. The house won't be inhabitable by the time I finish with it."

"I know how much you enjoy destruction, but try not to go overboard," Tristan said. "We may have to move back before long."

"Don't you worry, I know what I'm doing. It's not like I've never faked damage to a building before."

I was certain there was a good story behind that comment from the look on Greta's face, but I thought I heard movement down the hall and the sky had begun to lighten.

"You two should probably get out of here before anyone catches you."

"Of course. We'll see you downstairs in a bit," she said.

They disappeared out the door. Even though I strained to listen, I didn't hear them move to their own bedrooms.

I walked down to the kitchen later wondering if there would be time after school for Greta to show me a few things. As much as I'd enjoyed them, those lessons in Italian would've been better spent learning how to defend myself.

I found Mary and Agnes cooking a big breakfast.

"Good morning, sweetie," Mary said, brightening up when she saw me.

"Morning."

"Are you going to tell us what's going on before everyone else gets down here?" Agnes asked. For a moment I thought they suspected the brewing trouble, but then I caught the sly grin on Mary's face.

"I think you've been holding out on us," she said.

"You two have overactive imaginations," I responded firmly. Of course they would jump to the wrong conclusion.

"It just seems like the two of you have spent more time together lately, that's all. You know we think he's great."

"And cute. You should go for it Eva," Mary chimed in.

"How about I help with breakfast instead. And you two can just put that idea out of your heads."

A knock sounded. The three of us turned to find Tristan standing in the kitchen doorway.

"Good morning. Is there anything I can do to help?"

We stared at him in embarrassed silence. He looked completely innocent of what he'd interrupted. I told myself it was entirely possible he hadn't caught enough of the conversation to know what we'd been talking about. But still, I blushed.

Agnes was the first to recover, Mary right behind.

"Oh no, we've got everything covered here—"

"But it's very sweet of you to offer, dear."

"The food's almost ready, anyway."

"Why don't you help Eva set the table instead?" Mary suggested.

"Sure, I'd be happy to."

He walked out.

I rolled my eyes at Mary. "You're impossible," I hissed.

"Mmhmm. You're welcome."

I didn't know what to say to Tristan now, after everything. But as I joined him, Sebastian and Helen came in and caught us both up in an easy conversation.

Too quickly, breakfast finished. It was time.

Greta had told the others she needed to go into town, so she had an excuse for walking with us. She became focused once we were out the door, lost her light manner as she and Tristan carried on a hushed conversation. When we passed through the gate that marked the property line, the two of them fell silent. They moved to walk on either side of me.

Nothing was amiss in the woods, however. Though the weather threatened, the birds still sang, the small creatures going about their business like any normal day. I wished the same were true for me, too.

After the tense quiet of the woods, the town seemed bright and full of people. For the first time, I actually felt relieved to be closer to school, to be around other students.

"All right, my dears," Greta said in a low voice as we neared the steps to the front door. "Stick close to each other, stay watchful. I'll meet you right here when school gets out. Be careful."

She stayed behind while Tristan and I continued up. I hesitated at the top, glanced back at her. She gave me a quick smile with a reassuring nod.

I turned, followed Tristan through the main door, and fell in with the rest of the students. True to his word, he didn't treat me any differently than he normally would, though he did always manage to stay close.

The morning classes went by slowly, but I was less tense than I thought I'd be — I drew a strange sense of safety from the other students. It was odd to watch them go about their day, though, entirely unaware of the danger that had pressed in around the town in the night.

In my visions I'd seen what that man was capable of. I wondered if the same fate that had befallen those villagers was in store for the people here. I did not want to be the only thing that stood between him and them. Tension wound through me at the thought.

I hoped Greta was coming up with a damn good plan.

At lunch Tristan sat at his usual table, in the seat closest to me. Unlike every other day, I found myself relaxed. For once I didn't care what Molly and her friends might do. And when I caught Tristan's eye, the thrill that shot through me had a different quality to it — no embarrassment. It struck me that I knew who he really was, unlike any of the others. Even Lisbeth. It was a nice change.

After lunch I went to French, separating from Tristan at the door. I wasn't sure how he managed it, but I was certain he spent the classes I didn't have with him just outside in the hall. It was comforting, especially since I felt increasingly uneasy as the class went on, though I couldn't pinpoint a specific reason.

Then, just as the last class of the day began, the fire alarm went off — a loud, piercing sound that set my heart racing. The level of excitement rose as everyone got their things together, thrilled to get out of class. But I saw the apprehension on the teacher's face that meant this wasn't a drill.

Something was off.

I tried not to let my uneasiness grow into outright panic as I grabbed my things. The moment I stepped into the hall, Tristan was beside me. When our eyes met, I saw the same troubled look on his face. So not reassuring.

We followed the flow of students onto the front lawn. I don't know where Tristan's class lined up for the head count, but he said he'd taken care of it, so we didn't need to separate. Not that he would have left me anyway. We stood side-by-side, close enough that our shoulders touched. We watched everyone around us warily.

A group of teachers stood together talking, and after a minute, the principal separated from them to make an announcement. It took a minute for the students to quiet down enough for him to start.

"May I have your attention. The school is being checked just to be safe, but we believe this was a false alarm. If you have anything in the school you need to get, it will be a little longer before anyone can go back in, so I ask you to please be patient. Otherwise, since it's last period, you are all dismissed early."

A cheer went up. Whatever final comments he made were lost.

We still had about forty-five minutes before Greta was supposed to meet us and there was no sign of her.

I looked up at Tristan. "What should we do?"

"I don't know – I don't like this. We can't just stay here."

"So we make for the abbey?"

He stared down at me for a minute. "I think it's our best option."

"Then we're agreed. And I don't think we should waste any time."

Tristan grabbed my elbow, pulled me out of the way as some kids ran past, almost knocking into me. We were both jumpy, despite the happy atmosphere. We started off across the lawn, but someone called his name.

"Hey, Tristan, hold on a sec," Molly said, breathless as she came up beside him, clutched his arm.

I didn't want to stop, or be stuck standing with them so obtrusively, but our safest bet was to stay with each other. So I stood there, completely awkward, trying not to let my impatience show.

Molly eyed me, annoyance flitting across her face, before she turned back to Tristan with a smile.

"I've been looking for you. A bunch of us are headed down to the pier to celebrate. Come with us, it'll be fun."

"That does sound good," he said with a rueful smile, "but unfortunately I promised my grandmother I'd come home straight after school."

"Well just come for a little bit. You wouldn't be home for a while anyway so your grandmother would never know the difference." Molly's voice was sweet but her eyes flickered to me. She clearly wondered why the hell I was there, if I was his reason for declining, but she didn't want to be rude in front of Tristan. God forbid.

"I'm sorry, but my grandmother has been sick – I don't want to leave her alone any longer than I have to. Plus, she wants me to drop something off at the abbey for Father Blackwell. But maybe next time. I'll see you tomorrow, okay?" Tristan began to walk away.

I locked gazes for a moment with Molly. Her eyes narrowed. Anger warred with disbelief to twist her features as I turned to catch up with him. That was clearly not the way she'd expected the conversation to go, and she held me responsible.

I couldn't worry about her now, though.

Tristan and I increased our pace without a word. I concentrated on our surroundings. The further away we got, the more tense I felt. We were in the no-mans-land between the safety of the crowded school and the protection of Ragnarok. When we stepped off the road onto the path, we exchanged a look. He'd picked up on the eerie silence of the forest, too. It was unnaturally still.

A few feet in, I heard the low whistle that only meant one thing.

"He's coming through!"

We broke into a run, sprinting as fast as we could down the path. The sound grew louder. I knew we weren't going to make it. I couldn't even see the wall.

Then I felt the snap as the door closed, and the world reordered itself. I stumbled at the abruptness of it. Tristan grabbed my hand to steady me as we ran.

A moment later I pulled hard against his grip to make him stop.

"What is it?" he asked in a hushed voice.

"Can't you feel him?" I whispered back. "He's there, up ahead. Between us and the wall."

Chapter Twenty-Two

Tristan closed his eyes, concentrated. A second later they flew open. He looked down at me in horror. It was a little surprising Tristan had to put any effort into perceiving him. The winged man stood out to my senses like a giant bonfire raging before me.

We stood still, waiting. I heard nothing but the rasp of our own breathing. I squeezed his hand for reassurance, tried to come up with a plan. We couldn't be too far from the wall by now, but how could we get around him?

Tristan's breath caught at the same moment a spasm of fear shot through me.

The man who haunted my dreams strolled up the path ahead of us.

He paused when he was still a distance away. He wore an impeccable suit, his black wings folded behind, the familiar sense of power rolling off him. He stood unmoving, watching us with an impassive expression on his face.

I had no idea how long the three of us stayed like that, but the moment was broken when I caught sight of a black shape hurtling towards him. My heart dropped when I realized it was Stopha, diving to attack. Without a thought, I shot a strong gust of wind at the bird to push him aside. I damn well wouldn't let another one die.

The crow screeched as he was buffeted away, a loud racket in the otherwise silent woods.

Tristan had taken advantage of the distraction. He'd spun something in front of us I couldn't see but could sense. Now he flicked it at the man and yanked on my hand, pulled me with him as he raced into the woods, angling towards the wall.

I caught just a glimpse of the winged man struggling with what seemed like invisible ropes before I lost sight of him. Tristan and I sprinted, dodging trees and struggling through underbrush. I tried to pull my hand from Tristan's so we could move faster. But he only held on tighter.

"No, Eva, stay with me," he insisted.

I jumped over a tangle of roots to keep even with him, brushed past another tree, a searing pain suddenly shooting up my free arm. I didn't slow down. I had no idea where the man was now. All of my attention was focused on the ground in front of us.

A root yanked up abruptly in front of Tristan. It happened so quickly. Before I could get a word of warning out, the root snapped against his foot.

He tripped. The force of his momentum sent him flying away from me, tugged his hand from my grasp.

The moment he let go, fire sprang up between us, separating him from my sight. I slid to a halt, looking for a way to get past it as panic bubbled up my throat. But when I spun around, I suddenly found a wall of fire in every direction I looked.

I was trapped.

The fire stretched high, eclipsed all but the tree branches above. Though it flared and roared like regular fire, I felt no heat coming from it. A shiver of warning went up my spine. I turned slowly.

The winged man was there. I had nowhere to run; we were encased in the fire together now. Just as he had in every dream, he stood before me, watching me with utter calm.

I didn't know what to do. I was unprepared for this moment. There was nothing I was capable of that would stop him. I stared back into his strangely colored eyes, with the thin ring of yellow fire around the pupils, and I wondered if this was where it would all end.

He reached his hand out to me, a slow gesture of invitation.

"Eva Harroway," he said, his voice gentle, though it carried deep echoes of power. "Leave these others. Come with me now."

My mouth was so dry my reply stuck in my throat. I managed to shake my head. It might be safer to agree, but I couldn't. I had no idea what might've happened to Tristan on the other side of the fire — I didn't hear him. That terrified me.

"They cannot keep you from your destiny forever." His voice took on an edge. "I will tear down every protection around you if I have to. Come with me willingly."

"Never," I spat, fear driving my anger. I knew what he

must mean, who would fall if he couldn't get to me. Threatening the abbey, my family, erased any sense of curiosity he'd held for me.

Whatever he wanted, whatever his plan was, I wouldn't make it easy for him. I would fight with everything I had.

"It does not have to be like this," he pled, urgency bleeding through his composure.

For a few brief heartbeats, as his gaze searched mine, I hesitated. There was something in his eyes – it drew me in, caught at something buried deep within me.

"Eva!" Tristan's voice broke through my thoughts, and the moment was gone.

He shouted again in panic. He was close.

I had no time left; I had to make a decision. When Tristan called my name once more, the answer suddenly became clear.

He must have read the shift in my expression because his face hardened.

"No, wait!"

But I was already following my hunch. I threw myself at the wall of fire in the direction I'd heard Tristan's voice. The next second I was free of it, out in the woods and unscathed. Tristan was already beside me. He grabbed my hand as he shot something over his shoulder.

"This way." He pulled me, racing forward.

After only a few moments, I felt a strange sensation wash over me. The world around us was suddenly plunged into a white fog. We came to an abrupt halt. It was so thick I could barely see Tristan standing next to me.

In the new stillness he held a finger to his lips. I clutched tighter to his hand, uncertain of what had happened. But he didn't seem worried...he seemed to be waiting.

Something shifted in front of me and I jumped. Tristan squeezed my hand in reassurance, so I kept still, watched as a pair of shadows detached from where we stood. They became solid echoes of the two of us. They moved off to the left.

"Keep moving – go straight ahead." Greta's voice whispered in my ear as though she stood right next to me.

Tristan began to walk forward quickly, but silently. I made my way along with him, barely daring to breathe. Off to the left, I could hear occasional noises from our doubles...the snap of a twig, a whisper of movement. It was eerie as hell.

After a ways, the fog parted enough to show the wall.

Able to see more clearly now, we picked up our pace. When we got closer, I saw Greta on the far side, her eyes closed in concentration as her lips moved soundlessly.

An icy breath blew across the back of my neck, sent shivers of alarm down my spine.

I was afraid of what I might see if I turned around. Tristan seemed to have the same idea. We abandoned caution, sprinted the last few yards, leaped up to the top of the wall and launched off to the other side.

Greta stopped what she was doing the moment we were safe, and the three of us backed away quickly. I stared across the wall, saw nothing beyond the thick fog. But I could feel him on the other side, just out of sight, staring back at me.

Tristan pulled my hand, drew me further into the woods, towards the abbey, as my crow flew above us. My heartbeat slowed to normal, and I was finally able to think past the need to escape, the whole occurrence spinning through my head. It didn't make sense.

When I was trapped in the fire, I realized he wouldn't hurt me. Whatever it was he ultimately wanted, he didn't want to kill me, at least not yet, despite Greta's insistence he was a danger to me. That was why I suspected it would be safe to throw myself through the fire he built. The question was why. What was it he really wanted from me?

There was something more going on here that I didn't understand. But I was inclined to think Greta did.

"Well that wasn't part of the plan." Her dry words cut across my thoughts. "What happened? I was just on my way to meet you when I caught the thread of what was happening. By the time I got to the edge of the property, you two had separated. I couldn't do anything until you were back together."

"What were those things, anyway? Those weird ghost copies of us?"

"That was called a fetch — a bit like an echo of your spirit. It's rather tricky to sustain and control one, but they can be awfully handy. Now tell me. Why were you early?"

Tristan told his grandmother about the fire alarm. Nobody believed it was a coincidence. It worried Greta that he'd managed to set it off somehow without having come through all the way to our world yet.

We'd almost made it to the lawn. I didn't know how the afternoon would go, if I'd have a chance to confront Greta.

And that had been too close a call – I needed to know what I was really up against.

I stopped walking. The other two turned, focused twin expressions of interest on me.

"This doesn't all make sense."

"What doesn't?"

"I don't think you've told me everything."

Greta raised an eyebrow. I fought the desire to drop my eyes and apologize. But if I was the one in the middle of all this, I needed to know. No more secrets.

"There are too many things that don't add up. If everything around him dies, then why wasn't I hurt when I stood close to him? And if he's so powerful, why doesn't he do whatever it is he wants: either kill me or take me? Because back there he had the opportunity…but he gave me a choice. So what does he really want with me? I'm certain you know more about this than you said."

Greta's gaze remained steady. "That is true. I haven't shared everything with you."

"Why not?"

"Well, first of all, there have been more immediate concerns that needed to be discussed. Second of all, I wasn't sure it was safe. There are also things I wasn't certain were true. I've spent much of the morning pouring over old records, trying to confirm stories and lost legends. I can give you answers, but now is not the right time."

"You've been holding back information this whole time. I need to know the rest of it."

"Wait, forget about that for a second," Tristan cut in. "Eva, you're bleeding. What happened?"

I looked at my arm, saw that a deep gash extended down it. "Oh. I think I scraped it against the stump of a tree branch while we ran." I'd barely noticed the pain at first, but now it throbbed.

"That doesn't look good," Greta said. "We need to take care of it before we go in."

"When will you tell me everything else?"

She was examining my arm and responded absently, "If you really insist, then I suppose there will be time this afternoon." She ran her hand over the wound. The growing sting suddenly eased, a coolness spreading across it.

She glanced back up at me. I caught sight of that otherness in her eyes, that glimpse of something ancient and powerful. In the next heartbeat it was gone.

"What was that?" I breathed.

She cocked her head. "The healing magic?"

"No, what I just saw in your eyes. I've seen it before. It's like, I don't know...like a doorway into something...vast. Something otherworldly."

"Hmm, I've heard of the occasional person in the past who could see the magic sweeping through someone when they drew on it, but I've never actually known anyone who could do it. Perhaps that's what you saw. Very interesting."

The bleeding on my arm had stopped. It looked more healed over, though there was still an angry red line.

"You probably won't end up with a scar, but I'd like to put some salve on it once we're inside. Put your coat on for now so the others don't see it. Come on, let's get going."

Greta started off. I glanced at Tristan to find he watched me with a strange look on his face.

"What is it?" I asked as we fell in step together.

"I'm sorry I let go of you," he said in a low voice, staring straight ahead. "I shouldn't have let us get separated."

"Well, that was just as much my fault as it was yours. So don't worry about it."

"What happened behind the fire?"

"He wanted me to go with him. Same as before."

Tristan looked over at me, his brows drawn, his eyes intense. "Eva, whatever he said to you back there, don't listen to him."

I stared back at him, hoping he would say more. When he didn't, I turned my gaze ahead, picked up my pace.

Whatever they'd kept from me, it couldn't be good.

What was it about my destiny they were afraid I would find out?

*

"You kids are home early. What happened?" Sebastian asked, wandering into the foyer as we came in.

"There was a fire alarm during last period so they let us go," I said. I gave him a kiss on the cheek. "It was a false alarm though, don't worry."

"Very well then. Would you two mind if I stole Eva for a few minutes? Please make yourselves comfortable."

I followed him into his study, curious when he closed the door.

"So, Evie, I don't know if Greta told you already, but there was a lot of damage done to their cottage in the storm." At my nod, he continued. "It didn't feel right to let them go home without the electricity back on or any of the leaks fixed, so I've invited them to stay here until they can get someone out to see to the problems.

"I wanted to make sure that was okay with you. I know you have to go to school with Tristan so it could be awkward to have him here. If you don't feel comfortable with this arrangement, there's a place in town we can set them up in – it wouldn't be a problem."

"Oh, thanks for asking. But, really Basher, don't worry about me. Tristan and I get along fine so it won't be weird. Plus I'm sure it would be easier for them to stay close to their place in case they need anything."

"Good. The ladies were quite enthusiastic about having guests," he said with a smile.

I hesitated, but best to be forewarned, right?

"What about Claire and Margaret?"

"Don't you worry about them, I've had a talk with Claire. She won't be causing any more trouble. I made sure she understands her place here and if she wants to keep it she'll be on her best behavior – with our guests and with you. Besides, I think she's secretly afraid of Helen," he said, trying to keep a straight face.

I couldn't help but smile at that, which had probably been his goal.

"All right, then, off with you. I need to get some work done. Just check in with our guests once in a while if you wouldn't mind, make sure they have what they need. I think Helen and the others are busy and they'll be wanting to work on dinner soon, anyway."

I headed up to my room. A few minutes later, Greta

knocked on the door. She inspected my arm again, put some ointment on it before wrapping it in gauze. When she noticed me staring at her, she sighed.

"Tristan and I will be in the reading room; no one else is in there. Once you change into something with long sleeves, come down and I'll talk to you."

"You'll tell me what you've been keeping from me?"

Greta's look was heavy with regret. "If that's the way it must be, then I have no choice. This will have to be the time. I'll see you down there."

She left me alone, with uneasiness stirring in my belly. Slowly, I slipped into a different shirt, thinking all the while about how much my life had changed in the past two days. So much of the world was not as it had always seemed. And now there were more difficult things I was going to have to hear. I hesitated.

No, I wouldn't take it back.

I wouldn't give up knowing the truth about who I was, who Tristan was.

So enough already – I'd have to get on with the crappy part.

The two of them sat in the reading room, their heads bent together in conversation. I couldn't make out anything they said, their voices low and insistent, and as soon as Greta noticed me in the doorway, she broke off her sentence.

I sat down in one of the chairs facing the windows, tried not to fidget as she watched me, her expression inscrutable. Tristan wouldn't even meet my eyes, staring instead out at the ocean.

Okay, this should be fun.

Chapter Twenty-Three

I suppose I should start at the beginning. There are things you both need to hear if we're going to figure out a way to stop this threat."

She spoke in a low, even voice, but I couldn't help glancing at the doorway.

"Don't worry, my dear, we won't be overheard. Someone could come in here, stand right next to us, and they wouldn't hear a thing. I've taken precautions."

How handy. I nodded for her to go on.

"Tristan, you will have heard much of this before, though some of it only as stories and legends. Back before our history even began, there were many more creatures walking the earth like the one who's after you, Eva. They took care of the land, existed in peace, and nurtured the magic."

"Okay, sure," I said. So the storybook I'd found in the attic must really be a true history. "They were the guardians of our world and the doorways to other lands."

They both stared at me. Intently.

"How did you know that?" Greta asked.

Cautious now, I replied, "I read it in an old book I found. I didn't know it was real, but it seemed to fit with what you said."

"Hand-painted? I thought that book was lost," she mused. "It was all supposed to have been destroyed in the fire. Tell me, Eva, did you find anything else? It's important."

Wait – screw that. I was tired of being kept in the dark, pushed around by everyone who knew more than I did for their own ends. It was time for answers. I wasn't going to let Greta be sidetracked, not yet.

"We can get to that later. First you have to tell me the rest of it. And this time tell me everything. I can handle it," I added softly, meeting Tristan's unhappy gaze.

Greta reined in her excitement, got back on subject. Tristan and I reluctantly turned our attention back to her.

"Right then. Though much of the history was lost, from what I can tell, for a long time, our kind lived alongside them peacefully. But something changed. It's said they resented our growing powers. They turned on us. They killed many innocent people in their determination to wipe us out, but we came together, we grew stronger...we fought back. And so the war began.

"Once our kind learned how to kill them, everything changed. Their numbers dwindled until it seemed we would prevail. However, the last few remaining proved difficult to defeat. They went into hiding, most likely slipping through the gateways. All but one.

"For as far back as our history goes, he has been our enemy. The Immortal One. He hunted us, tried to destroy us. And then he disappeared for long periods of time, long enough that we grew complacent, so that eventually the secret of how to kill his kind was lost. Though still he sought to annihilate us."

A cold thread of fear slipped down my spine as I remembered the look in his eyes from my first vision. I had seen madness in his eyes. I had seen my own death reflected back.

"At some point, a very long time ago, our people found a way to weaken him. Nothing is known about what they did, but it turned out only partially effective. His powers were diminished, yes, but that only angered him further, led to more attacks as he tried to find a way to undo it.

"Finally, three of the most powerful of our kind came together to curse him. They corrupted his connection to the land, and therefore his magic, which, among other things, caused everything around him to wither and die. Because of this weakened state, the three of them were able to find a way to banish him, sealing him off in the Veiled Land, the land of shadows."

Greta's expression was solemn as her gaze drilled into me.

"So for many generations, he hasn't been a threat. He's been nothing more than a bedtime story. Until now."

A winged betrayer stalking my nightmares. He'd tried to destroy people with the ability to use magic since the beginning...now he'd come back and was after me. Awesome.

"One of the three who cursed him was an ancestor of mine. He would have been Tobias McGrath's great-grandfather. It was said he was the keeper of the knowledge: he kept records of how they managed it, and that secret was passed down through the family. Supposedly it was lost, along with one of the oldest histories telling the story of the war. Eva, if there's any chance his records are here with the book you found, they may be our only hope."

I regarded Greta for a long moment. Either the answers were in the trunk or they weren't. Leaving it a little longer wouldn't change anything.

"Why was I not affected by the curse?"

Greta blew out a frustrated breath, shaking her head. "You are stubborn, you know."

"So I've been told."

"The curse was intricately designed. The corruption wasn't meant to affect people, just the natural world around him. Otherwise he would have posed even more of a threat to us. But it seems he's grown strong enough to suppress that aspect of the curse at times. From what I can tell, however, the longer he stays in one place the more irrepressible it becomes."

"Tell me, please," I said quietly. "What does he want with me?"

She studied me. I wondered if I'd finally get the whole truth. Did she trust me enough?

"He doesn't want to hurt you, Eva. I believe he wants you to break the curse. It was humans who placed the curse on him, so it would have to be removed by one of us. Part of his choosing you may be because one of the original three who cursed him was an ancestor of yours. A Harroway, a McGrath, and a Moldovan. It was a very powerful working.

"But I suspect he wants you primarily because he believes you're the only one strong enough to break it. It's doubtless he recognized the portents about your birth, about how powerful you would become. That's why he searched you out...as we always knew he would."

"So you've known since I was born he would come for me. And that's really why the families are afraid of me? Because they believe he'll succeed in forcing me to break the curse on him?" Greta's expression held nothing but pity as she watched me struggle to understand. I was still missing something. "If everyone was worried about me eventually being caught and forced to help him, why didn't my grandfather keep me close instead of hiding me away? Why didn't your friends want you to teach me how to defend myself? What is it you haven't told me?"

"I don't know if he would be able to make you break the curse against your will, Eva. He isn't interested in hurting you or overpowering you. I think he visited you in your dreams, tried to connect with you, because he wants you to choose to help him. He wants you to join him willingly."

"And the families think I will," I said, my voice bleak as it became clear. *They cannot keep you from your destiny forever.* "Why is everyone so sure I'll join him? Now that I know who he is, why would I ever want to help him?"

When Greta didn't answer immediately, I turned to Tristan, hoping he'd smile, tell me I had it all wrong. But after meeting my gaze for a long moment, he went to stand by the window to stare out at the ocean.

I turned back to Greta, a sick feeling swirling in my stomach. This was what it had all been about from the beginning. Everything they'd held back centered around keeping me from finding out about this.

"Please understand," she said, "we didn't tell you because we wanted to protect you. I don't want you to second-guess yourself, especially now. We need to stay strong. I think it's a mistake to put any faith in something like this."

I couldn't find the voice to demand she get it the hell over with and tell me already.

She leaned forward, keeping my gaze trapped in her own.

"But I said I would tell you everything, and so I will. Before you were born, we began to hear of dark stirrings. Change was coming, and with it, something malevolent. There are a few among us able to catch glimpses of what is to come. Sadly, those who can, often lose their minds. Their sight is limited, their thoughts warped by what they see, so their words are frequently misunderstood.

"As the time of your birth grew closer, more and more of their foretelling focused around you. Perhaps it was because you were to be so powerful, you became something of a lodestone to them. Or maybe it's because the change they saw you bringing was so significant, there was nothing worth seeing beyond it. Either way, they spoke grim prophecies about you."

Greta fell silent for a while. I tried to wrap my mind around what it all meant.

"The council tried to keep them secret. They didn't want anyone to know the specifics of what was spoken...to suspect their power might be threatened. But of course, it wasn't difficult for Reed and me to get around them to find the truth for ourselves."

"What did the prophecies say about me?"

"Some simply pointed to your convergence with the Immortal One. Others said you would be the ultimate weapon in the war, though for which side it was unclear."

"That isn't all, is it?" I asked, sensing her reluctance. "There were other prophecies?"

Greta's look was dark with sorrow. "There was another that kept repeating." At my nod, she closed her eyes, recited the prophecy, her words falling heavily.

"A child of two worlds will be born with great power, power enough to beget our destruction. The fate of our kind will rest in her decision to betray us. She brings the dark victory in the war, a final end to it all."

When she finished, the room fell silent.

Oh god, I felt sick. This was why my grandfather had hidden me away, afraid of how I would threaten the lives of all his people. Greta said prophecies were often misunderstood, but that sounded pretty damned clear.

It was my destiny to help the enemy and destroy my own people.

No. I shook my head. This was ridiculous. I knew myself. I was in control of my life, and I would never do anything like that. I looked Greta in the eye.

"This can't be right." My fingernails dug into my palms. "I don't care what they saw. They don't know me. It's a prophecy, but I can change it, can't I? It doesn't necessarily have to come true, right?"

"Listen to me very carefully, Eva," Greta said in low voice. "Yes, they do unfailingly come true...it's just not always in the way we assume they will. They saw what they saw for a reason; if we were going to make different choices, they would have seen a different outcome. But you have to remember that prophecies are tricky. We don't actually know what they saw – we only know the words they spoke. Words that are so easily misunderstood and misinterpreted. We don't have the whole picture. There may be hope yet...a way around this we can't see.

"We cannot live our lives afraid of what is coming. We can only have faith in ourselves as we struggle to always do what is right. The council knows better than to believe so literally in something like this. But their judgment has long been clouded by fear."

I glanced over at Tristan still standing at the window. "So what about you two? You don't believe in the prophecy? That I'll betray you?"

Tristan suddenly hit the frame of the window, making me jump. He came and sat down, his frustration barely contained.

"No, we don't," Greta said simply, ignoring his outburst.

"Eva, please." Tristan drew my gaze back to him, his eyes intense. "The prophecy doesn't matter. I don't believe any of it and neither should you. We didn't want you to hear it because it doesn't change anything. It's just a bunch of bloody nonsense spoken by some ancient witches whose minds are shredded by their own magic – it's not to be trusted."

But as I stared at the two of them, I couldn't help the horror digging its claws into my chest. All this time they'd been trying to keep me safe from the winged man, what they'd really wanted was to keep me from being caught by him because of what *I* might do.

"Your grandfather never believed them," Greta said gently. "He knew you wouldn't become a danger to us. He only sent you away to protect you from what the families might do to you. I agreed to help because I believed as he did. His plan had always been to eliminate the threat, and then move to Fairhaven to be with you, teach you about your magic. When Reed died, I simply thought it would be best to leave you with the family you had here."

I wanted to know what had happened to him, the last family I'd had left, but now was not the time. I guess it was a comfort knowing he'd still planned to be a part of my life. But he was dead and gone now – he couldn't make any of this better.

"I promised him I would keep your existence a secret for as long as possible and protect you the best I could," continued Greta. "But when I came here, I had to tell a few chosen friends – I needed their help. They were wary, though. That's the real reason I wasn't supposed to teach you anything. They didn't want you to learn our secrets, grow more powerful, only to put that in the hands of the enemy. This all would have been different if Reed were alive. Together, we never would have let them get away with such foolishness."

"But even your closest friends are convinced I'll join him?"

"They were being cautious. It's not that they thought a granddaughter of Reed's would be evil. It seemed more likely the Immortal One would somehow find a way to work through you, not necessarily by your choice." She sighed. "Certainly none of us believed he'd find a way back into our world. But it doesn't matter – those things will not happen. The point is that those of us who know you, trust in you. That's what counts."

None of what Greta said made me feel better. And with the two of them watching me so closely, I began to fear I'd lose it. The pressure building inside me took up all the space, left me no room to breathe.

"I just need a minute, if you'll excuse me." I got up, fled from the room as fast as I could, not caring what they thought.

I hurried out onto the front porch, the crisp afternoon air a relief against my hot skin. The wind had picked up. Clouds scuttled across the sky as the sun slipped closer to the horizon. Darkness would come soon enough.

I stared out at the woods that closed around the abbey. All my life I'd tried to be good; I'd lived quietly, not experiencing much of the world beyond Ragnarok. But people like Claire and Margaret, not to mention the kids in town, had always assumed the worst about me.

Now it seemed they might have been right.

For a moment, hysterical laughter threatened to bubble up. It was absurd to think I was supposed to have that much power.

I'd always known the unlikely was possible. The things I'd seen, like visions of the past, were utterly real. So if I believed in my magic, how could I not believe in other people's magic, in their visions? How could I not be assured of the truth of the prophecy?

After a couple of minutes of brooding, I heard the door open behind me. I knew without looking it was Tristan.

He came over to stand silently beside me. I watched the trees sway in the wind, comforted by his solid presence. He'd said he didn't believe in the prophecy, but I wondered if, deep down, that was really true.

"Eva," he said finally. He put his hands on my shoulders as I turned to him. "You know we would never let him hurt you...or change you. We'll do whatever it takes."

I looked up at him, uncertainty swirling in my thoughts. I couldn't help but think how often in my dreams, despite my fear of the winged man, I'd felt drawn to him. He'd taught me a little magic and I'd been captivated. Was there something wrong with me? Why did he have this power over me?

"This whole time, you all have known I'm doomed to betray and destroy everyone, but despite your significant efforts, you weren't able to alter anything. The Immortal One still found me...it's all still happening. If it's inevitable, how am I supposed to stop it or change it? What if I can't?"

Tristan leaned forward, gently rested his forehead against mine. "I have faith in you."

"But what if you're wrong?" I whispered back.

"I'm not."

We stood like that, neither of us speaking, as the moments passed. My eyes were shut, but he was so close I could feel him all along my skin, breathing him in with every inhalation. Something shifted in the mood between us. Despite my worries, my heart began to race.

Tristan lifted his head from mine. He placed his lips softly on my forehead for a brief moment before pulling away.

"Come on." He walked over to the door. "We should get back inside. There's more we need to discuss with my grandmother."

He held the door open but didn't meet my eyes as I went by. Had something just passed between the two of us? Or had I imagined it?

Chapter Twenty-Four

I found Greta sitting patiently in the reading room. I sat down, met her gaze squarely, and tried to convince myself I felt more confident than I actually was.

"Eva, I know this has been a lot for you to take in. I've burdened you with far more than you should have to handle, without giving you time to process any of it. Please believe that I am sorry. This was not my plan.

"But now I have to ask even more of you. We have to make our stand. I need you with us and I need you strong, ready to fight. I know everything has changed very quickly for you, that finding all of this out can't be easy. But I think we have to act tonight."

"Are you sure?" Tristan asked. He looked calm except for a tightening around his eyes. "We need more time to plan, to prepare. It might be a good idea to wait since we have a safe place to hide."

"No, I'm sorry, I have to disagree. The defenses here will hold against him, but the longer we wait the worse things will get. It will become increasingly difficult to keep

Sebastian and the nuns on the property without drawing them into this, which places them in too much danger."

"She's right," I stated, the words sounding flat as I thought of what he said he'd do to get to me. "We'd put everyone else at risk, and we can't do that."

Greta regarded me a moment. "Yes, I'm afraid the more time that passes, the more desperate he'll become. He'll turn that frustration onto the townspeople and we can't protect them. Surprise is our best option."

So when it came down to it, I really would have to stand between him and the town. What would Molly think if she knew her life depended on me? If I didn't leave the safety of the abbey to face him, everyone would pay the price.

All those lives were my responsibility – that terrified me.

The thought was too overwhelming, I couldn't handle it. I needed to concentrate on what had to be done, what I would do.

Right, focus…well I'd be damned if I'd let some old prophecy tell me what my destiny was. I would go out and fight him, prove to everyone, myself included, who I really was.

That was a noble idea, came the bleak thought, but how were we supposed to defeat him?

"How exactly do you plan to pull this off?" I asked. "I've seen him fight in my visions of the past. He is…beyond strong. It didn't work when the townspeople shot him, or used fire."

"I wonder though." Greta gave me a speculative look. "*Your* fire might be able to hurt him."

"Why? Because of our connection? You really think that would make a difference?"

"I think it's possible he's using the connection he built with you to anchor himself to this world. That could make him more vulnerable to your magic."

Peachy.

"Let's hope that is actually the case because we'll need every advantage we can get."

I didn't like the idea of that man being connected to me, but if it proved helpful, I'd use it.

"Now, Eva, I think it's time you told me what you found that belonged to my ancestors. If they kept records of any weaknesses the Immortal One has, we need them."

"The book describing the war with the guardians is in a trunk in the attic. If there's anything useful, that's the place to start looking. But I don't know if now is the best time. If anyone saw us it would be hard to explain."

"I'm afraid time is not on our side, my dear. It won't be a problem to get up there without being seen, though. We do have a few tricks, you know."

"Right. Okay, then."

I went over to the door, listened in the quiet hallway for any movement.

"Don't just use your ears," Greta said from right next to me, making me jump. "If you want to know where people are, use your other senses as well."

I closed my eyes, cast my awareness out into the

building. Claire was the only one upstairs, but she was in her bedroom, so it seemed we had a clear path to the attic.

I nodded to Greta, grabbed a couple of extra candles, and started down the hallway. The other two followed silently.

The attic was dark, undisturbed since my last visit. I lit the candles, feeling a little shy about using magic openly in front of anyone, and brought them straight back to the trunk. I found the lock much easier to remove the second time. The odd shiver ran over me again as it clicked.

"A blood ward," Greta said, noticing the movement. "Only someone with the blood of one of the three families could open it." She pulled the lid up, drew in a sharp breath when she saw inside. Gingerly, she pulled out one of the journals, ran her hand over the cover.

"This was supposed to have been lost in the fire that burned down the original house here," Greta murmured. "It was thought the trunk, with all its treasures, had been destroyed. Of course it makes sense Tobias would have guarded this carefully, finding a way to save it."

"Do you know why the house burnt down? The records I found said the townsfolk never knew what really happened."

She gave me a measuring look. "The fire at the house was started by Tobias's brother, Jonas. He had the same kind of visions of the past you have, Eva. Just as visions of the future are traumatic to the mind, so, too, are visions of the past, especially without training – which is why you got so sick. Jonas couldn't handle the visions, and he went insane. He burnt the house down...and himself with it."

I shuddered, suddenly queasy.

"After I found you having that first vision, I was afraid to leave you alone," Tristan said, shadows flickering in his eyes. "I told her what I'd sensed happening, but all we could do was wait."

"It came as no surprise when I got word the following day that you were feverish. You were in more danger than you knew, Eva. We nearly lost you."

The fever had almost swallowed me. I knew how easy it could've been to lose myself like Jonas had. I didn't want to imagine what he must have gone through that night.

"But you pulled through. You didn't even seem affected the next time it happened. You have no idea how impressive that is."

"I didn't really do anything." I hunched my shoulders.

"I know. It's just a testament to the natural strength of your magic."

Time for a change of subject. I pointed to the journal. "Those aren't in English. I didn't recognize the language."

Greta flipped the book open, scanned the page. Her mouth quirked up in a smile. "Our family has always been big on secrecy – it's Gaelic." She pulled all the journals out. "I'll go through these as quickly as I can, hopefully I'll find something."

I replaced the lock. We headed back. Halfway down the stairs from the third floor, we froze when a door opened on the second floor. I held my breath as the footsteps headed our way. We'd be easy to spot when Claire passed the stairs. She wouldn't believe any story I told about giving them a tour of the abbey.

"Relax, Eva," Tristan whispered. "Just let yourself blend into the background."

I glanced back only to find I couldn't really focus my eyes on where I knew they stood.

"Concentrate." The word floated out of nowhere. "Feel what I've done. Mimic it."

Claire was almost to the bottom of the stairs. I centered all my attention on Tristan to sense what he was doing. An aura of magic surrounded him, showing me nothing but the background, allowing him to disappear completely.

I wove the same magic, drawing an invisible curtain around me.

Claire appeared in the hallway, glanced up the stairs as she passed. Her eyes slid over us without recognition. She turned and descended to the first floor without pause.

I let go of the breath I'd been holding. Claire still made me nervous, despite Sebastian's talk with her.

"Not bad, Eva."

"I can see how that could come in handy," I said, smiling back up at him.

"Just be aware," Greta warned, "if you try to hide from someone like us, it takes a lot more finesse than that. Now, let's get going."

We set up in the reading room. Greta settled at one of the tables, began to pour over the journals, while Tristan and I sat on a couch. We spread our schoolbooks on the coffee table for show while we brainstormed plans.

"We need to catch him by surprise."

"What about using something like what we just did on the stairs?"

"We'd never be able to shield ourselves sufficiently for long enough to sneak up on him."

"Okay, then, what if we try to get him right when he comes through the gateway?"

"That's what I was thinking. It seems you're able to pick up on his entry immediately, so we might have just enough heads up to make it there. My grandmother said he kept appearing – at least last night – in the same spot anyway."

"Then what? He may be weaker and hopefully disoriented as he enters...emphasis on the *may*...but what can we hit him with?"

Tristan was silent, his eyes unfocused as he thought it through. Then his gaze sharpened on me. "He'll come through oriented towards you. If we're set up in a triangle around him, we'll be in good position. The moment he's here, you'd have to hit him with fire...and pray Greta's right about your effect on him."

"Even if I can reach him, that won't keep him busy for long. What will you two do? Can you have something ready to throw at him if I keep him distracted?"

He cocked his head, green eyes assessing me. "We could lay out a binding spell beforehand. Greta and I can seal it while he deals with you. That should trap him."

"Trap him? How?"

"There are different types of binding spells. Among the strongest, there's one that'd keep him in place and keep him from using his magic."

"Then what do we do with him?"

"Hopefully we throw something big and brilliant at him that she's discovered in those journals."

Greta spoke up from her table, surprising us both. "It's not a bad idea to have a backup plan."

"She's right." I turned back to Tristan. "Supposing we can't hurt him, we have to try to weaken him further. If we can find his connection to the land that the others already eroded with the curse, maybe the three of us could somehow twist it or damage it more."

"If we work together we might. Then we'll be able to do whatever it takes to get rid of him."

We continued to go over the plan, flush out the details, and try to figure out what could go wrong. Tristan explained how the binding spell worked. He went over some basic magic that could be handy.

It grew dark as we talked. I was caught off guard when Helen walked in.

"Oh goodness," she exclaimed. "Have you been in here all this time? I'm relieved to find you haven't been outside like I thought. Dinner will be ready in just a couple of minutes. Eva, would you mind setting the table?"

I nodded. I went into the dining room with Tristan trailing behind. The interruption frustrated me. Greta had hardly said anything beyond an occasional suggestion, and I wondered what she'd found in the journals, if anything. Once this was all over, assuming it went well, I hoped she'd translate them for me.

I couldn't bring myself to think about what might happen if it didn't go well.

With my stomach so full of nerves, I had trouble forcing food down at dinner. Not to mention trying to concentrate on the nuns' questions about school. I just kept thinking in a few hours we'd have to face the man who was supposed to steal my destiny.

Tristan leaned in close to murmur, "You should eat." I gave him a look that made my thoughts clear on the subject. The corner of his mouth tugged up in amusement. "I'm serious. You'll need your strength. Just pretend it's any other night."

"Right, no problem," I said, with a rueful smile. But I made more of an effort.

The nuns were in high spirits, enjoying the company that brightened the normal routines of their day. But I noticed Claire studying me surreptitiously. Not like she waited for an opportunity to say something cruel, but rather like she wanted to catch a glimpse of something I had hidden.

I sighed. I had far bigger problems than Claire.

*

A murmur of voices drifted out of Sebastian's office. I walked down the hall, hoping to spend a few moments with him, but paused outside when I heard my name.

"Come on, you cannot continue to avoid talking about Eva, Sebastian. What should we do about that crazy...nightmare she had?" Helen asked.

"I'm not sure there's anything we can do."

"I know Greta said it didn't sound like anything to be concerned about, but...something isn't right."

"Has Eva had any more incidents?"

"Not that I've seen. But I doubt she'd tell us she had if nobody witnessed it."

"She seems to have recovered just fine," Sebastian said patiently.

"I know, but did you see her at dinner? And last night, too. She's been so jumpy, so distracted — I'm just concerned about her after everything she's been through. Maybe this isn't the best time for visitors. If they make her more nervous, if they upset her, they shouldn't stay."

"But maybe this gives her exactly what she needs."

"And what is that?"

"A friend. Tristan seems to care for her. Didn't you notice the way she was with him tonight? He calms her down, makes her smile. It's something she's never had."

"I'm afraid he'll end up hurting her."

"I know. I am too. But she's tough — she'll be okay, whatever happens."

"Of course, you're right. I just can't help worrying."

I quietly backed away from the door as they continued. I didn't want to be caught eavesdropping. I should've known Helen wouldn't let such a violent, strange episode pass without further fretting. But what could I do? I didn't have space left in my head to worry about that now.

I leaned against the wall, closed my eyes…tried to convince myself I wasn't terrified. With the setting of the sun had come the memories of so many dark nightmares that had plagued my sleep all my life. Once my nameless enemy knew I wouldn't join him, there was no telling what he might unleash on us.

I went back to the reading room to join the others, feeling no better than I had before. Mary and Agnes chatted with Greta, who managed the conversation while still taking notes from a journal. I sat down next to Tristan.

"Are you all right?" he asked in a low voice.

"Yeah, I'm fine. Why?"

He shrugged. "You look upset, that's all."

I hesitated. He watched me, nothing but sincere concern in his eyes. So I told him what I overheard, how I worried about hiding everything from Helen and Sebastian. He listened attentively, and the world shrank down to just the two of us.

"How much do they know about what you can do?" A teasing smile spread across his face, though his eyes held a touch of sadness. "I mean, I know I was a bloody nuisance with my magic when I was a kid. My mum used to threaten to bind my powers before I grew old enough to control them. It must have been...difficult here."

I wanted to ask about his mother, but I didn't want to pry. Even after a year, that wound...

"When I was little, visiting nuns thought the abbey was haunted. The chimes in my nursery swung and jingled even when the windows were closed. Toys floated into my crib. Someone would always wake when I was hungry – even though I hadn't cried. Helen didn't like to talk about it, but Mary told me by the time I was two, candles would light and extinguish without anyone being close to them. Apparently I wasn't fond of the dark."

He gave a low whistle. "That's a lot of power to demonstrate at such a young age. And I can see how that might be hard to explain to visitors."

"I certainly would've liked an explanation. Mary would tell me her grandmother's stories about fairy children left on the doorsteps of villagers' homes. How they would be raised as humans, but able to do inexplicable things. I can still hear her asking me, 'Is that what you are, little one? A fairy child?' I've never been sure if she secretly suspected that was the truth. Or what any of them really believed.

"Sebastian, Helen, Mary, and Agnes were the ones who took care of me from the beginning, so it didn't take them long to figure out I was the cause of the strange things that happened around me. But they just...accepted it. One thing they understood quickly, though, and were clear about, even early on, was the danger people posed. They were careful to keep me away from the other nuns as much as possible, even other kids. They were afraid I'd be taken away from them if anyone ever saw what I could do. I was lucky I didn't freak them out, lucky they protected me. They even helped spread the rumors this place was haunted."

I shook myself. I hadn't meant to get carried away and tell him so much. It was just such a relief to talk to someone without having to edit myself, or worry how he'd react if I said anything weird.

"That sounds terribly lonely," he murmured. "So you eventually figured out how to suppress your magic? As a form of self-defense?"

"I learned from an early age how right they were to worry, how important it was to hide what I could do. So I made it go away. I buried the magic as deep as I could, tried desperately to be normal."

"But it wouldn't stay buried. And that's a good thing, Eva. It's who you are. I wish we could've moved here so much earlier so you wouldn't have feared it."

"Somehow I don't think knowing I'd be destined to destroy everyone would've made growing up any easier, but thanks."

Tristan's lips quirked up in a smile to match my own and I was suddenly, weirdly happy we were in danger. Here, together.

I noticed Mary sneaking looks in our direction, so I pulled out my math book, pretended more convincingly to work. Mary was just a little too interested in what she thought might be going on between the two of us.

Eventually, Agnes and Mary excused themselves. Only a few moments later, Helen and Sebastian came in to say goodnight, make sure their guests had everything they might need.

I gave them each a hug, trying to shut out the bleak thoughts that kept popping up, unbidden in my head, like what they would do if I didn't return home tonight.

Helen gave me an extra squeeze and kissed my forehead. "Try not to stay up too late tonight, sweetheart. You need to get some rest."

"Okay, I'll try," I said with a smile. I forced myself to let go of her. "We just have some more homework we have to get done for tomorrow."

"All right then. Goodnight everyone."

A new, tense atmosphere settled into the quiet now that there were no more distractions.

"Okay you two," Greta began, sitting up a little straighter, "come sit down, there are things you need to learn. The journals proved to be at least partly what I'd hoped for. They confirmed that the secret of how to kill his kind was lost long ago, so sadly that's no help.

"They do give us another option, however. Each of the Lost Lands has a pathway to our world. Our ancestors sealed one once before, after shackling the Immortal One on the other side, in the Veiled Land. But, eventually of course, he found a way to break through. Now that we know how they managed it, we must force him back into the Veiled Land...only this time, we'll destroy the gateway behind him. He'll be trapped there forever. You, my dear, will be free of him."

I pulled her notes to me. "So how exactly do we do this?"

"Read through that, both of you. It lays out the specifics of the spell. We need to work together, each of us taking a different aspect. To understand how the parts fit though, you need to know the whole thing completely."

Tristan scooted his chair closer, leaned in to read.

It was complicated. And it required a tremendous amount of power. Greta would be the focal point of the spell, directing it, keeping it contained, while Tristan and I did our parts. I committed the details to memory, seeing it spin out in my head, and asked her to explain anything I didn't understand.

Once we finished reading, Greta went over the plan again and again, made sure we knew precisely how the spell worked without hesitation.

I had never used fire as a weapon before – it kind of freaked me out. But Greta had me practice building a wall of flames at a distance, showed me a few tricks. I didn't mention it was our enemy who'd shown me how to use fire in the first place...I was afraid it really wouldn't go over well.

"How will we know when to go out?" I asked. "He might not come through at all tonight, assuming we'll hole up here."

"It's likely he'll know the moment you step off the property. But if not, I have another thought as to how we might lure him here. You'll be our bait."

"Wonderful." Our plan suddenly seemed flimsy and ridiculous. We'd be attempting to recreate a spell that had already been used against him once, with no idea if it would even work. Not to mention the two of them would put themselves directly in the line of his wrath. For me. "Are you sure this is the only way?"

She regarded me with that piercing look that always made me feel uncomfortably exposed. "Eva, he's been reserved so far, played nice. But if he can't get to you, can't get what he wants, then he will go to war. He will turn his anger upon the world and no one will be safe. We have no choice – this is our only weapon. We have to seal him away to keep him from hurting us all."

And to ensure he never had the chance to turn me to his side so *I* could hurt them all...mustn't forget the real motivation. But she wouldn't say that aloud.

Damn. Of course we didn't have another option. I knew that.

A quick glance at Tristan showed resolve burning in his eyes – he was ready for this. I nodded.

"We're settled then," Greta said. "It's time."

The world dropped away for a moment. No more stalling, no more planning. There was nothing left but to go out and face my nightmare.

Chapter Twenty-Five

I tied my hair back in a tight bun, pulled on a pair of pants and a black sweater, the motions automatic. I grabbed the candles Greta had requested and went down to the reading room to wait, dread crawling through my belly. I'd seen this man kill people. He'd come close to killing me in that first vision.

When Tristan came in, I was pacing. Only a few candles were lit – I didn't want anyone to notice a light was on and come to investigate. The room was full of shifting shadows from the flickering flames, the hallway behind him dark.

"My grandmother will be down in a couple of minutes. She's just looking over some last minute things."

I tried to smile, but my face felt stiff. How was Tristan so relaxed?

The candlelight reflected strangely in his green eyes as he drew close to me. He searched my face, his brows drawing together.

"Everything's going to be okay, Eva," he said, his voice gentle. "You're so much stronger than you realize."

"But too much could go wrong. What if he does something to me, uses his power to change me so I don't even realize what I'm doing?"

"Even if he could do that...which he can't, I'm certain...my grandmother showed you how to shield yourself. He wouldn't be able to get through that. Besides, we're going to hit him so fast he won't have time to respond. You'll do fine."

"Holy hell, Tristan, how can you be so calm about this?" I asked, swallowing the anxiety that tried to swamp me. "Don't you have any reservations?"

His mouth curved in a small smile. "No, I don't. It's the only way to make sure you'll be safe."

"But it puts the two of you at risk along with me," I said quietly, dropping my eyes.

Tristan took my chin, coaxed it up until I met his gaze. He looked at me as if I was the only other person in the world, and my heart began to trip and stumble about. "I wouldn't have it any other way," he whispered.

He leaned down and kissed me.

Oh. Holy. Hell.

His fingers skimmed down my throat, his lips pressed softly against mine. I reached out to him, any sense of hesitation gone. His arms went around me as I slid my hands behind his neck. My lips parted, the kiss growing deeper.

The earth spun as I lost myself in the feel of him, his hand trailing down my back, my fingers burying in his hair. No one had ever touched me like this. I wanted the moment to last forever.

He pulled me tighter against him for a moment, and then, with a sigh, he moved to brush his lips across my cheek. He shifted back slowly and I opened my eyes. A hint of a smile lingered on his lips. "My grandmother is coming," he said, stepping away.

I dropped my hands, remembered to start breathing again as I stood there, trying to figure out what the hell just happened.

A few seconds later, Greta appeared. She walked over, her expression set, no indication she knew what had occurred. Thank god.

I couldn't look at him. My thoughts whirled too quickly to focus on anything, strange things fluttering around in my chest.

Tristan kissed me.

Holy crap, I hadn't just imagined that.

Now he stood there, watching his grandmother, all calm and collected, as though nothing out of the ordinary had happened.

I felt the corners of my mouth turning up and tried to smother a smile that didn't want to be repressed. This was a totally ridiculous time to be happy.

"Are you two ready?"

I saw Tristan nod out of the corner of my eye. Greta turned her sharp gaze on me. I suppressed a wave of giddiness, tried to focus. Was I ready to face him?

I pushed everything else out. Determination settled over me. Knowing what my destiny presumably held, I had no choice but to go out and face it.

"Let's go."

We gathered the candles, slipped out the back door. Outside, Greta paused. The air was chilly, the wind blowing in off the water. Above, the stars were thick, with only occasional clouds drifting by.

"It's the night of the dark moon," Greta murmured, looking at the sky. "It had been believed the night of the deepest shadows belonged to the Immortal One before he was locked away. I fear this isn't a coincidence."

"Greta," I said, suddenly curious, "what is the Veiled Land?"

"Very little is known of the Lost Lands," she replied, her voice whispery. "Legends claim they exist beyond our world, through doorways better left closed. The Veiled Land was said to be a world of eternal night, where nothing remained apart from the darkness, and creatures of nightmares roamed." She sighed. "Enough of this now – we need to get going."

She set off across the lawn. Once we reached the woods, she lit her candle with a thought. Tristan and I followed suit.

I picked my way calmly over the uneven ground. Now that everything was set in motion, I knew exactly what I was doing. I hadn't realized it, but a slow anger towards the winged man smoldered inside me. I was ready for a fight.

Greta was leading us to the place where he'd come through the night before, and after a ways, I noticed Stopha drifting silently above us. It took the rest of the walk to convince him to go back to the abbey to wait. I couldn't afford the distraction.

We finally reached the wall. Even with the dim candle-light, it was easy to see the small clearing on the other side. I could sense the residue of corruption he'd left.

"You stay on this side of the wall," Greta said, her hand heavy on my shoulder. "We're going to get started, but until we're ready, I won't risk him sensing you and showing up early."

She climbed easily over the wall, making me wonder again how old she really was. I leaned against the stones to wait as they discussed the boundaries of the spell.

The wind blowing through the trees made eerie sounds as the night pressed in around me. A chill crept up the back of my neck. So much for feeling calm. I reminded myself there was nothing out there to be afraid of. At least not yet.

Greta set the candles around the clearing to mark key places. The tiny flames flickered madly in the wind. She and Tristan walked patterns between the lights, the soft words of their incantation barely reaching me. Faintly glimmering lines trailed from their hands.

They separated to stand on opposite edges of the working. As Greta spoke, I felt the growing pressure of the power contained in the space before them.

She fell silent. She slowly bowed her head and the soft, silver-lit lines sank into the earth and disappeared.

The spell was prepared.

Greta raised her gaze to meet mine. Even with the distance, I could see the strange abyss shining out through her eyes. It was a powerful working. She beckoned me over and I tensed. This was it. Once I crossed the wall there would be no stopping it. I glanced over at Tristan, feeling the lives of everyone weighing on me.

He waited, both of them watching. It was up to me. Right.

Without further hesitation, I climbed over the wall.

When I landed on the other side, Greta raised her eyebrows. "Are you sure you're ready?"

"Where do you want me?"

She pointed. "Just behind that candle." I went to the spot farthest from the wall. They positioned themselves, made a triangle containing the working. "Now we wait."

I stood looking back at the other two, the wall stretched out behind them. My senses strained, my concentration sharpened. The minutes passed and the noises of the woods became magnified.

Still we waited.

I began to feel more and more edgy. Stray sounds made me jump. If he came through anywhere else, I'd know. But except for the rustling of the wind, the forest was quiet, empty.

How long would we wait? I looked at Greta. She held my gaze for a long moment, then shifted her eyes to Tristan, raising her eyebrow in a silent question. He nodded, resignation settling in his features. They both turned to me.

I got the distinct feeling I wouldn't like this.

"I'm sorry," she said. "If he can't tell you're off the property, we need to find another way to draw him. He's obviously able to sense when you begin to dream, so Tristan will guide you into one. The moment the Immortal One drags you into his slip-dream, he'll know you're not in Ragnarok. Tristan will pull you right back here and we'll continue as planned. Okay?"

Yup, I was right: I didn't like this at all.

The idea of losing consciousness sucked. Even if I was safe in the dream, I'd be vulnerable physically. I looked at Tristan. He would be my only way to get back.

He regarded me in silence, his expression revealing nothing. He wouldn't push me to agree. But, of course, I would. I wouldn't be out here if I didn't trust the two of them with my life. Besides, Tristan had been watching over me in my dreams since he'd arrived in Fairhaven.

I nodded. "What do I have to do?"

"Just try to relax, if you can." He looked at Greta, who shook her head.

"Do it from where you're standing. I don't want us to fall apart if he comes through too quickly."

"Okay, Eva. Try not to fight me."

Tristan closed his eyes. I felt something wrap gently around me. The pressure of his influence grew, and I let go, gave in to him.

I dreamt I stood in a hallway at school, unnoticed, a tide of students flowing around me. I felt a shift, turned to see Tristan next to me. He gave me a small smile that didn't reach his eyes and squeezed my hand. "I'll bring you back, I promise," he said. Then he let go, stepped away.

I closed my eyes for just a second. When I opened them again, I stood in the desert I'd visited so often in my sleep.

A flicker of fear stirred in my chest. I was alone.

I spun slowly. Everything was unchanged. The sand stretched away to the black line of the horizon and stars hung all around. But as the seconds ticked by, nothing happened. No one appeared.

Something wasn't right. I felt it itching along my skin as my heart hammered. If the winged man brought me here, why didn't he appear? And why hadn't Tristan pulled me out? What the hell went wrong?

I looked around. There was nothing here. I was stuck, with no way of knowing what happened to Tristan. Panic gripped me.

His words echoed in my head. He promised he would bring me back. I had to trust he was trying.

Okay, deep breath. I'd gotten myself out of here once before, I just needed to think. I also had to find Tristan. Damn it, if the Immortal One wasn't here, he may be interfering with Tristan. To get free without him wouldn't be enough...I needed to find a way to help him. And quickly.

I concentrated, tried to sense some thread of the magic Tristan had used on me to trace my way back to him. As soon as I caught the trail, I opened my senses further, straining to the fullest. Suddenly I touched on a furious struggle just beyond the dark world.

The two of them fought each other, Tristan trying desperately to get to me. There was nothing to see, all of it happening in some place beyond, but I could sense it. I knew his agony as he tried, and failed, to break past the winged man. I felt the danger he was in.

I screamed his name, the sound echoing heavily around me.

He wasn't going to make it. We'd lose everything if we didn't get out of here.

Focus, damn it. I closed my eyes, gathered myself. I latched onto the thread of magic still connecting us and threw myself along it, hoping if I could just make it to him, he could get us back to safety.

Everything happened so quickly. Suddenly I sensed Tristan with me, grasping onto me. The next thing I knew, I felt an unbearable heave and we were gone.

Chapter Twenty-Six

I fell to my knees in the clearing, looked over to see Tristan lying on the ground. Greta yelled my name as she rushed to her grandson, pulling him to her.

"I'm fine. Is he okay?" I climbed to my feet.

Tristan opened his eyes and gave his head a shake. He stood up, murmured something I couldn't hear. Whatever it was, Greta seemed reassured. She began to back away just as I heard the low whistle that sent panic shooting through me.

"Greta! He's coming through!"

She stepped back to her place, met my eyes with a fierceness in her gaze. This was what we'd waited for. I looked over at Tristan, worried he wouldn't be recovered. But his face was set with grim determination. He nodded to me. We were ready for this.

I tried to prepare myself as the noise grew louder. I could sense the door tearing open…only a few more seconds.

And then he was through.

He simply stepped out of nowhere, appearing before me with that same aura of power rolling off him. The gateway snapped shut, and the sudden change in pressure almost made me lose my balance.

There was no more time. I called up a spark, fed it with power as I hurled it at the man in front of me.

Only a moment after he appeared, he was engulfed in a pillar of flames. I knew it wouldn't hurt him, but I had to keep him distracted. I sensed Greta and Tristan begin to close the working they'd left unfinished.

I drew all the energy I could into the fire, fueled with urgency. It burned intensely, the flames such a bright white they stung my eyes. For a long moment I couldn't see anything of the man consumed by the blaze.

Slowly however, despite my effort, the fire began to recede. I blocked out everything else, saw nothing but the shrinking flames. Faster than I was able to build them, he suppressed them.

I caught sight of him then. His eyes were closed in concentration. Flames licked up around his calm face, his hair drifting about his head in drafts from the fire. He smothered more of the flames, and I saw a burn mark on his face. His suit was singed in places, too. I was surprised I managed to hurt him.

His eyes snapped opened and he looked straight at me, sending a jolt of terror through me.

I felt, rather than heard, Greta shout the final word to close the binding spell. The lines that had disappeared earlier rose from the ground, only now they burned a deep, fiery gold and twisted around in complex patterns.

He extinguished the last of my flames just as her glowing lines wrapped around him, keeping him in place when he tried to struggle. The spell was finished. He was finally trapped.

Relief flooded through me, and I readied myself for the spell that would send him out of our world. It would take everything we had. Greta and Tristan began the weave of magic. I tied myself into their working, letting Greta control the intricacies of it.

She laced our magic together, started to form a net around the man – a cage within a cage. Our combined strength would keep him from escaping, and keep his magic contained, when the binding spell was released so we could shove him through the passage.

We'd have to work as one to perform the complicated magic needed to open the gateway in the first place. Once it was open, the spell was designed to split our energies: I would keep the door from closing, while funneling power to Tristan as he strengthened the chains securing the Immortal One to the Veiled Land. Greta would break the binding spell and push him through at the right moment, preventing him all the while from interfering – no small task.

We would have to then obliterate the gateway behind him so it couldn't be opened again. Ever. I was certain we were strong enough to make this work.

Every aspect was burned into my brain, so while most of my attention was on what Greta did, I still kept an eye on the Immortal One. I noticed when he stopped struggling. I shifted my focus, staying peripherally aware of the working. He stood completely still, staring at me across the lines of the binding spell. A shiver went through me.

It was impossible to know if he was aware of what we were about to attempt, but his calmness set my nerves on edge. There was no way to hurry Greta, though. I silently willed her to finish, hoping it wouldn't take long.

He slowly lowered his head, seeming to draw himself inward. In that instant, I felt a flash of warning and tried to yell to the others.

But I was already too late.

He suddenly broke through the working, shattering the binding. For a brief moment, beyond the rest of the motionless world, I saw him raise his head, his black wings unfurling behind him.

In the next second, the backlash of his magic breaking the spell smacked into me, sent me flying. I hit the ground some distance away, and the impact knocked the wind out of me. I tried to get up as I struggled to fill my lungs with air, my chest aching. I couldn't see the others, but I knew they'd been hit as well.

Finally I managed to draw in a short, ragged breath, desperate for more. But panic crashed through me as the Immortal One stepped closer. He loomed over me, his black wings spread wide, his eyes burning.

There was nothing between us. I tried to scramble away, but I couldn't get my feet under me. I was totally helpless on the ground.

Out of nowhere, a rope of fire wrapped around his neck, pulled him back. He clutched at it, tried to yank it off.

Greta stood behind him, holding the other end. "You stay the hell away from her," she snarled.

Another rope slipped in, snaked around the man's torso, pinning his upper arms. Tristan had a hold of this one. I saw a trickle of blood drip down the side of his face from a cut on his forehead, but he ignored it as he struggled to hold on.

Blue fire flared at the winged man's neck, racing along as it burned out Greta's flames. When his fire reached her hands, she dropped it with a curse. He was already twisting to reach for Tristan's rope. The second he seized it, it snapped, hurtling back to lash Tristan.

Greta sent a new spell and I quickly got to my feet. With a thought, I floated a rock up, flung it at him. It struck the back of his head with a crack, but the second one I sent flying sank to the ground before making it anywhere near him.

A low chuckle reverberated around me, made the hair on the back of my neck stand up.

Tristan shot me a quick look then broke off a large branch above the winged man. As it whipped down, I ignited it, sent my fire burning along the wood. It crashed onto his head and shattered. Sparks burst out, lighting tiny flames on his clothes.

Greta was ready – she turned the ground to quicksand, the earth sliding beneath him, sucking at his feet.

He raised his arms. The sand rose as he did so, more filling in firmly under his feet. He threw the wall of sand at Greta. She barely got a barrier of magic up before it slammed into her, the force driving her to her knees.

Tristan and I both went at him from different sides, distracted him long enough for her to get back on her feet. But even as Greta and Tristan sent more spells at him, he fought off or dodged each one with hardly any effort. We couldn't keep it up.

So as the three of them continued battling, I closed my eyes, opened my senses. The journals had been vague about how exactly he was tied to our world, drawing his magic from it, but they did say damaging that connection so long ago had weakened him. I focused with everything I had, seeking out that bond.

I almost missed it. It was such an intricate and powerful web, even as corrupted as it was, that I almost didn't realize what I saw. I probed along it, tried to find a way to diminish it further, though I didn't know any specifics of the original curse.

Somehow the Immortal One sensed what I was doing. His head jerked around, his gaze pierced me. With a flick of his hand, he tossed me backwards, smacked me into a tree. I crumpled to the ground, unable to catch myself.

Though my head pounded, I wasn't badly hurt. After trying to get up, however, I realized he was somehow keeping me immobilized.

Terror raced through my veins as I sat, paralyzed, watching him face the others. The spells they'd been spinning suddenly died. Before they could defend themselves, he threw them like rag dolls, smashed them back against the wall.

"No!" I screamed. They just lay there, neither one moving.

The Immortal One turned to face me, and the scream died in my throat. I wondered why he'd played with us when he could've ended it at any point.

Slowly, he walked over. He grabbed me by the arms, lifted me as though I weighed nothing. He raised me to eye level, my legs dangling, and captured my gaze.

His eyes blazed, pulling me in until I saw things. All the hidden mysteries of the world burned in their depths. I saw stars die out and magic bloom, strange worlds unknown to man unfurling just beyond my grasp.

I struggled, tried to keep from being sucked in further. Tristan and Greta were out there – I had no idea if they were okay. They needed me. I couldn't be drawn into his world, losing my sense of everything here.

I set my will against him, dragged myself out with a groan.

But even as I managed to tear my gaze away, the Immortal One began to wrap us in darkness, a darkness far deeper than the night beyond. I squirmed in his grip, tried to loosen it. If I could just get away...but his hands were like iron bands around my arms. It was useless.

I looked back up, only to find there was no longer anything left of the world. I couldn't see the others. Nothing existed but the man before me, his cold blue fire licking up on all sides – the only light to see by.

Neither Greta nor Tristan would be able to save me now. And there was nothing I could do for them. My heart sank.

We had lost.

Everything we'd hoped for was gone. I was left with nothing but the shadows he wove. Had this outcome always been inevitable? Perhaps he'd been right: they could not protect me from my destiny. I looked at the winged man, wondered what would become of me.

"You are the one I have searched for," he said, his rich voice rolling through me, full of echoes of ancient power. "The one to help me bring an end to it all."

I stared, fear quaking deep in my belly. I wasn't ready for this. Oh god, Tristan had been wrong. He was going to change me, make me forget myself somehow. There was no way to stop him.

"Do not fight me. None of what happened here is of consequence anymore."

Tears rolled down my cheeks. I would disappear into the shadows, lost to everyone. Now that he had me, he'd turn me into what everyone feared. There would be nothing left of who I really was. A wave of despair washed through me and I wondered if it would hurt.

He regarded me in silence.

I knew I had to ask. After a moment I found my voice, though it came out shaky and weak. "What about the others?"

"Forget them. They were only a vexation while they stood in the way. I came here for you."

So he'd leave them alone if I cooperated. But how safe would they be once I gave him what he wanted? How safe would anyone be if I set him free of the curse?

"If I refuse to help you?" I whispered. "What will you do to me?"

"You cannot change who you are, Eva. You will choose to stand by my side – just as it was prophesied." He set me on my feet, but kept his grip firm on my arms as he gazed calmly down at me. "This is only the beginning."

Pressure built behind my eyes. The beginning for him, the end of me. He believed everything foretold about me. Everything I had hoped to deny. The Immortal One believed he didn't need to change me, to force me to side with him, because he was as certain as the families were that I'd choose him on my own. They saw only the prophecy.

Ever since I heard the damned prophecy, I worried I wouldn't be strong enough to stand against him, that I'd somehow betray myself along with everyone else, some unknown demon inside rising to overwhelm me. But if that was what he waited for now, it wasn't going to happen.

I didn't know what might occur in the future to change me into what had been foreseen, but I was not that person yet. This would not be the night it came true. My resolve hardened.

His eyes narrowed as he noticed the change in my expression. I held myself still, wary of his wrath.

His grip tightened. "You listen to their fairytales. You believe they are righteous," he said, the power in his voice beating against me. "They will not be able to save you when the darkness comes. Your world will fall down around you, and there will be nothing you can do to stem the tide of destruction."

An image rose before me of my crows lying dead. The picture changed, the black shapes became the bodies of the nuns. I saw the whole town laid to waste. That was what he'd bring upon me if I didn't choose the way I was meant to.

My fear slowly drained away, replaced by something unfamiliar. His words ignited it, but it was fueled with far more than just his threats. I was sick of being afraid of everything...of being afraid of myself. And I was sick of feeling powerless. I began to fill with a new, searing rage.

The fury burned through me as I finally realized the truth of what they all believed. The Immortal One was certain I was powerful enough to do what even he couldn't. The families feared the strength of my magic so much they would've killed me as a baby if they'd had the chance.

It all had to mean I was stronger than I knew.

I stared into his otherworldly eyes with that knowledge thundering inside my head, and I knew, one way or another, I had to end this. I would rather die fighting him tonight than risk drawing out the confrontation, knowing I might somehow change enough over time to betray everyone. I would never be free if I didn't stop this now.

The certainty that I was strong enough blazed within me.

I knew what I had to do. It was reckless and crazy, but it was the only way I could think of to save us all – I had no choice. I had to do this for everyone who'd been stolen from me, and everyone else I couldn't bear to lose.

I reached deep into that place where I'd buried the magic for such a long time I hadn't even known it was still there, and I let loose the rest of it...not what had begun to leak out so many weeks ago...but all of it.

I glared up at him, my blood beginning to boil. The shadows pressed in closer as he fought to draw me further from my world, tried to use the force of his will to capture my thoughts as he had before.

But that no longer worked on me. My magic rose up, wrapped around me in defense. I would not let the darkness consume me.

Fire raced through my veins. The pressure inside me grew, building to a shrieking pitch, just waiting to be released. I smiled at the Immortal One – I knew what was coming.

His eyes widened as he suddenly sensed the power streaming through me. Before he had a chance to react, I exploded with magic, a scream ripping from my throat. Fire burst out of me in every direction. It blasted the Immortal One away, burning up his shadows.

All I could see were blazing white flames, tearing through the world, but I reined in the fire with a thought. It wouldn't be enough.

The Immortal One had tumbled away across the clearing. He stood up now in the sudden stillness, raised his head to meet my gaze. His eyes reflected flickering echoes of my power.

He held up his hand, about to speak, but I didn't want to hear any more. My ancestor had cursed him so he corrupted the world around him and I wouldn't be corrupted along with it.

I drew forth my power, felt the magic pulsing through me. It saturated every inch. I quickly threw together the traces of Greta's binding spell, strengthening it as I went. With a flick of my hand, the new binding tied around the Immortal One to hold him in place. It was easy.

I turned my focus to the spell I began to construct. The details had already been laid out for me...I just had to make the original plan work. It took only a brief thought in Greta and Tristan's direction to sense they were still unconscious.

I'd have to weave the entire spell myself. There was no other way.

I cast out my magic, constructed a new net for the Immortal One. It was obviously needed to help keep him secure within the binding spell, and it would be the only containment when I removed that spell to push him through.

I tossed the faintly glimmering, transparent net over him, found ways to loop it through his own defenses to keep him from breaking through. This wasn't something the journals mentioned, it was something I did by instinct.

The Immortal One struggled against it. I sensed him desperately trying to find a weakness in my cage...only there wasn't one. His mouth moved as he tried to shout to me, but I was beyond hearing him. Fear shone from his eyes for the first time.

To make this work, I'd have to divide myself now to take up the other parts of the spell. With the amount of power surging inside me, I was confident I was strong enough.

I also knew I might not come back from it.

It had to be incredibly dangerous with so much magic under my control, but I didn't care. As long as I banished the winged man, whatever happened to me would be better than living out my days waiting for some dark destiny to catch up with me.

I closed my eyes, inhaled. Softly, I chanted the words to reveal the entrance to the Veiled Land, keeping a firm grip on the spell that contained the Immortal One. The magic took hold, and the words stung my lips as I breathed them into the working.

I opened my eyes to find the gateway. It shimmered on a different plane, with an otherness that hurt to look at. The door could be passed through from anywhere in our world, but you had to know where it existed in the space beyond to access it.

I was so close.

A spasm of fear clutched me, but I shrugged it off. There was nothing to do but continue on. I poured power into the spell and slashed through the borderlines of our world. Whispered words of the incantation swirled around me as I threaded my magic through the weakening seals beyond, slowly forcing the door open.

A low whistle grew as the slit to the other side lengthened. The pressure in the air changed. I sensed the unbalance in the world around me that the opening created, but I had to focus – there was more to be done.

I left part of myself entwined in the spell keeping the gate open and concentrated on re-forging the chains that bound the Immortal One to the Veiled Land. It was the strength of these shackles that made it difficult for him to stay in our world for too long now, though every time he came through he seemed to weaken their pull further.

So I wove my most potent magic through them, all the power I could summon flowing into the spell. Even as I worked, I knew they'd be stronger than when they were first made.

All this time, a part of me fought off the Immortal One's struggle to break free, while still holding up the other elements of the spell. I began to lose my sense of where I was in the working. So much power raced through me, stretching too much of me in different directions.

I was getting lost in the immensity of the magic.

I had to keep going...before it was too late and I disappeared completely.

I whipped away the remains of Greta's binding spell and re-knit the tether around him, adapting the original spell to secure his chains deeper. The moment I began, he fought fiercely. But his magic was contained within the net, and I'd become too strong a force for him to overpower, like an avalanche gaining speed as it tumbled down the mountain.

The weight of the endless night on the other side of the opening had begun to leach through. It carried an iciness that was utterly terrifying as it stretched out to touch me.

Everything was set, though. Already I felt the clutch of the spell in the other world trying to drag him back. The Immortal One felt it too. As I gathered the last of my strength to push him through, he stopped struggling. He stared at me, at the small part of me still able to recognize him.

In that moment, I saw something in his face that made me pause long enough to catch the words he spoke. Understanding hit, and I almost faltered. But the spell pulled at me. I had to go on with it, regardless of what I heard, if the others were to have any chance.

Before the pressure of the Veiled Land became too strong, I raised the Immortal One and hurled him through the door, using every ounce of strength I had to snap his grip on this world.

He slipped a last burst of magic out past the net...maybe to break my hold, or maybe just to hurt me...but it was too late, he was already through. I was vaguely aware of a flash of pain in my shoulder as his magic hit me, but I was too far gone to pay it any thought.

Once he disappeared to the other side, I quickly spoke the final words of the spell. The completion of it fortified the working, kept him from forcing his way back out.

There was only one thing left to take care of. The magic still roared through me, making it difficult to hold the last of myself together, but I turned my attention to the gateway.

I closed the tear up over my only glimpse into the world of shadows and sealed the door, following the instructions Greta had made us memorize from the journal. With a last surge of power, I finished what we'd set out to do. I destroyed the gateway, eradicated its existence altogether. The flash from so much magic was almost blinding as it burned through the space before me.

There was a sudden stillness in the clearing.

It was over. He was gone.

*

The temptation to just let go now, to lose myself in the magic, was staggering. It swirled through me, drew me out along paths far from my body to places there would be no coming back from. I was tired. It would be so easy to drift away...all I wanted was to let go.

But some last, lingering connection tugged at me: I wasn't supposed to let the magic overwhelm me.

Wisps of thought threaded through of the people who waited for me. Barely aware, I somehow pulled who I was back together. I threw myself into my body with everything I had left, cut off the flow of magic. The wrench as it withdrew from my mind was a searing agony ripping through me.

I couldn't stop screaming.

I took the only escape I could find, slipped into the dark bliss of unconsciousness.

Chapter Twenty-Seven

Eva! Can you hear me? Talk to me, please!" A panicked voice stretched through the emptiness.

I ignored it. I floated along, wrapped in the comforting void, untouched by any suffering or fear. This was where I wanted to stay. It was nice here.

The voice became two voices, though, and they were insistent. Their words pounded against me.

"She won't wake up. What should we do?"

"I don't know, Tristan, with the amount of magic she must have used...I've never heard of anyone being able to do that, let alone come back from it. There may not be anything left of her in there."

I recognized the voices. Suddenly the need to find them flooded through me – there was no longer comfort in the darkness. I tried to swim towards them, struggling against a heavy weight that sucked me back down into the deep black sea of senselessness.

"I think we should try to get her inside."

"I can carry her," Tristan said. Then, so much closer, he

whispered, "Come back to me, Evie. You have to try – I know you can do it."

I pulled harder, fought to reach him. But the closer I got, the more I felt the pain.

"Wait Tristan, put her back down. Look. I don't know how it's possible, but she may be coming to on her own."

Everything hurt. My mind felt shredded. My shoulder throbbed so severely I began to fear my arm had been ripped off by the blaze of magic the Immortal One loosed at me. I thrashed around in horror, trying to feel my arm, my eyes still squeezed shut. The movement sent new pain exploding through my body and a scream tore its way out of me.

"Eva, stop! Help me hold her down!" Greta shouted. She crouched on one side of me, Tristan on the other, both trying to keep me still.

"Can't you put her to sleep? She's going to hurt herself."

"No. It's too dangerous just yet. We don't know how damaged she is. If her mind is shattered…it will only make things worse."

I couldn't stop convulsing as the aftermath of the magic ravaging through my body took its toll. Fear gripped my heart. A fiery torment swept across me and all I wanted to do was slip back into unconsciousness, away from my body, away from the memories of the world I saw beyond the doorway.

Then Tristan laid his hand on my forehead, his skin soothing against mine. "Easy now. You have to calm down, Eva," he said, his soft voice easing some of my panic.

"We're here now. You're going to be all right, just stop fighting us."

"Good, that's helping. Now listen to me, Eva," Greta said. "I know it hurts, but you have to relax. Follow my voice, concentrate on this place, here and now. Come back to us."

I stopped struggling, slowly forced my jerking muscles to hold still, though the pain was too difficult to shut out. I tried to breathe evenly as I opened my eyes to find worried faces leaning over me.

"Oh, thank goodness," Greta murmured, her shoulders sagging in relief at what she saw in my eyes.

"Eva?" Tristan stared down at me, worry etched in his face. "Are you okay? Can you sit up?"

I tipped my head slightly, not trusting my voice. They helped me sit up, and I kept my teeth clenched against the pain. My shoulder still ached with an agonizing intensity, but my arm was intact and working, so I tried to ignore it. I wiped at something wet on my face. When I pulled my hand away, it was bloody. My heart sped up, my hands started to shake.

"Your nose is bleeding," Tristan said.

"You had too much magic flowing through you," Greta explained. "I don't even know if training on how to control it would have helped. Your body couldn't handle it. You're incredibly lucky it only knocked you unconscious and gave you a nosebleed. How do you feel?"

"Awful." It came out as a breathy whisper. "He hit my shoulder."

"Let me take a look." Greta pulled away the neck of my shirt, gave a low whistle. "That's a nasty mark, Eva – he managed to scorch your skin without even touching your clothes. It's serious enough that I don't want to try anything out here; I need to take care of it properly. Can you make it back to the abbey?"

I nodded, gasped at the sharp knives suddenly shooting through my body from the movement, my head pounding as I almost blacked out.

"She can't walk like this. Can you give her any relief now?" Tristan asked Greta quietly. She nodded. "Okay then. Eva, I'm going to carry you back." I tried to protest, but he insisted. I didn't have the energy to argue.

"It's safe to sleep now that you're back from the worst of it, Eva," Greta said as she stood up. "Don't fight it. You can tell us what happened later."

Tristan pulled my hand over his shoulder, slipped one arm beneath my back and one beneath my knees. He stood up, carrying me with him, my face pressed against his neck. I felt his body shifting as he walked to the wall. I breathed in the comforting smell of his skin.

He set me on top and climbed over. Then he gathered me back up in his arms to follow behind Greta.

"I can walk," I mumbled.

Tristan's chest vibrated against me as he chuckled softly.

I slipped into the dark void again, helped along this time by Greta's influence.

*

The world faded in and out. I knew when we reached the abbey, felt it when they cleaned me up. Greta treated my shoulder and the sudden relief was enough of a shock to bring me fully awake for a moment.

Softly, from somewhere beside me, Greta said, "Magic poisoning. It's going to take a lot more than this to heal you, I'm afraid. More rest will help."

The words drifted across me...I floated away again.

That was when the nightmares began.

A storm raged around me. I dreamt of the magic burning me up from the inside, of the pain and emptiness as it left me. On an endless loop I saw darkness and death spread, feeling helpless as I watched.

I strayed in and out, aware of others always nearby. Thunder rolled through me, flashes of lightning imprinting scenes from my dreams in my mind.

And on I slept.

*

Eventually the pain eased. I came back to the world slowly. The light outside was gloomy and dim, so I had no idea what time it was. Rain lashed against the windows, a fierce wind blowing.

Greta gazed at me from a chair next to the bed, her face unreadable.

"I thought you'd be waking around now so I insisted the nuns all take a break. I wanted to talk to you alone first." She looked at the door. A second later it opened.

Tristan slipped inside, gently closed the door behind him, and took the other seat. He had dark circles under his eyes, but as he looked down at me, his mouth curved in a slow smile. "Welcome back."

"Thanks. How long have I been out?"

"It's Sunday morning," he replied.

Just over two days. Damn. I pushed myself up, waved them off when they tried to help. But, though it felt good to move, my muscles trembled with the effort. I felt raw, fragile.

"First thing's first," Greta said. "I knew you'd be out of it for a while after such a display of power, so that next morning I told Helen you hadn't felt well when you went to bed, to prepare her. Unfortunately there was nothing I could do to speed up the healing – you needed time to recover.

"But I couldn't explain that, so they're all very worried. The doctor came, but of course he had no idea what was wrong. You ended up spending the past few days in a rest-less sort of sleep. At this point, however, you've gotten the aftereffects mostly out of your system – you'll be weak for a while, but you'll be fine. And now, if you wouldn't mind, I'd like to hear what happened after we got knocked out."

So I went through everything. Greta wanted as many details as I could tell her about the magic I performed – how I managed to hold onto the different aspects of the working, how I was able to cobble back together her bind-ing spell (something that apparently shouldn't have been possible). Much of it was difficult to explain, but they were patient.

I told them everything I remembered…except for the moment right before I sent him through the gateway. I wasn't ready to think about that yet.

"With all that magic running through you after it was over," Greta said when I finished, "you simply came back to yourself and closed it off?"

"It wasn't that easy," I murmured. "I think it nearly killed me."

She stared at me for a long moment, her gaze intense. "I daresay you're right. I don't know how you managed any of it. No one else could tap into that much magic. Not even close. And even if they could, they would have been ripped apart by it. To be able to work that spell by yourself, then come back from it...you're more powerful than any of us believed."

I felt a chill run up my spine. There was something about the way Greta looked at me, something guarded about her expression. It made me wonder if she'd begun to fear I really would become a danger to them.

"But we're really lucky you are," Tristan said. "You saved us."

"Indeed," Greta said. "And the Immortal One is once again locked away where he belongs...for good this time. You, my dear, are finally safe. Now it's just a matter of filling in the council on what transpired."

The chill I felt deepened.

"The others are up. Helen is on her way. They don't know about your shoulder, Eva – I managed to conceal the wound. I'm afraid it will scar, though. You were seared by a powerful bit of magic. There was only so much I could do."

I nodded. "Thanks for taking care of me." My shoulder felt tender, which was far better than it had been.

"Just be sure you tell me if you don't feel well in any way, no matter how minor. I want to be extra cautious about this."

The door eased open. Helen came in, her eyes puffy

and red. But as soon as she saw me awake, her face brightened.

"Oh, Evie, you've had us so worried," she exclaimed, rushing over.

"And absolutely no magic, Eva." Greta's words whispered in my ear as she and Tristan slipped out quietly.

Helen sat down on the bed, wrapped me in a hug.

"It's okay, Helen. I'm fine, I promise."

"That's what you keep saying." She pulled away to look at me. "But you keep getting sick and having these violent nightmares. What's really going on?"

Helen's eyes were full of concern as she searched my face, waiting for an answer. I was afraid a time would come when, regardless of my wishes, the nuns would be pulled into all this. When that time came, it would be such a relief not to have to keep these secrets.

But until I had no other choice, I would protect them from this darkness.

"It was only one nightmare," I said with a smile, forcing my voice to be light. "And I don't know why I got sick again. It's probably from being around so many other kids these days – I'm sure I just caught something at school. Greta said it's out of my system now, so don't worry."

Helen's brows were drawn. She narrowed her eyes at me, but before she could say anything, Mary and Agnes entered with Sebastian in tow. The mood brightened as everyone chatted, catching me up on the last two days.

Unsurprisingly, it sounded like nothing but shifts of watching me sleep. Greta and Tristan had rarely left my side. They kept the nuns from panicking, assuring them

Greta's medicines were the reason I was so out of it, which was a good thing because it meant I was getting better.

And apparently, thunderstorms persisted the entire time I'd been sick. Of course.

I spent the afternoon trying to prove to Helen I didn't need any more rest. Eventually, I managed to persuade her to let me eat downstairs. Catherine joined us for dinner, which was cozy and lighthearted, despite the bad weather that persisted.

Being allowed downstairs was one thing, apparently, but convincing Helen I was well enough to go to school was another matter entirely. This time, it wasn't even easy to get Agnes and Mary on my side. I certainly wasn't better and hiding that took a lot of effort, but there was no way in hell I could sit around the abbey all day, with nothing to do but dwell on everything that had happened.

"Come on Helen, I'll go crazy stuck in bed another day," I said as everyone finished eating. "I've rested enough, I promise. And if I feel unwell at all, I'll come right home. Please?"

"You were out of it for two days. We don't even know what was wrong with you," Helen replied, her fears putting an edge in her voice.

I looked at Greta for help. The nuns needed to believe there was nothing wrong with me.

She cleared her throat, drawing Helen's attention. "I know you're concerned about her health, but the medicine did its job. She slept off whatever made her sick. For what it's worth, I think it would be perfectly safe for her to go to school."

Helen didn't look totally reassured, but she trusted Greta after everything the woman had done for me, so she was reluctant to argue with her.

"What was in that medicine you cooked up anyway?" asked Agnes.

"Just an old family secret," Greta replied, a small smile on her lips as her gaze met mine.

"I don't know, Evie, I'm worried about you," Helen said.

"If it makes you feel any better," Tristan said, "I'll be with her the whole time at school – I can keep an eye on her."

Helen hesitated, glanced over at Sebastian. He smiled warmly at Tristan. "Well, I think that sounds wonderful. We'd certainly appreciate you looking out for her."

That settled it. With Sebastian agreed, Helen yielded, content that someone would be there to watch over me. Agnes and Mary were delighted with his offer, of course, exchanging significant looks with each other.

I didn't care, as long as I was able to go to school. I only hoped Tristan wouldn't be overzealous about sticking with me.

I hadn't had a minute alone with him since everything happened, and I was trying not to freak out about it. Was the kiss a one-time thing? Everything had been so uncertain as we were headed off to face the Immortal One...what if Tristan had just been swept up in the moment?

The walk to school together would give me a chance to figure out how he felt. The thought set my nerves skittering about. No – don't panic, one thing at a time.

I didn't want to admit it, but I was exhausted by the time Mary served dessert. After everything, I still felt shaky. So I said goodnight and, insisting I didn't need help, left the warm, bright room. On the way up the stairs, I let myself lean heavily on the banister since there weren't any witnesses.

I'd pulled my sweater tighter against the chill and begun to make my way down the hallway, when Sister Claire stepped into view. She stood staring at me from her doorway, the room behind her dark. The beads of her rosary were wrapped around her pale, bony hand, and she clutched them tightly to her chest.

"You might have the rest of them fooled," she said, her eyes burning with a feverish intensity, "but I know what you really are. Mark my words...the evil inside your soul will take you over. It will infect everything around you, until we're all destroyed. I will pray for you."

Claire made the sign of the cross and disappeared into her room.

I stood there a long moment. Sebastian had already threatened her. She believed deeply enough in what she said that she was willing to risk her home here to say it.

I crawled into bed still hearing her voice. A shiver ran over me. She didn't know anything about the prophecy, but her words eerily echoed it.

Chapter Twenty-Eight

The abbey was hushed. The rain had let up, but the mist was heavy, turning everything gray and insubstantial. At breakfast, everyone seemed tired still, the mood subdued.

"It's too bad the weather has been so poor," Mary said quietly, her gaze darting to me. "This can be such a lovely time of year."

Greta tilted her head, raised an eyebrow at me in silent comment. Of course she knew I hadn't let go of the storm entirely. I wondered if it worried her. I certainly wasn't doing it on purpose.

"Well, I'm sure it won't last much longer," Helen said in a firm voice, giving Mary a look. "Are you kids almost ready? I have to go into town this morning. I'll walk with you."

So much for having a chance to be alone with Tristan. I sighed. Helen had watched me like a hawk since I came to. It would take her a while to get over this latest incident. Not that I was complaining. I was incredibly lucky she cared that much, that they all cared that much.

From the other side of the table, Tristan studied me, his green eyes sharp. He shifted his gaze to Helen. "Sounds good. I just need to get my bag." His eyes found mine again as he got up. I was about to follow – I just wanted to know, either way, how he felt – but Helen stopped me.

"If you wouldn't mind waiting for a moment, Eva, I'd like to speak with you. Maybe Tristan could get your bag while he's up there?"

"Of course," he said.

Helen and I went into the reading room.

"I just want to make sure we're clear," she said, crossing her arms, "if you feel even the least bit unwell, you're to go the nurse's office immediately and call us." I nodded, resigned. "And no library after school. I want you to come straight home, all right?"

There was no point arguing. She was just being protective, suspicious something more was happening that I wouldn't admit to. Really couldn't blame her for that.

"I promise. I'll come right home."

"Thank you." Helen gave me a hug, with a few more cautious warnings.

Tristan waited for us in the foyer when we came out. The others discussed their plans as he walked over, held my coat up for me. No one paid us any attention.

When I finished slipping into the coat, Tristan's fingers brushed gently against mine, his touch lingering. Surprised, I glanced at him. His mouth curved in a soft smile as he met my gaze, sending a thrill through me.

I stared up at him, some of my anxiety fading. He knew exactly who I was and he liked me. Standing next to him in that moment, my fingers twined with his, the rest of it almost didn't matter.

He gave a nod towards the others and we separated. A moment later Helen turned. "We should head out. I don't want you to be late, especially since you both missed school on Friday. Greta will join us as well."

When the four of us crossed through the gate in the wall, I held my breath. But, of course, nothing happened. I told myself I was being an idiot and tried to concentrate on the day ahead. School still held the same hazards as before.

Greta and Helen left us at the steps, watching with solemn expressions as we joined the other students headed inside. In the hallway, we hesitated. I wished we'd gotten a chance to talk about how things would go in school.

"Tristan!" Molly called, rushing over. "Hey, where were you Friday?"

With his attention on her, I ducked away. I could only deal with so much.

I walked into class, trying to ignore the growing ache in my shoulder. Tristan came in shortly after and shot me an exasperated look, but he went to his seat without saying anything. As he'd promised before, he kept up the pretense throughout the day that we weren't friends. It sucked, but it made things simpler.

At lunch, I spent my time catching up on assignments, trying not to look over at Tristan. Every time I did, he sensed my eyes on him and returned my gaze, amusement tugging up the corner of his mouth. It took a lot of effort to keep my attention on my work.

When the bell rang, I went to my locker. I put my

books on the shelf, and as I pulled my hands away, the door slammed shut, making me jump.

Molly stood there, her blond hair pulled neatly back with little red clips, her expression cold.

"Don't think I haven't noticed you staring at Tristan, following him around like a pathetic puppy dog."

I froze, feeling caught.

Her mouth twisted into a sneer at my silence.

"You know he's only being nice to you because he feels sorry for you," she hissed. "He doesn't understand yet that you're a freak."

Suddenly something snapped, everything realigning in my head. Screw her. After all that had happened, I realized how ridiculous it was to be intimidated by her.

She watched me with satisfaction in her eyes. "But don't worry, it won't be long before he realizes what a loser you really are. And deep down, you know it."

It took all my control not to slap her in the face for everything she'd said and done. She so deserved it.

Instead, I took a step closer, put the force of my anger into my stare.

Molly shrank back, the confidence bleeding out of her.

"I would be careful if I were you," I said in a low, even voice. "You don't know me. You have no idea what you're talking about. As for Tristan, you wouldn't want him to see what you're really like, deep down, would you? See how ugly you are underneath it all? He may be willing to pretend you're a nice girl...for now. But I know better. I am done putting up with you." I stared at her for a moment, watched her face turning white. "I'm warning you, stay the hell away from me."

I stepped back. Molly moved away, her eyes wide, her shoulders rigid. I was probably going to regret that, but still...it was totally satisfying.

By the end of the day, I just wanted to get home. I felt trembly all over, the pain in my shoulder a steady throbbing. We got back to the abbey to find everyone in the foyer. Greta explained that the damage to their house was less severe than they'd thought, and after a few minor repairs that morning, they could move back in. Imagine that. I'd gotten used to their presence here, though, and okay, I knew there was no reason for them to stay, but their departure still felt abrupt.

Everyone began their farewells. Greta gave me a hug, said in a low voice, "I left a jar of ointment for your shoulder next to your bed – it should help with any pain. We'll talk again soon."

When Tristan finished saying goodbye to Mary, he turned to me. "Well, I guess I'll see you tomorrow," he said, his lips quirked in a smile. "I promised Mary I'd walk you to school – to make sure you get there safely." He winked at me and I couldn't help smiling back. "So I'll meet you in the morning."

He followed Greta and Sebastian out to the car, while I stood watching them with the nuns. There was no way to know what would happen with Tristan. Now that I was no longer in danger, I wasn't even sure if they'd stay in Fairhaven.

I sighed. That was a problem for another day. I was just happy I'd see him again tomorrow. Hopefully, Helen would let the two of us walk to school without an adult escort, and we'd finally have some time alone.

"Well, this is a little sad," Mary said. "It'll be lonely here without them now."

"We'll have them back to visit soon, don't worry," Helen said as she started down the hallway, the other two trailing behind her.

I felt a bit lost now with everything settled. The pain in my shoulder eased up some once I put Greta's ointment on it, and I went outside to the back porch, anxious to avoid any overzealous ministering of the nuns. Stopha flew down to the railing, called out as I went over.

After soothing him, I sat down on a rocking chair. I pulled my knees up, wrapped my arms around my legs and stared out at the ocean. I thought of Tristan's eyes as he smiled at me, and something inside relaxed. I finally eased my grip on the last of the storm, sighing with the warmer breeze that swept past me.

With a clearer head, I thought about what had been weighing on me. All my life I'd been plagued by nightmares about what was coming. When we set out to face the Immortal One, I'd been certain that was the moment my dreams led to, what they'd all been about. But what if it wasn't?

Greta and Tristan believed I was safe from the prophecy coming true now with the winged man imprisoned in the Veiled Land. I knew better.

His words kept echoing in my head, the words he uttered just before I shoved him through the doorway.

Do not let the magic overwhelm you now, and heed my words: the shadows hunt you. This will not keep me forever, Eva...your blood calls to me. You cannot fight your destiny.

I'd seen the truth of it in his face. Somehow, I was certain, it didn't matter that I'd destroyed his only way back to this world. He would come for me again one day. It was a promise.

And when he did, something inside me was supposed to twist, make me betray everyone, make me join him. If he was right, and the prophecy came to pass, I could destroy everything. *If* it came to pass. I had a lot riding on that little word.

As for the rest of it...had his words helped me keep hold of myself as the magic burned through me? I wasn't sure I wanted to know. Nor did I want to dwell on his warning about the shadows.

I'd planned to tell Greta what the Immortal One said, but the way she'd been looking at me after my display of power made me hesitate. I just wanted more time without them wondering when it might happen, worrying about me. Afraid of me.

I didn't know how many years I had, though. Someday, I'd have to warn them he was coming back.

The dark tide still swept towards me.

My gaze drifted out along the ocean. In the distance, as the fog broke up, the sun made shifting patterns of light on the water. I reminded myself that things were different now. I reminded myself that Tristan believed in me.

The thought made me smile.

I knew where I belonged. I had people who would stand with me. The Immortal One would return eventually, but I'd already stood up to him once, already defeated him.

I would keep growing stronger. The next time the Immortal One came for me, I would be ready. For today, though, I could just look forward to my walk to school with Tristan. And I could be myself.

I knew who I was now. No prophecy could change that.

Acknowledgements

There are so many people to thank for helping me get to where I am today.

To my family, I want to say I love you, and thank you for always being there for me. I could not have asked for better, or more loving and supportive parents. You all make me laugh, and you let me be exactly who I am. I would be lost without you guys.

Jade, Anneke, and Jay – you make my heart happy. I have the most amazing people in my corner. You've seen the best of me and the worst of me; still, you root for me. You always manage pull me back from the brink of insanity.

I want to say a huge thank you to Dana for her cover art and unfailing enthusiasm for the project. I completely lucked out in being able to work with her.

I had the good fortune of getting plenty of help along the way. I owe a lot to everyone who read drafts and gave notes, or precious words of encouragement. The advice, support and input from people throughout the process were invaluable. Thank you to Kate C., Kaitlyn, Heather A., Heather T., Ron Koertig, the Writing Pad, Aviva Layton, M. Riley, and the teachers who encouraged me over the years.

For all the friends who have been with me through good times, and been solid rocks to lean on through bad times, I can only thank you and hope to always be there for you in return.

CPSIA information can be obtained at www.ICGtesting.com
Printed in the USA
BVOW08s1933050516

446956BV00003B/107/P